CREATURE OF THE NIGHT

ANNE STINNETT

For those of you who keep me sane.

Emily ran a hand over her already smooth hair and took a deliberate breath. She didn't look like her typical self today because today wasn't a typical day. Except for occasions (and if appearing on the highest rated series ever didn't qualify, what would?) she wasn't one to bother much with makeup, or fancy clothes, or doing anything more complicated with her hair than brushing it and throwing it into her signature ponytail. Did people have signature ponytails? Still, she looked good. Good but not threatening. Not bad for a librarian. *Former librarian*, she reminded herself. It was fascinating how deeply one's career touched the definition of oneself. But that life was over now; whether it was with a bang or a whimper remained to be seen. She had researched all she could in preparation for the coming days, but the distinction between theory and practice was going to be made brutally clear in less than twenty minutes. Assuming, that is, that they started on time.

She wiped her palms on her pant legs. Her hands trembled. She couldn't remember the last time her hands had trembled. *Untrue*, she corrected herself. She could always remember; she chose not to. The past was past. Now was the time to push her terror aside and focus on ensuring she had a future. Because, in the immortal words of F.D.R., the only thing to fear was fear itself, and she clung to the banal comfort because, well, any port in a storm. Oblivious to the cascade of helpless adages, her hands continued to shake. Frankie D's judgment was suspect. He had been spared the excruciating knowledge of the things that go bump when they come to kill you in the night. Those things had not lurked outside his bedroom. *As far as you know*, Emily amended. Nevertheless, she had signed the contract, deposited the check, and Emily did not believe in second-guessing her thoroughly mulled decisions. She wouldn't turn back if she could.

Everything she was about to endure would be worth it, as would all she was poised to inflict. Every action that tarnished her character would eventually fade in her memory until the prize she was about to earn made any remnants of regret insignificant. Knowledge was Emily's god, and there was no more devout disciple.

One thing she would do when this was over would be to look into the history of the house. Her bedroom alone sported a pair of gargoyles perched on pillars to either side of the walk-in fireplace. It was a bit much for Emily, who had grown up in a ranch house indistinguishable from most of its neighbors. On the other hand, the Manor might have sprung from the union of an uptight Victorian and a sprawling Southern Plantation, with a touch from a creepy Roman uncle during the formative stages. Emily suspected this was some architectural mishmash created just for them. She would soon have time enough and more for that and any other lovely mystery that caught her attention.

Emily checked her watch again. Sixteen minutes to eternity.

Madeline scowled at her outfit and wished she were back at the Manor, preferably cowering under the four-poster bed. The producers had put her in pink, for fuck's sake. She could have forgiven the wardrobe people for wanting to make her appear a bit more mainstream, but pink, that was downright sadistic. She felt like she was eight years old again, bored and sweaty in her Sunday dress, waiting for her parents to drag her to church. Madeline loved her parents, as much as she could love anything so foreign, but these people were different.

She had come here planning to be nothing more or less than herself, and they had rendered her unrecognizable. *They can pry my eyeliner from my cold dead hands*, she had thought, smirking at her cleverness. Madeline's hands were still warm and quite alive, but they had scrubbed away her black eyeliner. Ironically, she was wearing more makeup than she ever had, but now it was *tasteful*.

Such is the price we pay for our dreams.

At least they hadn't lasered off her tattoos. As far as she could tell, they owned her body (if not her soul) until the final, "Cut." But none of that mattered. Current styling choices excepted, Madeline had always stubbornly done things her way no matter what indignities life (or her peers) threw at her, and she would ride that stubborn wave to victory.

She knew she was meant to be here. Some people were born dark and brave and destined for extraordinary things. Eternal things. Madeline knew what she was, and soon the world would be forced to accept her truth. She had already started referring to herself as "Mistress Madeline," sometimes aloud, much to the discomfiture of anyone in her vicinity. These third person references invariably led to snickering, often disguised, sometimes not, but Madeline didn't give a shit what other people thought. In fact, not caring was her thing.

Of course, that intrepid attitude came with a price, but again, it didn't matter now. There was one unassailable truth in which to take comfort: Madeline would never have to pay that particular price again. She would never have to go back.

She might never *get* to go back. Even though, maybe someday, a visit wouldn't be so bad. She was free again to be herself. Looking herself was another matter.

Madeline understood these imposed changes reflected some perceived deficiency. But, she knew how to meet derision with defiance, and she would defy everyone who had ever judged her for being different by winning and becoming the epitome of Madeline. Mistress Madeline. Unfortunately, she had felt more like that dark and beautiful creature back in her room at the Manor.

A week of living in gothic splendor hadn't led her to anticipate the sterility of her dressing room. Her room at the Manor looked as though mysterious drafts were the preferred method of climate control and a spider's web might inhabit every corner. Although these authentic touches were regrettably absent, the ambiance was there, and that was important. Here, she was surrounded by earth tones and daffodils.

And the outfit. For the outfit, someday, she would make them pay. The thought of future revenge fortified her resolve, much of which had disappeared along with her familiar clothes and painted face. There were a lot of people on Madeline's revenge list.

Mistress Madeline sat on the couch in her pressed khakis and pink sweater set to wait. Thirteen minutes to go. Lucky thirteen.

Twenty floors up, Little P finally gave up on waiting for The Voice's secretary to acknowledge his presence, cleared his throat for courage, and spoke. "Is he in?"

Rose didn't bother looking at Little P. "He's in."

"Is he..." *In a good mood? Already drunk? Waiting for someone, anyone, to walk into his office so he could fire them?* None of these things could be said to Rose, although they were all valid questions.

"Is he what?" Rose had been with The Voice for a decade and had abundant disdain for Little P, who, despite being the right hand of The Voice, was too recent an acquisition to merit her respect.

Little P went with a different approach. "Can I go in?"

"He *is* waiting for you," Rose said.

The Voice, aka Executive Producer, aka God, hit Little P with a question the second he walked into the office. "What are you going to do about the lineup for the girls' intro? I'm not happy with it."

Little P stole a look at his watch. The lineup would be a matter of history in less than ten minutes. "What would you like me to do, Sir?" Little P averted his eyes from The Voice's basilisk— like glare and tried to focus on the printout being waved vigorously under his nose.

"I want you to fucking fix it," The Voice said. "I don't want the boring one to be first up. It'll set the wrong tone."

"Of course," Little P said. "Which one would you like–"

"The crazy one, of course. It's always good to lead with crazy."

"Absolutely," Little P agreed. "I'll take care of it."

"What about the other thing? Are they here?"

"Yes, sir," Little P said, noticing The Voice's handmade suit had acquired a splotch of mustard. "They are."

The Voice raised a shaggy eyebrow and stared at his subordinate. "All of them?"

"Well, all of them that we expected to be punctual." Little P had to take his victories where he could. "And he's not one of the regular judges. We don't need him until—"

"Find him." The Voice didn't raise his, but his displeasure was clear. "I want him here when we start."

Little P goggled at the impossibility of the command. Nevertheless, he answered back with a peppy, "Yes, sir!" On his way out, he caught Rose rolling her eyes and wondered if she had been listening or if his mere existence provoked her scorn.

Cassie was feeling good today. Strong. She'd been doing everything in her power to keep limber without overdoing it. Her current workout routine included baby stretches and other gentle moves. Moves that a year ago, and with a certain amount of affectionate condescension, she had encouraged her grandmother to do.

Feeling good was to be expected. In spite of the devastating diagnosis her doctor had spouted, glibly, as though it wouldn't ruin her existence, the rigors of everyday life weren't yet a problem. She could still walk to the grocery store or tackle a couple flights of stairs with the best of them. The problem was her career. It didn't mix with her disease.

She was going to fix it. And if she couldn't fix it, it wouldn't matter. There were only two possible outcomes, and that meant simple. Easy-peasy, lemon squeezy. She smiled at her reflection and nodded firmly. She could do this. She'd worked all her life to be strong in mind and body. Her body was doing its best to fail her, but her mind had worked out a solution, a way to keep her dreams alive.

Beneath her surface confidence lurked a swirl of dark dread, but she had labeled it stage fright with some anticipation of formidable competition thrown in—both of which she had dealt with countless times. The only difference here was there would be no other chances.

People who've lost everything are best prepared to make the most of whatever chance they get, and Cassie had lost everything except her determination. Sure, her life looked okay on the outside: she had a nice boyfriend, a cat that was as devoted as a cat could be, and a beautiful apartment all waiting for her return. She could still teach. This splashy, last-ditch effort to return to her previous existence, her healthy existence could turn out to be a waste of everything she'd ever done, a waste of everything anyone had ever done for her.

She examined those subversive thoughts and dismissed them. Again. It didn't matter that there were scraps of her life that resisted destruction. Whether she was in the mood to call it God, or fate, or chance; something had blasted to smithereens the life she had chosen for herself. Everything that was the essence of the person she had worked so hard to become was gone for now. Maybe it was gone for good.

There was a tap on the dressing room door followed by a voice calling, "Five minutes."

"Thank you," Cassie whispered.

Portia. It wasn't the name her fanatically traditional parents had bestowed, but it had been hers for the last fifteen years. Fifteen years of no big break, minimal encouragement, and being the envy of no one, but perhaps that was too much resentment to hang on a mere name.

Life was about to change. There would be no more doing theater for snotty (literally and figuratively) little shits who, for the most part, were more in need of a good belting than of an afternoon watching Portia play Peter Pan.

Which hadn't even paid scale.

And there would be no more waiting tables. Portia was never going to touch a plate again after this, not even her own. There would be people for that. She'd have someone to cut her food and fork it right into her mouth. She could hire someone to chew for her if she wanted, but she wouldn't, of course. That would be going too far.

As ridiculous as this was, it would put her on the map. In fact, that stardom would soon be in her well-manicured clutches was guaranteed once you factored in the bonus benefits. This was the big-time. In the next few minutes she would be a household name. All she had to do was win, and then it would be back to the movies, but this time there would be luxurious trailers and a bevy of underlings. She'd be in the Hollywood issue of Forbes, and the world would adore her. Then, she would tell Charles he could go fuck himself. Portia was sick of his endless support that did nothing but remind her she was a failure. Being on a fucking soap didn't grant him license to pity his wife.

It wasn't as though Charles had ever starred in a movie. She had. It hadn't won an Oscar, but it had gotten her a SAG card. The ad in Backstage West had referred to the film as "artistic." The thirty-three thousand five hundred and seventy-two people who had seen it understood it to be soft porn in spite of its noticeable lack of eroticism.

Would they be calling "action?" She had three minutes left to wonder.

Mandy came out of the bathroom with Mason perched on her hip. She loved the way he smelled after she'd given him a bath. It reminded her of when he'd been a true baby. He wasn't even two yet, and already she could feel his childhood slipping away.

Her husband Seth was in the living room prospecting with the remote control. "Hey, *Creature* is about to start," he said.

Mandy settled next to him with Mason on her lap. "Fantastic." She fiddled with Mason's plump toes. "Do you think they're really going to do it?"

Seth laughed. "You mean the full monty?"

"It's a little more serious than getting naked."

"Things are different since last season. Legally, I mean."

"Yeah, I and the rest of the world are aware." Mandy set the squirming toddler on the floor. Mason half crawled, half walked over to the television and reached a stubby fingered hand out to touch the face of the blond vampire on the screen.

Once upon a time, Chaz would have taken a deep breath before going onstage. Now he didn't need to, and it wasn't just because he was no longer a breather. It was impossible to be nervous in front of a bunch of humans. You might as well be nervous because a colony of rabbits was looking your way.

Some time ago, Chaz had been a rabbit. Now he was closer to being a god.

And then, he spoke. "It's been a long time coming, but we are back! Welcome to the first episode of what is going to be the best season yet! I know it's been too long since you've gotten to see me, but I'm here now and you, my friends, are about to get what you want! Are you ready?"

The crowd screamed in response. They were ready. Chaz preened around the stage while the crowd reached out with their voices and their hands, trying to grasp or even momentarily catch the attention of the beautiful creature parading just out of reach. They shouted his name, they roared endearments, they even offered up veins. For Chaz, the adoration was the best part. He didn't need the rest of the show.

"For the two of you at home who don't know, I'm Chaz Hunter, and this is *Creature of the Night*. Everybody wants to be a vampire, right?"

Emphatic cries of "Yes!" and "Please!" and "I'll do anything!" warred with wordless screams of assent.

"Well, you can't all be," Chaz said. "Because then what would we eat? Besides, you guys tried to eradicate us."

Delia watched Chaz rile the audience from backstage and sighed. *"I miss the war."* For vampires, the war had been like an endless buffet. For the first time in millennia self-control could be abandoned. For the older ones it had been a time to remember who they were. For Delia, who had been born again in the war, taking what she wanted was natural.

Beside her, Nodin snorted. *"You were in your element."* Just out of sight of the audience, they had gathered to await their entrance.

"I don't remember you turning your nose up at the feast," Delia said. *"It was too bad you missed it, Ed."*

"The point of remote living," Edmund said, *"is to avoid such trivialities."*

"Listen to them." Nodin nudged Edmund who sneered at his eagerness. *"Humans. There's nothing trivial about killing them. Every disposal made the world a bit better."*

"Speaking of disposals," Delia said. *"Our fourth, have you seen him?"*

"Him being The Imp–"

"Yes," Delia said.

"I didn't realize you were so close," Nodin said.

"We're not," Delia said. *"But there's always a bond, don't you think?"*

The elder vampire considered his own maker. A brief infatuation had led to his rebirth, but not long after that she had left without a word. *"No."*

"Then chalk it up to how nice it always is to catch up with the one who plucked you from humanity and gave you an army." Delia fluffed her hair and basked in the knowledge that her maker was famous. A lurking stylist scurried over to straighten a lone lock that had been disarranged by Delia's self-congratulatory primping.

"Sentiment," Edmund said, *"is a weakness of humanity. Of course, since you and your thousand newborn siblings were created only to serve us in the war, I understand why you still cling to human tendencies."*

"Do you sound so distressed for any particular reason?" Delia said.

"I do not sound distressed," Edmund said. He could not allow the others to glimpse any inappropriate emotion. His role was very clear. *"Perhaps your inclination to cling to your human weakness caused me to be overcome with shame."*

The crowd was chanting and clapping in time. *"Eradicate! Eradicate! Eradicate!"*

Onstage, Chaz waggled a finger and said, "Naughty, naughty." The audience lost it. They howled with laughter, remembering the days when humans thought they could kill a bunch of creatures that could disappear with a *poof* and were mostly immune to killing. No hard feelings here.

Cyri Newton scooched another increment closer to her father to avoid the moist arm of the gentleman to her left. "I can't believe we're going to be here for a week," she said. What she really couldn't believe was that her mother hadn't vetoed her attendance.

"I know. Who has the best dad ever?"

Cyri thought it might be some girl whose father hadn't just sprayed saliva on the back of a stranger's head while chanting, "Eradicate!" Cyri overlooked the spit and offered her father a smile because he did try hard, but her dad's attention had gone right back to the vampire host.

"Being elite beings, we like to *stay* elite," Chaz was saying. "That's the purpose of this show: we give people who might be worthy a chance to prove it. To the judges. To the world. And, much less importantly, to you. One of the twelve contestants you're about to meet will be the newest chosen one. The other eleven, well, they've gotten their affairs in order. But the winner! The winner will be transformed into an infinitely superior being, and you get to watch every step of the journey. And I do mean *every* step. Remember to take a peek at the contestants when they're in the house. They've waived their right to privacy."

"Bathroom cam! Bathroom cam! Bathroom cam!"

Chaz shook his head at the audience. There were times when he was charmed by humans, but they were rare, and when exposed to them in large groups, he ended up fighting the desire to drain every last one of them.

Finally, the catcalls and whistles dwindled, and Chaz could continue. "You and everyone watching at home can vote for any contestant at any time. Those votes will be tallied after each challenge, and you will have the opportunity to participate in a poll clarifying the results. That is, you'll have a chance to vote on why you hate a contestant so much you elected to ruin their dream. Then the judges will assess the contestants and make their decision. They may, or may not choose to honor viewer votes."

Chaz paused for more cheering, although he noted it shrank from ear splitting to a reasonable din a few seconds faster than the initial roar had. No stamina. Humans were such pussies.

"Are you guys ready to meet our judges?" Chaz cupped a beautiful hand around an equally beautiful ear and leaned forward. "I can't hear you!" It was a lie. Vampires in the next state could hear them, but the crowd tried harder. Chaz nodded in satisfaction.

"*Everybody ready?*" Delia asked as she adjusted herself in her corset for maximum effect. Nodin nodded. Edmund bared his fangs in one last practice hiss.

Vampires, being the showy fuckers that they were when not in hiding, couldn't just pull up a few stools. An altar rose above the audience and on it sat three thrones. Each was composed of human bones and overlaid with gold. They gleamed in the studio lights as they waited for their occupants. Like office cubicles, the thrones had once been identical but had since been individualized for their users.

One was adorned simply with only the top half of a skull on each arm positioned to serve as a handrest. Another had been enhanced by an abstract iron rendering that suggested wings unfolding from its back, and the throne in the middle sported ornately embroidered cushions on its seat, back, and arms that looked old but were memory foam. And pink.

Chaz was halfway through the judges' introduction. "Look to the altar, and you'll see our distinguished and beautiful panel, all returned from wherever they scatter when we're not filming just for you. Let's meet them now." The altar was empty, and then it wasn't. The judges appeared as though they were one, all in the same instant, and it was like The Beatles and the Super Bowl all rolled into one.

It always was.

Two males and one female now occupied the thrones. All eyes turned to the female. Wherever she was, no matter the company, all eyes were drawn to this female first. As always, Chaz bowed to the inevitable. "Please welcome the mesmerizing Delia. Men want her; women want to be her. Except for the women who want her."

"I believe, dear Chaz, that you forget about the men who want to be me," Delia said. The crowd cheered her wit. They were, of course, really cheering her beauty.

"Oh my god," Cyri said. Her seat was so good it was hard to miss a single word no matter how she might long to.

Her father was too busy wanting Delia to answer.

Chaz bowed. "In addition to welcoming Delia back to the show, let's congratulate her on her newlywed status!"

Delia inclined her regal head. "Thank you, Chaz. Thank you all. My beloved husband and I appreciate the support."

"Lucky number, let me think, it's only eleven, isn't it?" The judge to Delia's left raised a lip to sneer, letting a fang slip out.

"He is lucky, yes," Delia agreed. She was resplendent and unflappable. "And you are correct; he is only my eleventh husband. Of course, I try not to marry more than once a century or so. But Marco is not to be resisted, and he is doing very well. Thank you for asking. He brought home a lovely little model for us to share just last evening."

"Your human mother spat you out in 1971," Chaz said to Delia. *"What is this 'centuries' nonsense?"*

"I just like the sound of it," Delia shot back, managing to imbue her mental tone with shades of Nicholson.

"Don't be a tease, Delia," Chaz said aloud. "This model, was she good eating?"

"*He* was not for eating, only for nibbling and, of course, sex. Marco is adventurous. But please, enough about me. I think you better introduce him, Chaz." Delia indicated a Norse-god type to her left. "He's feeling unappreciated."

"Please welcome Nodin," Chaz prodded the crowd, who had been hanging on every word of the tiff, unwisely hoping for an outright scuffle. Nodin nodded his blond head in recognition of the cheers. The sneer disappeared. Nodin had walked the earth before Christ and spent centuries hiding what he was, but the perks of being on television were sometimes undeniable.

"And last, but not least, say hello to Edmund!" The crowd greeted Edmund with only slightly less enthusiasm than it had

Delia. Edmund was a traditional vampire fanatic's vampire. Chaz had long suspected Edmund's widow's peak had been surgically achieved.

Chaz knew Edmund hated the show because he hated humans. Chaz had always figured Edmund had hated himself when he'd been one. He was here because he took his duties as a guard of vampiric purity seriously. Edmund waved a hand at the crowd to shut them up and thought he couldn't possibly manage another season. Chaz shuddered at the sight of Edmund's fingernails. They were old school pointy and disgustingly thick and yellow. Chaz had indulged in a mani/pedi that afternoon.

Undead didn't have to mean unkempt.

"Do you know what happens next?" Chaz asked the audience. They didn't let him down.

"Fresh blood! Fresh blood Fresh blood!"

Chaz had come up with the chant the first season. It always gave him such a tingle to hear it chanted he forgot he was, in effect, getting validation from human beings.

"That's right!" Chaz beamed at the crowd. A teenage girl in the front row fainted. Chaz was, as vampires tend to be, gorgeous. "Time to meet this year's contestants. Let's start with the ladies!" The crowd expressed their love for ladies, particularly ladies who might soon be in a position to drain them dry.

"Ladies! Ladies! Ladies!"

"I love you!" someone screamed. Chaz flashed a pointy smile and waved in the direction of the shout, assuming, as always, that the outburst of affection was meant for him. Besides, the ladies had yet to appear.

Cyri slouched in her seat and let out a disgusted sigh no one heard.

Poised to step onstage to meet Chaz and be presented to the crowd, Emily let out a similar sigh. She was so absorbed in anticipation and dread that not until she'd been dragged twenty yards and bustled around a corner did she realize she had been seized by a pair of tall blonde vampires. Of course, to give them their due, her hijackers had moved quickly.

"Thank you," Little P said to the vampires who melted away without reply.

"What's going on?" Emily said.

"Just a small adjustment to the lineup," Little P said as though it were self-evident. "You'll go on fourth right after the dancer. Cassie, her name is."

"Why?"

"No reason."

"You sent the vampire brigade to yank me over here for no reason?" Emily tried to keep her tone polite. Little P didn't strike her as the average lackey. "Is this because I'm not crazy?"

"Absolutely not." Little P thought all the contestants were crazy. "It's because you're not *blatantly* crazy."

The audience was putting their hands together to welcome Madeline as she made her way across the stage to join Chaz.

"That's what they think of meeting this season's first *Creature of the Night* contestant," Chaz said when the crowd stopped screaming. "How does it feel to know all that was for you, Madeleine?"

"It's a dream come true, Chaz." In spite of her excitement, Madeline was a little appalled to be standing in front of so many people. She kept her focus on Chaz. She thought she might just fall into his eyes; they were so deep and dark. All those people, the ones who said vampires don't have souls, had never looked where she was looking. Madeline was ashamed to be standing before him in a cardigan.

Chaz wasn't showing off his soul, but he was assessing Madeline's emotional state. There was something fanatical about the gleam in her eyes.

"A dream come true," Chaz repeated. Like they'd never heard

that before. Another season or two and things were going to get tedious. "How ridiculously fantastic, Madeline. I'm happy to be part of your dream. And so are the judges." Madeline waved at the judges. "And so is the world!" Madeline waved at the camera. "We want to hear your story. Tell us about yourself in thirty seconds or less."

"Why must they tell us about themselves as though they are not all the same?" Edmund said, trying to entrench himself in character.

"They are not alike in every way," Delia said.

"The show is for humans," Nodin said, *"and they think of themselves as unique."*

Madeline had seen the show and had prepared for this part. She didn't have words to describe herself in all her complexity, but someone else had. Madeline ran her tongue over her lips to moisten them and found them still sticky and moist with gloss. It was her mouth that was dry. *You can do this,* she told herself. *You were born to be one with the night; this is just to make it official.* Her recitation started out as a croak, but gradually, she worked it out and produced a steady if not inspiring rhythm.

"Speak Mary-words into our pillow. Take me the gangling twelve-year-old into your sunken lap. Whisper like a buttercup. Eat me. Eat me up like cream pudding. Take me in. Take me. Take."

"Are you a big fan of Sexton?" Delia pinned Madeline with her gaze. "She was an interesting woman. It was tragic, her death. I would have been happy to turn her."

"It is possible a human, one that took her own life, would not have been interested in extending it eternally," Nodin said. *"Not to mention she was dead before you slithered from your mother's loins."*

"I wouldn't say immortality is the same thing as eternal life," Delia said. *"I've read her work, which means I know her in spirit. And I'm starting to think you have a problem with women, Nodin."*

"A problem with women spewing slithering spawn?" Edmund wondered.

Chaz hoped he wouldn't have to break up a brawl this early in the competition. Delia hadn't moved, but she had tensed, changed in a moment from basking in the adoration of the fans to being coiled to strike. "And the Catholic Church, among others, would agree."

"Are we so incapable of thought that we must claim The Church as an ally in our discourse?" Nodin said.

Delia threw back her head and laughed. Every male in the audience, plus or minus ten percent, responded with an erection. "No," Delia said. "We are not. Madeline?"

"I am, yes. An admirer." Madeline was congratulating herself on being a person of such depth that she had already snared the interest of the judges.

Every year. Chaz gave a nearly imperceptible nod in response to The Voice coming through his earpiece.

"So, Madeline," Chaz said. "Tell us about the time you recently spent in Happy Mountain."

"It was good, Chaz. Really good."

"For those who don't know, Happy Mountain is a sanatorium catering to the violent and severely delusional."

"The staff there is wonderful," Madeline said.

"Yet I understand you didn't go willingly."

"Absolutely not, Chaz." Madeline smiled and added, "Although now, I highly recommend it. Unless of course you're one of those happy people, and then I don't think there would be any point."

"Seriously?" The Voice was pissed. Chaz shrugged. Mental illness wasn't a big deal these days; the stigma, along with the thrill, was gone.

"That was fantastic, Madeline." Chaz threw an arm around her shoulders. Madeline quivered. "Are you guys excited to see what she's going to do throughout the competition?" The crowd was. "All right, you head off with the girls, and we'll see you for the first challenge."

The girls steered Madeline away, one of them leaning close and inhaling her neck. They were very much alike, both tall and blonde, both newly turned. Around set, they were sometimes referred to as "the twins." Their names were Rylie and Kylie, but no one could reliably tell them apart. Madeline thought them beautiful and let herself be led offstage with no sign of fear. Chaz was doing his best to monitor them since being newly turned meant they had an unfortunate tendency to want to sample the contestants.

"I'm so sorry, sir, but we had to start without him." Little P braced himself for The Voice's reaction to his failure. "He's just nowhere to be found."

"Yeah, no shit," The Voice said, gesturing at the monitors covering an entire wall of his cavernous office. "Fuck it. He'll show up eventually."

Lola's in the house bitches! Though technically, they'd brought her over from the house an hour ago. It was a badass house, and she planned on returning to it in glorious victory. Lola thought the Manor nearly worthy of, well, Lola. It had twelve fucking bedrooms for Christ's sake. Lola's had a canopy bed and a claw-foot tub, both things she'd coveted as a child but never experienced. Lola had gone without a lot of things growing up. In fact, the dressing room she stood in now, which paled in comparison to the Manor, would have looked like paradise contrasted with her childhood abode.

For Lola, the discrepancy between what she wanted and what she could obtain disappeared the summer she turned fourteen and worked out how to use her brand new body. Soon enough, there would be nothing she wanted and didn't get. Fuck that, soon enough wasn't. She was getting everything she wanted starting right fucking now.

She felt she was going mad with anticipation. The rules of

separation, enforced by rigorous supervision, had prevented her from catching even a glimpse of the others staying in the Manor. Even the trip over from their current home hadn't provided any opportunity for interaction. They had been ferried over individually and shut in their dressing rooms. If anyone could thwart the lockdown protocols, Lola would be the girl to do it, but for now, the rules should be followed. Not that Lola followed rules for the sake of obedience, but she might have been caught. A fresh failure would not put her in the proper mindset.

Even with minimal knowledge of what she was up against, she saw herself winning. Lola had made up her mind to win. It didn't much matter what that entailed. *"Whatever Lola wants, Lola gets..."* Lola threw back her head and laughed. As long as there wasn't a singing competition, she'd be just fine. Although she was probably better than she thought. Too bad *American Idol* had finally gone off the air. Otherwise, she'd do that next. Lola was good at life, which was funny to think of now.

She smiled at herself in the mirror, pleased with what she saw. Of course, Lola had a tendency to be pleased when she looked in the mirror. Framed by a fall of sleek black hair were a generous mouth and hazel eyes. She tried the smile again and considered whether it might come off as cocky. She pulled out her girl-next-door grin, the one that got her favors, gifts, and other gestures of friendship or lust. Sometimes, these tokens were followed by a period of hurt feelings when Lola failed to reciprocate, but she dealt with that easily by bestowing another smile, a lingering touch, a promise of more to come.

Lola snapped out of her reverie and cataloged one more time the white teeth, the dimples, the eye contact that meant she was a person worthy of trust. Check, check, check.

Some lackey knocked on Lola's door with her five-minute warning. Lola got dressed.

22

Onstage, Chaz addressed the audience. "Are you ready for your next contestant?"

The crowd screamed affirmations.

"Then let's meet Portia." Chaz extended a hand to Portia, who was crossing the stage with all the poise Madeline had lacked. The crowd quieted when she reached him; they were over the first craze of excitement and were settling into a routine.

"How are you, Portia?" Chaz said. She placed her hand in his and leaned in to exchange cheek kisses.

"It's a beautiful night," Portia said, "and I feel fine."

She was a beautiful girl, Chaz noticed. But she was a girl on the cusp of looking more woman than ingénue. She had already developed the habit of not smiling too hard to keep the crow's feet at bay. From the beginning, they'd gotten more applications from actresses of a certain age than from every other demographic combined.

"Are you ready to tell the world all about you?" Portia nodded and smiled her careful smile, lots of teeth, minimal eyes.

"My name is Portia, and I'm an actress."

"That's why I recognize her," Cyri's dad said.

"I do a lot of children's theater, which is the most rewarding thing in the world, and as you can hear, I'm from South Carolina. Don't worry, casting directors, I can lose or change my accent anytime." Chaz rolled his eyes. Actors just could not help themselves. He remembered they were live and switched to looking entranced by Portia's narrative cum audition for the world. "I'm thrilled to be a part of this, and I'm going to make sure you guys get the show of your lives!"

Edmund cocked his head. "How will you make sure?"

"Do you have to fuck with them so soon?" Delia said.

"Are the cameras not rolling?" Edmund said. *"Besides, we all have our raison d'être."*

"Um..." Portia's smile held but abruptly became strained. "By being the best competitor I can be."

"I hope she gives it a hundred and ten percent," Cyri muttered.

"Yes," Edmund said. "I imagine you'll give it one hundred and ten percent."

"Why do you come here if you hate humans?" Delia said to Edmund.

"Because I don't trust the judgement of those who do not." Edmund flashed his fangs for punctuation.

"And yet," Delia said, to Edmund only, *"you just repeated for all what a human child in the audience uttered to herself. How unfitting."*

"I thought it might be beneficial to our kind to promote someone worthy this season." Edmund desperately ignored the gibe about the girl. "Surely, we don't want a repeat of last year's little fiasco."

"Let's punctuate that," The Voice said in Chaz's ear.

"We're looking for some action here," Chaz passed along for the judges' benefit.

Nodin bared his fangs, but Delia was already straddling Edmund, her claws sunk deep into his neck. Cyri came to attention.

Delia gave Edmund a little shake. "We do not discuss last year's little fiasco, Edmund," she said.

"Someone must be aware of the dangers of bestowing sudden power on the unworthy." It was a painful remark for Edmund to get out, and not because of Delia's death grip on his throat.

"This season's winner will be closely supervised unless said winner has demonstrated an extremely high level of sanity," Chaz said. "Loss of human life can be upsetting."

"Apologies," said Edmund, who was still dealing with his upset. "I got carried away."

"You're bleeding," Delia said.

"You could pull your claws out a bit," Edmund said. Delia complied.

The Voice covered the mouthpiece connecting him to Chaz and asked Little P, "Is the massacre trending?"

"Yes, sir," Little P said with pleasure. They were off to a good start.

The Voice nodded. "Hard to believe we ever thought a massacre could be a bad thing."

Little P agreed. It was hard to believe. There had been twenty-seven killed when last year's winner lost her mind, but you couldn't buy press like that. "Yes, sir," he said.

Still onstage, Portia was barely breathing. Chaz could hear her pulse throbbing in her neck. She froze like a smiling deer in the headlights, but Chaz was willing to bet she was infinitely tastier. Chaz signaled to the girls, thinking that as long as the vampire twins could resist making a snack of her in her heightened state, Portia would be safer offstage. Besides, the twins eating her offstage would be better than having her ripped apart on camera because she'd ended up in the middle of a fight scene between Delia and Edmund.

The vampire put his hand on Portia's back to let her know she was exiting the stage.

"Hang on," the Voice said. Chaz felt his eyebrows crawl up his face as he listened.

"Just one more thing," Chaz said. "I'm being told you were quite active politically during all the controversy surrounding vampire-human marriage. Tell us about those days."

Portia nearly screamed. She was trembling with the need to be away from vampires. She hadn't even made it through her introduction before a potentially freaking deadly (to Portia) vampire skirmish broke out. And now she was expected to explain her political proclivities?

She forced her best smile. "It was a long time ago. I think many of us have strong opinions when we're young, and I don't believe anyone should hold those youthful opinions against us later in life."

"Shall we take that to mean your thoughts on vampire–human marriage have evolved?"

Portia squirmed under Chaz's gaze. She thought any human stupid enough to marry a vampire deserved what they got. "This is embarrassing, Chaz," she said, "but the truth is there was a guy." She was telling the truth. There had been a guy. Portia had dragged him to protests until his brain managed to override his penis, and he dumped her.

Fascinated by the bigotry, Chaz was prepared to delve deeper, but the Voice tickled his ear again, and he dismissed the actress.

Portia was led away by the twins who weren't twins, and the first hurdle was past. She managed to give a practiced wave as they took her away. She notched up the smile to go with it. She congratulated herself on her poise and threw up as soon as she passed the curtain. She fucking hated vampires.

There were a few moments of complete silence while Delia and Edmund worked things out; Delia's nails embedded in his neck the whole time.

"Let's move on," The Voice instructed.

"He says, enough," Chaz told Delia.

Finally, when half the audience was on the verge of passing out from holding their breath, Edmund narrowed his eyes and nodded as well as he could. A feat that isn't as easy as it should be when one has an enraged vampire poised to tear one's neck open. Delia released him and resumed her throne.

"That was Portia," Chaz reminded everyone. "Next up, we have another showbiz veteran. Say hello to Cassie!"

Portia had turned once she was safely offstage and past the puddle of her own sick to ascertain whether some freaky vampire war was about to break out. Therefore, she was in a position to get a glimpse of Cassie. Cassie was cute, thin but muscular. Light brown hair, not as pretty as Portia, but at least ten years younger. Portia felt a surge of resentment for Cassie's youth. The vampire twins let her glare for a moment then took her firmly away.

Onstage, Cassie trotted out, waving to the crowd the whole way. She made it to Chaz, met his upturned hand with her own, but deliberately stayed too far away for kisses.

Chaz ignored her reticence and pulled her in for a hug, which she returned gamely enough once she didn't have a choice. "How are you, darling?" Chaz asked.

"Great, just great," Cassie told him, turning to include the audience at the last moment. "I'm thrilled to be here."

"A female immune to Chaz's charm?" Nodin wondered.

"Inconceivable," Delia added. *"Besides, it looks more like she's afraid of him than immune."*

"Go ahead and tell the good people why you're so thrilled." Chaz knew she was this season's hard-luck contestant, so far. They'd always had one. Last year, it had been an orphan. Chaz couldn't see the tragedy of not having parents once one was an adult, but the audience had loved her. Still, a dread human disease was almost as good.

Cassie nodded. "I'm a dancer, and my doctor —not to mention the doctors I went to for second and third opinions —recently diagnosed me with Rheumatoid arthritis. I want to win this competition, so I don't have to give up my career. I've been dancing since I could walk, and I hope to be dancing forever. I live with my fiancé and my cat Bella."

"Way to sacrifice the male vote," Chaz said.

"I think the arthritis pretty much killed her chances of being this season's fantasy girl," Delia said.

"Her family," said the Voice. "They don't speak."

"Tell us about the rift with your family," Chaz said. "What's it like to be on the verge of an experience that will change you forever, with no support from your loved ones?"

"I do my best not to think about it," Cassie said. "And when I can't manage that, I think about why I deserve to be without them. It's the same reason I deserve to win this."

"The audience isn't following," Chaz said.

"Four years ago, I declined the opportunity to donate bone marrow to my little brother."

"And how is he doing now?"

"He's dead."

"I understand your decision had something to do with your career," Chaz said.

"It did." Cassie's chin was defiant, but her eyes were spilling tears.

"Which is going to be over regardless, if you don't win this," Chaz said.

"Yes."

Edmund pounced. "Why should we change you when you are weak and flawed?" *Weak, flawed, and foolish,* Edmund thought, but inwardly he smiled at the bravery.

"She can't help it," Delia said. "She's human."

"That's true," Cassie said. She looked at Edmund and raised her pointy little chin. "We are all weak and flawed. To you, I'm sure it seems we humans are especially so, but we are not the only ones. And I am doing everything in my power to overcome my weakness, although I imagine I will still be flawed. And I think of my brother every day. What else can I do?"

Chaz was ready to launch himself in front of the girl if Edmund attacked. He hoped Delia would rouse herself to assist. She was clearly up for a fight. The twins were in the wings, but they were so new Edmund could command them to stand down as easily as he would separate Cassie's heart from her chest. Instead, Edmund laughed. "I wish you well," he said.

"That seems out of character," Nodin said.

"*Right?*" Delia said.

The Voice squawked in Chaz's ear.

"Well wishes from Edmund," Chaz said. "I'm sure none of the other contestants will be able to tell that story. How about you skedaddle while you're ahead?"

"Skedaddle?" Delia said. "*Are you my grandmother?*"

Cassie nodded once in acknowledgment of Chaz's advice, waved brightly at the audience, and trotted off toward the vampire twins.

Celeste knew it should never have come to this. It was funny in a sick, sad way that her failure had brought her here, into a situation where the same failure would be virtually impossible. But it was finally good to be different. To be the one who understood happy endings are bullshit and pursuing them is futile. Which meant, that unlike the other contestants, the odds were staggeringly in her favor. Soon everything would be as it should have been all along. Today was going to be a good day. The best day—in fact, the day the waiting was over. Unless it didn't happen today. Celeste wasn't sure about the timeline, but she knew it would be soon, and that was enough.

She paced around her dressing room, concentrating on the thud of her boot heels. She had been unconvinced heels were appropriate, but no one had cared. In addition to the boots, she had been given pants and long sleeves to cover the scars. Celeste had sensed pity as they'd primped and styled her, but their pity didn't matter. She knew she was getting what she wanted. She knew because she'd always wanted it. She wondered some more about the other contestants. Would any of them be here for the same reason she was? Probably not. But that was fine. Celeste had made peace with who she was. *Made peace*, not given up like her parents had accused. There had been months of weeping and recriminations. Celeste felt bad for her parents; she believed they would miss her, but the time had come when she had to do what was right for her. She had learned that when they sent her to therapy.

Of course, she knew they loved her, but she suspected part of their fierce objections was the shame factor. Decent people don't do things like this, and they certainly don't do them in front of everybody. And most of the world surely counted as everybody.

Celeste had listened to their objections, duly considered them, but she had already known which way she would jump. She was ready. There might be obstacles, there might be hearts broken, but in the end, she was going to have what she wanted. And no one would stand in her way.

It was almost time. It was almost over.

"You've got to love a girl who doesn't overestimate the need for talk," Chaz said, as Cassie scampered offstage. "All right, people. Here comes Emily!"

Emily's hair shone under the lights. Chaz watched her big dark eyes as she crossed the stage. She reached him and leaned in to touch her cheek to his. She smiled around, and Chaz could see she wasn't simply submitting to observation. She was an observer. He was surprised to notice she was shaking.

"Emily," he said. "What must we know about you?"

"I don't know about *must*," Emily said. "But what I'd love for you, and of course everyone watching, to know is I'm a librarian, and what attracts me to immortality is having the opportunity to continue learning forever. Also, my favorite cuisine is Indian, and I'm a Pisces."

"You have composure," Delia said.

"Thank you."

"Would you lose your composure if I told you that if you do not win the first challenge, I will drink you to the brink of death every night for a year and then finish you?"

"I probably would," Emily said, "if I hadn't read the contract." Not that what she had read was much comfort. True, the legalese translated to, *could* be killed in competition, as opposed to *would* be, but Emily's extensive research had revealed modifications in the language for this season, their purpose to open the door to more intentional mayhem.

Chaz was impressed. Delia smiled. Hardly anybody read the

contract.

"Tell us about dropping out of college," Chaz said.

Emily considered before saying, "There's not much more to tell."

"You did eventually graduate, though?" Delia said.

"Yes."

"From a lesser school." Emily shrugged. It was a matter of perspective. Chaz cocked his head to study her. "You were so dedicated, on a scholarship at what most would consider a prestigious university, and you were able to let it go from one day to the next without regret?"

"No," Emily said. "I have no regrets. I would do it again."

"I'm told we may come back to this at a later time," Chaz said, after processing the information flowing from his ear bud. Emily shrugged. One didn't dwell on the past when the future was happening.

"I used to be a Pisces," Nodin said, dragging the conversation back to trivialities. "In the seventies. Do you think this is significant?"

Emily took a moment to assess Nodin. "I don't. It's just a bit of trivia so you and the audience can get to know me."

"Tell me, baby," Nodin said in perfect imitation of a hippie he had eaten in the sixties. "How does the shattering revelation of your sign help us to know you?"

"It doesn't per se," Emily clarified. "What you know is I made a poor choice in choosing a fun fact about myself."

"No one said it wasn't fun," Chaz said.

"*Shall I?*" Edmund said.

"*You missed the moment,*" Delia told him.

"I believe you have far more entertaining facts at your disposal," Delia said.

"I'm a librarian," Emily said. "The interesting facts I could share aren't about me."

"Why does this one believe she is entitled to tell us what we know?" Edmund said.

"You're such a dick," Delia said.

Emily turned her face to Chaz and lifted the eyebrow that the judges couldn't see a fraction. Chaz took it as a scream for help. "I'm Chaz, and I'm a Taurus," he said.

"Hi, Chaz!" The crowd screamed.

"And this is Emily the Pisces." Emily dutifully waved to the crowd. "Go see the girls, Emily."

Emily swept past the vampire girls, leaving them to trail in her wake. She had only wanted to avoid their touch, but to most of the audience, it appeared an audacious– if bitchy– move.

"Are you ready for Lola?" Chaz called to the audience. They cheered Lola as she crossed the stage to Chaz. Lola paused to pump both fists in the air and bent down to high five a couple members of the audience on her way.

"Lola," Chaz said. "Talk to us."

"Hi, Chaz. Hi, audience. Hello, esteemed judges." Lola had every ounce of wicked composure a human could contain. She wasn't nervous. She was laughing at the spectacle of the show, but she had slapped on her ear-to-ear, good-girl grin.

"Are you glowing?" Chaz said.

"Just happy to be here," Lola shot back.

"And, I imagine, happy the lawsuit has concluded," Chaz said.

"My body, my choice," Lola said. "The jury agreed."

"I'm told the lawsuit was about breach of contract," Chaz said after the Voice clarified. "The one you had with the parents? After all, genetically speaking—"

"Vampires kill people all the time," Lola said. "I don't understand why you care about—"

"We do not care," Edmund said. "We scarcely consider you humans sentient beings."

"Which, I imagine, is why Lola is here with us this evening," Chaz said. "To be all she can be."

"I want your votes," Lola yelled at the audience, "but I'm here to

CREATURE OF THE NIGHT

win. I don't care what anybody thinks. Whatever I have to do, I'm going to fucking do! I am your new Creature of the Night, and my name is Lola! Watch me, support me, and I will make you lose your minds when you see what I bring to the competition. See you soon!"

"Such big talk," Delia said.

"Such big b–"

"Really, Nodin?"

Lola grabbed Chaz and planted a kiss on his lips. There was no chance Chaz would fight off even a reasonably attractive woman, and Lola was far higher up the scale than "reasonably," so he returned the kiss with interest. The crowd screamed. The judges made various expressions of disdain.

When Chaz and Lola broke apart, Lola's lip was bloody, and her eyes were shining with triumph. She flashed her sweet grin one more time, and it looked sincere even to Chaz, though he knew it wasn't. Chaz smacked her on the ass and sent her off the stage. "Did things just get interesting, or did they just get *more* interesting?" The crowd damaged some vocal chords as they agreed things were getting interesting.

"I will wager three virgins on that one to take it," Nodin said.

"I'll take that bet. And make it five," Delia said.

"Done."

Chaz laughed uproariously. "Nodin, we don't wager virgins anymore. He's kidding, folks."

Sometimes virgins were wagered but not with the frequency of earlier times. Virgins these days were more likely to be socially awkward and pimply middle school kids than the ripe, supple, beautiful young men and women preferred by any self-respecting nightwalker.

"I think Lola might expend too much energy trying to appear as she is not," Delia said. "An unfortunate consequence of finessing what one wants from others instead of simply taking one's due."

"Did you never finesse before you became powerful?" Nodin

wanted to know.

"I don't believe I did. Of course, I can hardly remember." Delia smirked at the crowd. "My point is that one will never win," Delia said. "Please make sure my virgins are comely and capable of pleasing me."

"Control the judges," The Voice snapped in Chaz's ear.

Edmund sneered. "She means hung like a–"

"Okay–! It's time to move on," Chaz said, interrupting Edmund. *"Seriously, you guys, enough about the virgins."*

So this was how it worked.

Lola studied the man in front of her, the man who had been waiting to pull her away from the girl vampires who'd escorted her offstage.

He didn't look like much. But he acted like he was something, and she was inclined to believe him.

She didn't say anything. Instead, she nodded as though she was on the same page, because if there was one impression she was getting, it was that she had better be on the same fucking page. And it was a page that made sense for her. More sense than pretending to be sweet and adorable. It felt like fate. That they saw the bad-ass bitch she was and thought she was a winner. Although, suit guy hadn't said, "winner," but the gist was clear to Lola. She probably would have thought of it herself if they had just given her room to work.

"It'll be your brand for the duration of the show." Little P studied the girl to see if she was getting it. Talking to the contestants was the worst part of his job. "If you win, your brand can be the tooth fairy for all the fucks we'll give. Got it?"

"Got it," Lola said.

Onstage, Chaz extended a hand to Celeste and proclaimed with sweeping enthusiasm, "Now, here she comes, last but, as they say, not least, meet Celeste!" The audience roared their encouragement. Celeste, however, took so long mincing across the stage that by the time she fetched up against Chaz, he was ready to snap her neck.

"How are you?" Chaz could see how she was.

"I'm good," Celeste said. "Happy to be on the show."

"I can tell," Chaz said. Someone in the first row let out a nervous giggle. Chaz leaned in close. Her reaction to his nearness would give her some pep. She smelled like dinner. Celeste had been tearing at a fresh scab with those ridiculous pointy, black fingernails. Chaz knew the others would be able to smell it too. A room inhabited by vampires wasn't the place to be walking around smelling of blood.

"*Unless she wishes to be dinner,*" Nodin said.

"Hi, everyone," Celeste said. "I'm excited to be here, and I can't wait to get started." Chaz believed her. Her type could never wait to get started.

"Are you worried about the competition?"

"No," Celeste said with perfect honesty. "I'm looking forward to the competition, and I can't wait to get to know the other contestants."

Which was a lie, Chaz knew. "Do you like meeting new people?"

"Doesn't everybody?" Celeste said. She wouldn't look at him. Chaz knew she must be deeply absorbed by something internally because what better view was there?

"Maybe you'll meet your new bestie right here on *Creature of the Night,*" Chaz said. Celeste crossed her arms and moved her gaze from his knees to his shoes. "And the good news is those that bond on our show tend to bond for the rest of their lives."

Celeste managed to bring her gaze up to his chin and nod. Chaz decided to wrap it up. She'd done enough to fill her spot, however lackluster it might be. He looked forward to seeing what would become of Celeste. Her type was sometimes good for a surprise along the way.

Edmund leaned forward and inhaled deliberately. He had also caught the scent of blood. At Chaz's silent urging, Riley and Kiley swooped up to hustle Celeste offstage, and it was time for the guys. "That was the last of our lovely ladies," Chaz said. "We'll be right back with more!"

"Okay, what are their names again?" Nick said, hugging a bottle of bourbon to his chest, and hitting the mute button on the remote.

"What the fuck are you talking about?" Mike wanted to know.

"I can't remember which one is which," Nick clarified.

"Jesus, man. They've been promoting the shit out of this for months. There are two hot ones with dark hair, right?"

Nick nodded. "Sure."

"The one with big tits is Lola. She's the slutty one. And the one with the perfect handful is Emily. She's the smart one. Got it?"

"Got it," Nick agreed. "What about the crazy one?"

Mike had to consult the *Creature* app on his phone before answering. "The crazy one is Madeline. She looks like your mom if she had tattoos. The average looking redhead is Celeste, who I don't think is crazy, but you never know."

"I like the blonde," Nick said.

"Yeah," Mike said. "That's Portia. She was smokin' hot, like, seven years ago. She's an actress. Not bad." Mike was one of the thirty-three thousand five hundred and seventy-two, but he hadn't been disturbed by the lack of eroticism; the nudity had been enough.

"I'd still do her," Nick said. "And the little cute one too."

"The dancer?" Mike shrugged. "Eh. She has arthritis or something. She's probably not that flexible."

"I'll help her flex," Nick said with a laugh. "What's her name again?"

"Cassie."

Ollie had been taken over by a down-the-rabbit-hole sensation. The city was crazy; the house was crazy; the whole idea of this competition was crazy. Maybe Ollie was crazy for being here. But like Ollie's dad had said, he'd made his bed, and now he was getting ready to lie in it. Speaking metaphorically, of course. He had gotten out of his actual bed after spending the night tossing and turning and nursing regrets. And now he was here, waiting to be called onstage for the world to judge him.

It was all just nerves, he told himself. Nerves meant nothing. He would win, or he wouldn't and there was no shame in either. Just shame in not doing his best and he didn't intend for that to happen.

True, he was way out of his comfort zone, but that didn't mean everything wasn't under control. There had been a contract laying everything out; it was all aboveboard. Ollie hadn't done much more than run his eyes over it, but he assumed the lawyers for a set up this fancy knew what they were doing.

Ollie wished his dad could be here with him, which was impossible for a number of reasons. His dad would be watching though; he had promised, and that meant the world to Ollie. There was a time when Ollie had believed his dad would never speak to him again, but it seemed that thought had never occurred to his dad.

Ollie had spent a lifetime feeling not quite unloved, but as though he were a curiosity, inexplicably showered with fondness by those close to him. Winning wouldn't mean he suddenly fit in with his family, but he had grown accustomed to that alien feeling. What had driven Ollie for the last six months was the possibility that this was the beginning of a new adventure that would lead to real manhood and his permanent niche in the world.

From that niche, he would be able to make amends.

Physically, Ollie knew he was up for most anything. He wasn't a huge guy, but he wasn't scrawny either. He had grown up playing football and helping his dad out on the farm; he was healthy and strong. He wasn't feeling confident about his outfit; they'd dressed him up to look like a city version of a cowboy, even though at home he hadn't dressed like a cowboy at all. One hint of a Middle America accent and you end up the token hick. In this case, he was the token hick in a pair of two hundred dollar jeans.

Ollie wiped his sweaty hands on his denim-clad legs and realized his remaining time could reasonably be counted in seconds.

Stewart had spent half the night hugging the toilet and not due to his customary drowning of the sorrows. Last night had been all about good old-fashioned fear. (For fear, read "shit-your-pants-terror".) Fucking kids, the love of those little bastards was going to be the death of him. If he'd been able to come up with any other way to win them back, he would have done it twice, but he had been labeled an absentee father, which was true enough, although not entirely his fault. That was hard to overcome. Marcy, his bitch of an ex-wife, incessantly plotted against him, never missing an opportunity to point out who was the good parent and who was the deadbeat piece of shit.

He had been warned, by his camp and hers, he was marrying up; he was taking on a wife who had expectations. Stewart had expectations too; they consisted of modest comfort, football on the weekends, and kids who made it to college without getting pregnant or hooked on drugs. Marcy's expectations were so far beyond Stewart's, their marriage-to-be began to unravel the moment they met.

Stewart knew Marcy had plans to change him. Marcy had always loved a good project, and he was fine with being one of them, even happy to be. What he hadn't envisioned was his future as a *failed* project, and Stewart never expected the girl who had been a virgin on their wedding night to cheat on him with not one but two other members of the club they couldn't afford. Rather, the club he couldn't afford because Marcy was a fucking *Stay-At-Home-Mom*. Not that the kids had stayed at home with her since they had started preschool and begun padding their little resumes with extracurriculars.

Nor had he expected Marcy to gloat about her extramarital adventures over dinner. The savage announcement the night she'd thrown him out had included a detailed list of indiscretions punctuated with the fun fact that she had already been pregnant when they married. Stewart, who had believed wholeheartedly in her premarital virginity, had been left speechless and unable to retaliate.

So much for the memory of their romantic whirlwind elopement.

Now here he was, making the big gesture, trying to win back the tolerance of his fucking children and damn the biology. Stewart checked the clock again. His attempt would begin in less than two minutes.

"Okay people," Chaz said. "First, we met our lovely ladies. Now, it's time to meet some equally lovely gentlemen!"

Ollie was first up. He jogged out and offered Chaz a hand to shake, sweeping his fall of sun-lightened blonde hair out of his eyes with the other.

"What brings you here today, Ollie?"

Ollie laughed. "The show brought me, sir." The truth was Ollie had also applied to be on *Paradise Fought*, *The Bi-Bachelor*, and *What Would You Eat?* Among others. *Creature of the Night* hadn't even been in his top ten. Ollie was desperate for something, *anything*. "I want to be just like you."

Perish the thought. Chaz forced a smile. "Tell us more about you."

"Well, I grew up on a farm, and my dad, well, he always wanted me to help him out with farm stuff and follow in his footsteps, maybe. But it wasn't for me. It always made me too sad, eating some animal I'd been taking care of, you know? Although I did earn my allowance fixing fences, maintaining equipment, and such."

Chaz's head was nodding along, but his attention had fled at the first mention of farm life.

"I'm here to make my dad proud since I couldn't do what he wanted. I feel like if I win, well, that isn't exactly what he wanted for me, but me choosing my path and going after it and succeeding, *that* will make him happy."

"I find it charming that you seek to honor your elders." Delia's smile of approval had the same effect on Ollie's complexion as a good public shaming. Delia had honored her father with exsanguination the day after she'd risen. It was her favorite auto-anecdote.

"So then, you must not miss your family farm," Edmund said. "Did your father find it as easy to let go?"

Ollie looked stricken. "My dad is still there. We don't own the land anymore, but if I win, we'll get it back. I promised my dad."

Nodin laughed. It was a grating, rusty sound and sent chills even along Chaz's spine. The vampire twins cast furtive glances Nodin's way as they came to escort Ollie away.

It was almost time to go. The anticipation was almost too much to bear. He had spent most of the day trying to distract himself by playing Lord of the Manor, a fantasy impossible to maintain in the generic cube of a room he currently occupied. It had been easier to keep calm in the Manor that had been home for the past week with gargoyles flanking the fireplace and a four-poster bed. Jeff and every girl he'd ever slept with could have climbed into the bed all at once. Jeff lost a few minutes dwelling on that. Followed to its logical conclusion, the fantasy ended with the girls turning on him.

He must be nervous to be this unfocused. Chalk it up to jitters and focus on the plan. The plan wasn't too specific; specifics were hard to nail down when you didn't know what was coming, but he'd done his best. Besides, most of *The Plan* focused on after Jeff had won, when he would venture out and make the world a better place.

Jeff wasn't entirely clear on what he would do to make the world a better place, but he believed deeply in his vision. Jeff was a sucker for a cause. In college, he'd clocked more hours protesting than studying. When this was over, he figured he would make sure there were no more starving kids, and everyone would have clean water. It would probably be best for everyone to practice the same religion too. Jeff didn't much care what religion; he just knew it would solve a lot of problems if everyone prayed to the same God.

The fair thing would be to draw straws or something.

Jeff did a few jumping jacks to get his blood flowing just like he did before a softball game or a bowling match. The spirit of competition was strong in Jeff, although he was known to be as gracious in defeat as in victory. But he never planned on defeat.

A tap on the door alerted Jeff to the fact that he was on deck.

"Let's hear it for Stewart," Chaz said. *The Vampire Stewart?* Chaz would bet his last virgin Stewart wouldn't make it to the final challenge. Maybe he could sucker someone into taking that action. To atone for his inner doubt, Chaz signaled the crowd to cheer harder for Stewart.

"Not a chance," Delia said.

Stewart made it all the way across the stage with his hands sunk deep in his pockets and came to a stop beside Chaz without bothering to remove them. "How goes it?" Stewart said.

Not well for whoever had instructed Stewart on his entrance. Chaz offered a hand for Stewart to shake just to force those hands out of their pockets and disrupt the picture of uptight suburbia Stewart was projecting.

"Let me guess," Chaz said. It wasn't a guess. Even if he hadn't had The Voice's intelligence in his ear, he could almost smell the divorce. "Your wife threw you out, and there are kids who prefer not to see you."

"One girl, one boy," Stewart confirmed with a rueful smile. "Best things that ever happened to me."

Humans always said their children were the best things in spite of evidence to the contrary.

"Hi, Audrey. Hi, Logan," Stewart said. "They love the show, so it'll be like we're spending lots of time together while they watch me this season. I don't get to see them as much as I used to."

Pre-divorce, Chaz knew. He wouldn't see them much after the show either. But without misguided dreams, there wouldn't be reality television.

"So all you kids out there, give your dad a hug," Stewart said. "He loves you more than you know."

"Do you believe that your offspring will be suitably impressed with this gesture?" Nodin regarded Stewart with what Chaz would have taken for sympathy on a human face. "It is a potentially expensive gesture."

"Of course they will," Stewart said. Not even Stewart believed it.

"Give the overachieving dad one more round of applause and let's meet Jeff!" The wave of cheers lasted long enough for one contestant to be replaced by another. Jeff arrived and took Chaz's hand in both his own, doing a half bow and grinning so hard Chaz could count his molars.

"I love you, Chaz," Jeff gushed once Chaz had convinced him it was acceptable to stand upright. "I love all of you." Delia smiled as though she expected nothing less. Nodin nodded solemnly.

Edmund sneered.

"I've wanted to be on the show since season one. When you guys went public, I marched for Vampire rights. I was at the Million Fang March and everything." The Million Fang March had, through a somewhat glaring oversight, taken place during the day, so all the participants had been human. Although the vampire community had by and large appreciated the support, many of them hadn't forgiven the fact that all the protestors had sported fake vampire fangs.

"I'm ready for whatever you guys throw at me and winning this competition would be the proudest moment of my life." Jeff was so overcome with glee he was making Chaz jittery.

"And our pride be damned," Edmund said. He had not been a fan of the fangs.

"I don't think Edmund should be a judge next season," Delia announced. "You must approve of someone. A winner is necessary."

"Such a simplistic view may be all we can expect from you, Delia," Edmund quipped. "For me, it's about choosing the least of a dozen evils." A snicker came from someone in the audience followed immediately by a whispered apology. "And that one wore fake vampire fangs. Very racially insensitive. You wouldn't be defending him if he'd marched in blackface."

Delia ignored Edmund to address Jeff. "Your enthusiasm becomes you." Delia bestowed her praise like a precious gift; Jeff received it the same way.

"Although it is rumored that enthusiasm has gone awry in the past," Nodin said.

"They have no self-control," Edmund said. "These things are bound to happen."

"It was an accident," Jeff said.

"We've all done worse," Delia said forgivingly, "and Jeff's little friend did walk again."

"It is fascinating what they're doing with prosthetics these days," Chaz agreed and sent Jeff on his way before Edmund could berate him further for his humanity.

One minute to go. Donovan was ready to wipe the floor with the competition and go home. Well, not home. His wife was there with her sniveling and her endless *I'm the mother of your children and I deserve respect* crap. He was ready to go somewhere better.

On the face of it, this wasn't his sort of thing, but it was a way to get to what *was* his thing. Lately, Donovan had been thinking his thing wasn't sitting in an office forty hours a week, foisting his work off on subordinates, and occasionally firing one just to keep everybody else on their toes. His thing, he had decided, was swilling beer on the beach, somewhere with topless natives and college girls going wild.

Donovan was sick of providing for his ungrateful kids, and he was over going home to a wife full of quiet resentment. He had busted his ass for years to give them a house and cars and some goddamn status; their end of the bargain was silence in the matter of their trivial dissatisfactions.

Fuck them. It was his time. There was no reason a couple of teenagers and a forty-year-old woman couldn't fend for themselves. The gravy train was pulling out of the station, and if you didn't have a ticket in the form of twenty-year-old boobs, you weren't going to be on it.

They'd thrown him a party at the office like he was never coming back. He wasn't of course, but he hadn't told them. Judy had cried. Stupid bitch. He'd banged her once, and she'd gone so batty he'd had to have her transferred to another department.

It had been worse at home. The kids hadn't given him any grief, but Tara had cried incessantly.

Their concern was stupid. Like he'd have any trouble beating out the kind of losers that were going to be here. Those fucking emo *I heart my emotions* types had no understanding of what it took to dominate. Still, it was going to be a fucking awesome thing to be a—

The door opened. It was time.

"Next up, Donovan," Chaz said as that overgrown specimen made his way across the stage.

"Chaz," Donovan returned. Chaz paused the handshake when he noticed Donovan was squeezing full force. Chaz gave back one quick squeeze and felt the bones in Donovan's hand shift.

"Sorry, man," Donovan said hastily extracting his hand when Chaz allowed it. "Got carried away."

"So, Donovan," Chaz said. "What about being on the show appeals to you?"

"I want to do what I want when I want for as long as I want," Donovan said. "I mean, I got the first two handled, but I want to make it that way forever. Being a vampire is so prestigious nowadays. You know what I'm saying?"

"We all grasp your profound message," Edmund said before Chaz could comment.

"I'm psyched to get started. Ready to wipe the rest of these jerks off the map. Oh yeah, and I wanted to say hi to the wife and kids."

"Consider them greeted," Chaz said. "All of them. That's a big *Creature of the Night* hello to Tara, Vincent, and Tiffany. But, we can't forget little Sara Jane Wilson, who just came screaming into the world at seven pounds three ounces, and just for fun, let's also give a big hello to her mother, Shiela."

Donovan stiffened, and the crowd cheered. One of the vampire girls produced a cigar which Chaz presented with mock reverence to Donovan. "Congratulations. Head off toward the girls and we'll see you shortly for the first challenge." The crowd voiced their approval of the upcoming challenge or perhaps, of Donovan.

"Is it me," Rose said, nudging Dani with a toe to get her attention. "Or does the Donovan guy seem kind of date-rapey?"

"Totally," her dorm mate agreed. "And I bet he's on steroids too. Ollie is cute, though. I love his eyes."

"The farm guy?" Rose asked. "He has a good body, but he'd probably call you 'Ma'am' in bed."

"Better him than the whiny dad," Dani said.

"I feel bad for him," Rose said. "I bet his wife is a huge bitch."

"Yeah, but would you fuck him?"

Rose made a face. "He probably cries after sex."

It was time for some action. Kannon was pleased to be out of the Manor. As far as he was concerned, the gentle beige of the dressing room was far superior to his assigned bedroom which contained all the trappings of *The Tower of Terror* at Disney World. The Manor oozed money, with which he was familiar, but everybody knew money couldn't buy taste. Proof of that had been present in his surroundings for the past week.

He understood there was a theme. However, there was such a thing as going too far, and whoever had been in charge of decorating the place had raced full throttle across the line of good taste and never looked back.

The things we do for our parents. Although, truth be told, he hadn't been entirely against the idea, in spite of a brief period of *reconsideration*. But his father had explained the long-term benefits far outweighed any other consideration, and because his father's explanations were forceful and relentless, Kannon had found himself here.

Kannon had vowed one thing: he would not be a disappointment to his father. Now that he was here, he was fully committed, and he intended to win. There was no other option.

Besides, it was going to be pretty badass. Victory wasn't something money could buy. The opportunity to be here maybe, but the prize itself, no. The gold, no. Fuck gold—gold was for peasants. The platinum medal was something Kannon would earn, and once he'd earned it, the dynamics of the world would change.

The eldest son is about to make good. Something that wasn't fucking easy when you've spent your life being compared to your fuck-tard younger brother. The idiot who'd enlisted, in spite of being born into wealth. The golden boy who'd gotten his shit blown off the face of the earth while saving some loser. The shithead Kannon's brother had died for was a fucking mechanic now. If it had been up to Kannon, his brother would never have been allowed to sacrifice his life for that of some blue-collar grunt. It was maddening.

What the fuck was money for if it couldn't buy immortality?

One of the endless production assistants knocked on the door and informed him he was needed. Kannon swallowed his wordless rage and followed.

Brett was so fucking excited he could die. He had been bouncing around his room at the Manor like a bunny on a hotplate; his arrival at the studio had only amped him further. And he was stone cold sober; that was the funny thing. Not that Brett was much of a drinker. Here especially. Bad things could happen when you let yourself get wasted in a house full of strangers. Not to mention the abundantly stocked bar came accompanied by the proviso that to show up inebriated would mean dismissal. Rules didn't matter at fucking all to Brett because soon he would be restriction-free forever—but there was no point in being a rebel without a cause.

Brett had plans, big ones, for after. First, he was going to spend a long time banging Playboy Bunnies. *God Bless Hugh Heffner,* Brett thought, throwing a salute toward the heavens where presumably his idol was cavorting with the souls of promiscuous, yet pious, hotties. *Rest in peace, brother.*

Once he banged his way through the centerfolds of recent years, Brett was going to become a fucking rock star. Rock star Brett would graduate to banging Victoria's Secret models while the rest of the world worshiped him. (This would take some getting used to for the rest of the world, which had looked down its collective nose at Brett for years. That is, when it noticed him at all.)

The thought of all the artistically waxed pussy that would be his for the taking resulted in such a surge of glee that a high-pitched giggle erupted from his lips. Brett clapped a hand over his mouth and shook his head, admonishing his mirror self. *Not cool, Brett man. Not cool.*

It was time to get his shit together; he was finished being the outcast. He was no longer the loser wearing guy-liner or the creep who was fascinated with things best left to teenage girls. He had grown up. He was tall, he was nearly blonde, and most importantly, Brett was the guy who had been right to believe. He was the guy who was on the verge of snatching everything he'd ever wanted.

He could do this. He knew he could. When no one else believes in you, you believe in yourself. And once you're an immortal rock god, swimming in money and girls, you make every fucking naysayer who ever shit on your dream sorry they hadn't gotten on board. That was some heady stuff.

Someone knocked on the door with the five-minute warning. There was totally time to beat off again before they got started.

"Two guys left to meet," Chaz told the crowd who let loose another wave of appreciation. "So, let's bring out Kannon!"

Kannon was a beautiful specimen of human beauty and virility. Chaz was oblivious to these qualities. The only male virility he was concerned with being his own, but the women in the audience responded to Kannon in a way that made it unmistakable. It was, to a lesser degree and minus the fear (or love) of death, the way they responded to Chaz.

"Satisfy my curiosity," Chaz said. "How did your parents come up with 'Kannon?'"

Kannon rolled his eyes. "Our family name is Ball. They thought it was exceedingly clever. I've gotten used to it."

"What made you want to do the show?"

"Well, I just finished up my MBA. Originally, I was going to take a year to travel, but this seemed like a good option too. Since my parents were more supportive of my doing the show, here I am."

"So becoming a vampire is the new backpacking across Europe," Chaz said. "Good to know."

"Are you a virgin?" Delia asked.

"What difference would that make?" Edmund asked. *"There is no history of depravity that would deter you."*

"If they're not virgins, they may as well be skilled," Delia said.

Kannon shook his head and laughed. "But looking at you, I wish I was."

"All this talk of virgins is making me nervous," Cyri's dad said. "Stay close."

Cyri awarded her parent a patient smile and decided he was better off worried than reassured.

The smile Delia gave Kannon was more predatory. She made sure he got a good look at her fangs.

"No eating or fucking the contestants Delia," Chaz cautioned. "Rules are rules. Besides, I want to ask Kannon if he's heard from the Marquez family since they were deported."

"I don't know them," Kannon said.

Chaz waved a dismissive hand. "You might not, but you know people who did. Your brother died saving Manuel Marquez's life, and one of your old fraternity brothers had the rest of the family deported."

"They say it's a small world," Kannon said.

"Make them hate him," The Voice said.

"They do say that," Chaz said to Kannon. "It seems to be even smaller when you have money and the proper connections."

"Wouldn't it have been more reasonable to simply kill Manuel?" Delia said.

"Say goodbye, Delia," Chaz instructed.

"Goodbye, Delia," she said. A *ba-da-da* came from the band in the corner that, somehow, no one had noticed until now.

"I'm going to kill somebody," Edmund said to the room at large, leading Chaz to dismiss Kannon and announce the last contestant. The parade of humans needed to be wrapped up before one of the judges lost it.

Brett smelled of semen and hair gel. Chaz blithely avoided shaking his hand by instructing him to wave to the audience. "Tell us about yourself, Brett."

"The first thing you gotta know about me is I fucking love vampires," Brett said. "I mean, I love everything; I'd be a werewolf too if I could. Are there werewolves? I would be so stoked if there were werewolves. Don't get me wrong—vampires are the best. You guys have the sex appeal going. I mean, Delia, I love you. You are a goddess, seriously. I always fantasized about you guys when I was a teenager, and when it turned out you were real, man, best day of my life. But now *this* is the best day of my life. And the day I win this thing and get turned, *that's* going to be the next best day. By that, I mean the new best day in my chronology, not the second best day. What the hell was I saying?"

"That you're happy to be here," Chaz told him. "And we're happy to have you." Being a good show host often meant forsaking honesty.

"Head backstage and get ready for our first challenge. Let's have a big cheer for all of our worthy contestants who are getting ready to prove which of them is the most worthy of all!"

The crowd created such a din with their clapping hands and

screaming voices Edmund disappeared off the altar, which only encouraged the audience to take it up a notch.

"I'm going to marry him," Rose said.

"Not creepy loser guy?" Dani said. Brett would have been crushed to hear her assessment of him. "He looks greasy."

"No. Kannon." Rose hugged herself and let out a small sigh. "He's beautiful."

"He's okay," Dani said. Pretty boys weren't her thing. Pretty vampires, on the other hand, were. "But, Chaz is crazy hot."

"Chaz is scary," Rose corrected. "What about Jeff? He seems like your type."

"He's cute, I guess." Dani inspected her toenails to see if the polish needed repair. "But I don't think he's fun. His girlfriend probably has to go on protest marches every weekend."

"Yeah, that would suck."

Let Them Drink _ _ _ _ _.

When the clamor of the audience settled to a dull roar, Chaz grabbed their attention. "Okay, people, while they set the stage for our first challenge, let's dive into our first Friends and Family segment. As you know, someone is chosen from each contestant's life to give us a little background and insight. Or to let us in on an embarrassing secret. Let's all take a look at the screen and meet some people significant to Brett and to Cassie. First up, we'll see what Brett's friend Jonas had to say."

Heads swiveled toward the two jumbo screens on either side of the stage.

"Hey, man!" Jonas chortled from onscreen. "I can't believe you made it, man; you're so gonna die! But seriously, dude. I can't fucking wait to watch you on the show. I never thought you'd make it. None of us did, so just goes to show you, I guess. But I'm rooting for you, and I got your back, and when you're ear deep in pussy, throw some my way, dude. Throw some my way as long as it's not your leftovers. Yeah!"

Jonah disappeared from the screen. "Brings to mind 'birds of a feather', doesn't it?" Chaz said. "Let's check in with Cassie's friend Milay."

"Hi CassCass," said the previously recorded Milay. She might have been preparing to dance a solo at the Lincoln Center or performing La Bayadere with the Joffrey Ballet she was so heavily and flawlessly made up. "Just wanted to let you know, the other dancers and I are missing you much here at the company. A lot of people are hoping they let you come back, if you win, I mean. Well, some people are hoping. Including me, of course. It's too bad they're comparing vampire abilities to taking steroids, isn't it? Although, I guess it is unfair to those of us who have nothing but our talent. But don't worry, Cass. Everyone supports you so much, okay? Love, love, love, honey. Bye."

"Well, that was Milay, Cassie's close friend," Chaz said. "That seemed quite heartfelt."

"Humans are puny," Edmund said. "They lack even the fortitude to express their true disdain for each other. It is morally pathetic."

"Let's welcome Edmund back to the stage," Chaz said.

"Do not dare!" Edmund commanded. The audience immediately fell silent. Cyri grinned.

"Time for the fun to begin," Chaz yelled. "Behind me now is a table. At the table are twelve chalices, one for each of our fascinating contestants."

"Holy crap, Mildred, get out here!" The beagle had been asleep on the floor until Hal's outburst. He raised his head and blinked reproachfully at his human before rousing himself to check out the smells coming from the kitchen.

"I'm waiting on the popcorn." Mercifully, the microwave dinged.

"Hurry up; you're gonna to want to see this." *Un-fucking-believable*, Hal thought. *How did they get away with this shit?*

"Pause it, why don't you? I want to add some more butter."

"It's already buttered. Movie theater butter. You don't need more butter. You know I like to watch it live. Geezus, woman."

The floor creaked as Mildred came back from the kitchen. Old house, big wife. "What's going on?"

"They're gonna make them drink **blood**," Hal said.

"Well, it is a vampire show," Mildred said.

"It's human blood."

"It is not. It's chicken blood or something. Maybe pig blood. You'll see."

"Contestants," Chaz said from the television. "Join me for your first challenge!"

Hal and Mildred watched the twelve contestants file across the stage and take places behind the long table. They had already decided on their favorites; officially, Hal was rooting for Ollie because Hal too had grown up on a farm. Unofficially, Hal thought Lola was mighty interesting and hoped she'd be around for a while. Mildred was rooting for Cassie, who struck her as a nice girl.

"As everyone knows," Chaz was saying, "vampires subsist on blood. Any kind will do in a pinch, but since it became legal for consenting adults to offer themselves to us, there is no need to bother acquiring a taste for the swill."

Holy crud, Ollie thought. *They're tossing us in the deep end.* But like the vampire host said, the blood came from consenting adults, so nobody was hurting anybody. This wouldn't be any worse than choking down two helpings of Aunt Patty's blood-beef stuffing every Thanksgiving just to make her feel good. (To the consternation of his father, Ollie was a vegetarian the rest of the year.) He could do this.

"This is a simple challenge," Chaz said.

I can't believe they think this is a challenge, Lola thought. *Blood in a cup? Big fucking deal.* If they weren't going to make it harder than this, they might as well just declare her *Creature of the Night* right now. That way, everyone could forgo the boredom of watching them stand in a room packed with crosses or something equally lame. *I wonder if I get to keep the chalice. I could get a fortune for it on eBay.*

"In keeping with the spirit of the competition," Chaz went on. "We wanted the initial challenge to be something integral to vampire life."

This is great, Jeff thought. *This is classic.* You had to love vampires. Except some people still didn't, but Jeff dismissed those people as racist. Or maybe it was speciesist. It didn't matter. Jeff didn't approve of bigotry by any name. This challenge was fitting. It was clever, and they had dished up the blood in bejeweled cups like the contestants were royalty. Jeff had spent a lot of time in college working on his binge drinking. He could swallow the contents of a full Solo cup in 3.2 seconds. This was going to be great.

"And there is nothing more integral to us than blood."

Talk much? Cyri thought. Her dad grinned with excitement and patted her knee.

This is gross, Portia thought. *Where the hell did they get the blood?* It wasn't as though the contestants had vampire immunity to any blood-borne nastiness a donor was harboring. She would have called this whole endeavor a mistake except here she was on the set of a worldwide fucking phenomenon. Everybody was going to know her name. Portia reminded herself to smile.

"We chose all of those who donated blood for tonight's challenge from our studio audience," Chaz said. "So let's give them a round of applause." The crowd clapped obediently. As they cheered, they assessed their neighbors for telltale signs of blood donation.

Bunch of pussies. Donovan rolled his eyes. *All these assholes are getting squeamish over a little blood.* As though none of them had ever ordered a fucking medium rare steak. So what if this blood came out of a human being? If a mild ick factor was all these loser vamps had to bring, this shit was going to be his. *Donovan, Creature of the Night* and, more importantly, free fucking man.

"Each chalice contains sixteen ounces of blood," Chaz said.

Smells like copper, Emily thought. Although *smells like how copper tastes* was more accurate. It could be the cup. Could it be the cup? Did metal have a smell? A coppery smell? How had she never noticed whether or not she could smell metal? Walking into the biggest challenge of one's life without even knowing what one's nose was capable of was, well, there was no other word but slipshod. *Stop. It's unlikely that there will be a smelling competition.* Even if there was, the time to think about it would be then not now. One little cup of blood. The trick would be to disregard how disgusting this was, just like when swallowing anything else that had come out of a fellow human being.

"To complete the challenge, you must consume all the blood in your chalice," Chaz instructed.

I wonder if it will taste the same. Madeline drummed her fingers lightly on the table in front of her chalice and contemplated her advantage. Everyone else would probably have to get used to the thickness, the taste, the knowledge they were drinking human blood. A few months ago, Madeline had been invited to a party where those who were so inclined had gotten together for some ceremonial blood sharing.

They hadn't been graced with the presence of a real vampire, but with the help of a Swiss Army Knife, Madeline had exchanged blood with an incredibly sexy and complex second-grade teacher. She had been disappointed when he never called, but maybe it was meant to be one of those special nights that could never be duplicated, only savored. And it was enough to know he would regret not calling once he saw her on the show.

The main thing was, ever since she'd been green-lighted for the show, she'd been practicing. Madeline had already tasted blood today; she tasted blood pretty much every day, and the only thing new was this wasn't her own.

"Please don't spill," Chaz said. "That tablecloth is an antique." The audience laughed.

In for a penny, Cassie thought. She was trying to get through as much of this as possible on autopilot. *Don't think of the blood,* she instructed herself. *Do think of being able to dance forever.* Not that she was judging. She was focusing. To reach the goal, you had to envision the goal, and maybe try to get through the little things that stood between you and your goal without dwelling on them too much. *Pretend it's Kool-Aid. With a little ketchup mixed in for texture.*

"For added motivation," Chaz said, "we have a special surprise planned for every contestant who completes this challenge."

No big deal, Stewart told himself. He thought of how his kids would react when they saw the challenge and smiled. Audrey would roll her eyes and swear she was embarrassed every time she brought her dad's antics up to her friends. Logan would brag unabashedly and hope to grow up to be like his dad. Stewart would cheerfully do a lot worse than drink a little cup of blood for that. Marcy would hate every minute of the kids adoring Stewart, but she wouldn't be able to keep from watching with them. Maybe somewhere along the way she would remember old feelings, the ones Stewart still hadn't managed to forget.

Chaz told the contestants, "You twelve were handpicked from the millions who wanted to be with us this season."

"Who did the picking?" Delia asked.

Chaz nearly snorted. *"I think you know."* Aloud, he added, "So remember, there is a reason each of you is here."

Fucking savages. Kannon was beginning to doubt he was on the optimum path to making something of himself. Jeweled chalice or no, this whole thing felt about two rungs up the ladder from shooting crack in a whorehouse. *Did one shoot crack? Maybe not.* Kannon had friends that would know, but they had neglected to educate him on the finer points of crack. Kannon knew he was considered something of a prude in his circle, indulging only occasionally in a coke-fueled social weekend.

But that wasn't the point. There was nothing classy about

CREATURE OF THE NIGHT

bodily fluids; *that* was the point. But he would rise to this challenge as he would rise to those ahead. Kannon was determined that, when this was over, he would answer to no one.

"We see something special in each of you," Chaz said.

"They should have listed their special qualities in the program," Cyri said. "So they wouldn't be such a secret to the rest of us."

"There's a program?" Her father fished out a twenty. "Get two."

Chaz continued his hype. "The world is rooting for you."

This is lame, Celeste thought. *Where's the danger in having a beverage?* If you couldn't expect a little more peril from a freaking vampire reality show, what was the point? And the audience was salivating like a few cups of blood were a big fucking deal. This was why she couldn't deal with people. They were always so happy about nothing. This was infuriating to Celeste, who was never happy about anything.

"This is the moment when you reach for immortality," Chaz said.

Yes, I am a creature of the night, a drinker of blood, a bringer of your darkest desires. Brett was practicing the conversation he would have with the incredible girl in the second row the minute they crowned him *Creature of the Night*. There might not be an actual crown. Brett couldn't remember seeing a vampire sport a crown, but that didn't mean he couldn't have one made. It was about individual style after all, and his style was going to be heavy on crowns and hot women. Brett approved of this challenge. He knew destiny when he saw it, and he was squirming in his seat at the thought of being seconds away from his first taste of immortality.

"So tonight," Chaz paused for emphasis, "when you raise your cups, you will have the privilege of toasting with the blood of mankind.

"The first contestant to finish the contents of their chalice will be declared the winner of this challenge. Any contestant who does not finish will be eliminated from the competition," Chaz concluded. "Are you all clear?"

"It's simple enough, even for humans," Edmund said.

"Will you never be silent?" Delia asked.

Eleven hundred miles away, Mildred frowned.

"I told you!" Hal said.

"Quiet, I'm trying to hear." Mildred steadfastly ignored Hal's rightness. "I don't like the judge." Her words were garbled by the glut of popcorn she was pushing into her mouth. The beagle pressed against her leg, hoping to remind Mildred that he liked popcorn too.

"Him or her?"

"Him."

"Yeah," Hal said. "There they go."

"I can see just as well as you." Mildred forgot to guard her popcorn against the dog as she watched the contestants seize their cups and commence guzzling. The girl in pink hesitated before drinking. "Look at that one; she smelled it first. You never want to smell strange food before you taste it. Everybody knows that."

"Not everybody," Hal said. "The other one smelled hers too."

"You smell your food," Mildred pointed out. "I see you."

"It's gonna be a guy that takes it," Hal predicted.

"Yeah, because men don't care what they put in their mouths," Mildred said, pushing the dog's head out of her popcorn. "Look at the slutty girl, though."

Lola hadn't stopped for breath, and her cup was nearly upside down over her face. A moment later, she slammed her chalice on the table and shouted, "Done!"

A second chalice hit the table. Then a third and fourth. They belonged to Donovan, Emily, and Jeff respectively. Two seconds elapsed between the moment Jeff's chalice hit the table and the one when the bloody contents of his stomach joined it.

The remaining contestants kept swallowing gamely while they

edged away from Jeff.

"I'd get that back in your stomach if I were you," Chaz advised. Jeff visibly heaved again but managed to keep anything else from escaping his body.

"That is some hardcore stuff," Mildred said. Hal was too absorbed in watching Jeff put his lips on the table and start slurping to answer. Everyone had finished except for Jeff and Madeline. Jeff was reclaiming the contents of his stomach one slurp at a time. Madeline was taking one tiny sip after another, all the while looking as if she was struggling not to follow Jeff's vomitous example. Madeline emptied her chalice just before Jeff took a final tongue swipe across his bit of table.

"Congratulations, contestants," Chaz said. "One big hurdle down." He paused to watch Lola complete a slow back and forth sway and then topple out of her chair. "And that is one contestant down. We'll see you after the break with the little surprise I mentioned earlier."

"That was incredible," Mildred said.

"You think she's dead?"

"Nah." Mildred heaved herself up and headed for the kitchen. "You want some of the guacamole on chips?"

"Why not?"

Delia licked the last drop of blood from her lips and regarded the body of her late husband fondly. He had been a beautiful creature—he still was—and he had been so pleased to be summoned to visit her tonight. But it was better to say goodbye when things were at their best. Mediocrity and resentment were the forte of human beings and never for her. Delia had learned that many husbands ago.

Delia had given Marco a precious gift when she had chosen him, and the price of his privilege had been paid today. Delia could not allow a human who knew her secrets to return to his former existence. As nice as catch and release sounded, it was highly impractical. Marco, once made hers, would never have been the same if she had severed their connection, and she couldn't bear to have him underfoot while he lived out his natural life.

So, no more Marco, but Delia felt sure that if given the chance, Marco would have made his choice again and again.

Delia checked the mirror to make sure she hadn't bloodied her outfit. She was, of course, still perfection.

"And we're back," Chaz said. They had prepared phase two of the first challenge, the real challenge. The twelve contestants were still onstage, but now they were all unconscious.

"While it's true that most of you humans find drinking human blood a bit off-putting, it's not really a big deal. Especially considering we so graciously put it in cups for the convenience of our contestants.

"So, we wanted to add a little something extra to the first challenge. Undead life can be full of surprises, and in the spirit of surprise, we drugged the contestants' blood so they wouldn't have time to prepare."

The audience cheered the drugging. *"Drug the blood! Drug the blood! Drug the blood!*

"As I said, we already did." Chaz held up a hand to quiet the crowd. "We hate to cater to stereotypes, and I don't know anyone who sleeps in a coffin, but tonight, that's what our contestants will be doing. They are tucked in their coffins, snug as bugs, although they may not sleep particularly soundly.

"It's dark in there, so when they come to, they won't be able to see anything, and they won't be able to hear much more. Hang tight, friends; they should be waking up shortly."

"I said, turn it off!"

"No way, babe. This is the best show ever."

"They're torturing those people." Gina crossed her arms and glared at her hot boyfriend who was currently not so hot on account of being a super-douche.

"It's not torture," Brad told her. "You do know that, like, millions of people auditioned for this show, right? One of those people gets to be a real fucking vampire."

"Someone is screaming," Gina said. "How is that not torture?"

"I think it's that Kannon guy," Brad spoke with a bit of resentment. He had applied to be on the show but had never heard back. "The Richie Rich one."

"It is him, and you're a jerk." To her credit, Gina was mainly concerned with the general brutality of the show. Only a small part of her was upset they were being mean to the hot guy.

"I can totally see up the librarian's nose," Brad said. "Those coffin cams are amazing."

"I'm leaving," Gina said. She told herself she was never coming back. It was something she told herself once or twice a week. "You make me sick."

"Babe," Brad said, but Gina had already slammed the door behind her. "It's not my fault. It's right there. I can't *not* look."

"We learn a lot about our contestants during the challenges," Chaz told the audience. "Like right now, we're learning Kannon does not enjoy small spaces."

The crowd watched the monitors where they could see Kannon pounding and clawing at the lid of his coffin and nodded wisely. They could indeed perceive Kannon's aversion.

I'm dying. I'm fucking dying. Kannon continued to pound on the lid of the coffin. "I can't breathe!"

"Scary stuff, huh, kiddo?" Cyri's dad said.

Cyri only nodded.

"He's fine," Chaz told the audience. "We did a test run with one of the interns. He made it for two days with minimal permanent damage."

Emily had pushed and prodded her way around her coffin with no results. Since no one but Donovan resembled the Hulk, it seemed they were meant to spend some time confined to their lovely mahogany resting places. Although there was no way to know if the coffin was mahogany. Pine was a lot cheaper, and there were twelve of them, although the budget for the show had to be huge. *Not the point.* She was in good shape; she was comfortable enough, but she wished whoever was screaming would get a grip.

There's probably a fucking camera in here, Portia thought. She worked an arm up and smoothed her hair. She pasted on a serene smile. *Is that right? Is it believable to smile? Maybe I should act scared and then overcome it.* This was bullshit. Someone could have provided at least minimal direction. Was she surprised? Had she seen it coming? *I should try to get out,* Portia thought. "Help!" she cried and performed a few gentle thumps on the lid of her coffin. She hoped the angle of the camera was flattering.

Chaz listened to Cassie sob. He would have thought she'd do a bit better after the way she had stood up Edmund. It wasn't PC to say, but humans were weak. Once you'd turned four, there was no excuse to be afraid of the dark.

"First rule of *Creature of the Night,*" Chaz said to the audience. "Don't be afraid of the night."

Don't be afraid was exactly the point Cassie was trying to make to herself. *You're fine. This is just like being in bed at home.* The coffin was easily as comfortable as her bed at home, but at home, she had the comfort of light spilling from the closet. And the freedom to get out. *Nothing in here but you,* she told herself. *Be brave.* Cassie closed her eyes and tried to pretend there was light behind her lids.

Chaz could hear Portia reciting something. He finally placed it as one of Eleanor's monologs from *The Lion in Winter*. Nodin had known the real Eleanor of Aquitaine. Chaz had always envied him that.

Donovan was getting a cramp. He wasn't a pussy like whatever bitch he could hear crying, but he was a big guy and this was getting uncomfortable. He pounded on the sides of his coffin for a while to vent some frustration but stopped when he realized he had bloodied his hands. There was no point in fucking himself up. He needed to be in peak condition to win this thing, assuming they ever offered a challenge that was actually a challenge. So far, they'd had something to drink followed by forced quiet time. They might as well be in preschool.

"Looks like Donovan has given up," Chaz said. "He's going to have to buy the coffin now that he's gotten it all bloody."

"He is strong," Delia said. "For a human."

Edmund sneered. "For a human, indeed."

"I see someone is completely relaxed," Chaz said. Ollie had woken up briefly, addressed his situation, and gone right back to sleep. Chaz identified Ollie for the crowd.

"Wake him up! Wake him up! Wake him up!"

Chaz leaped to the top of Ollie's coffin and rattled the contents. "Five more minutes," Ollie mumbled.

Chaz steeled himself to endure an uneventful night.

This is awesome, Brett thought. He had already decided he would sleep in a coffin every night once he was a vampire. It would have to be bigger though. There was plenty of room for one person to be comfortable if you weren't claustrophobic like the dude down the line, but Brett planned on having company. He would have something made custom. It would have room for Brett and several flexible young ladies to cavort in comfort. *Creature of the Night! Whoo!*

Portia had gotten tired of performing for an audience that possibly couldn't even see her. Instead, she practiced her Awakening. She would be lying peaceful and lifeless, her hands folded beautifully over her heart, and then her eyes would open and she would be reborn, ageless and mighty. She couldn't work out whether her eyes would pop open all at once or languidly, taking in the world that would seem brand new, savoring each tiny increment. She parted her lips slightly and tried again.

"And that," Chaz said gesturing to Portia's monitor, "is why we don't tell them about the cameras."

Jeff was grateful to be lying in the dark. He didn't know or care whether he was being observed. At this moment, the fact he didn't have to deal with anything that had come out of another person was enough. *At least I tried. Who cares? Everyone tried. But only I puked. Not being able to drink blood might be a deal breaker; although, it's probably more appealing after the change.* He lay quietly with his arms crossed over his chest and replayed his embarrassment over and over. The audience mostly ignored him, and Jeff would have been glad to know it.

Celeste remained unimpressed. She had put everything she had into getting here, and here sucked. And not in the literal vampy way she'd anticipated. Celeste had been dreaming of fangs for a long time, fangs that were not her own, fangs that would bring her peace. Still, this was peaceful enough for now. She could ignore the hum generated by the throng of thousands that was the audience and enjoy being alone in the dark. Celeste liked her coffin. It would probably be even better when it was for real.

Lola was fuming. Not at the incarceration, but at the duping that had been employed to get them there. Anyone who was too cowardly to climb in and pull the lid shut behind them shouldn't be here. It wasn't a big fucking deal to stay put when you had no choice. She would have shown everyone she didn't flinch if she had the chance, and she would have pointed out that perhaps a more active demonstration of their worth would be appropriate. But there would be other opportunities. In the meantime, she would occupy herself.

"Chaz, darling," Delia said just as Lola achieved a satisfying rhythm. "Would you mind?"

The Voice and Little P sat in the high corner office and watched Lola in her coffin. The Voice tilted his head and leaned closer to the screen. "Is that what you told her to do?"

"Not exactly," Little P admitted. "She put a personal spin on the instructions."

"Numbers?"

"Strong. And counting."

"Until the censors step in, leave her to it," the Voice commanded Chaz. "The live SM content is unbelievable."

Onstage, Chaz checked the monitor. Across one of the screens, various social media updates posted by fans scrolled.

"You can't see much," he said to Delia. "She hasn't taken her pants off."

"Yes, but what do the censors say?" Delia smiled. "I find it hard to believe the parental warnings mention sexual situations."

The audience perked up at the mention of sexual situations. Cyri's dad thought about covering her eyes, but then Delia stretched.

There was a pause during which Chaz tensed for action, the audience craned their necks, and Lola carried on.

Finally, Riley and Kiley appeared from backstage. They spoke to Chaz in perfect unison. "The censors say to make her stop."

Chaz swore and sprang onto Lola's coffin. He banged on the lid and told her to get her hand out of her *fucking pants*. "There are children watching." Chaz pitched his voice so Lola could hear, and hopefully the audience could not. *Fucking humans.*

"At least it is only the one," Nodin said.

"So far." Delia smiled to herself. *Humans.*

Two down, Stewart told himself. Technically, the coffin challenge was still happening, but Stewart knew he'd be fine. He'd slept in worse places. Although, he should try to stay awake. He'd heard the audience chanting a while back, and he'd gathered they were expected to endure their incarceration in wakefulness. It was tough, after such a big week, not to relax into the satin pillow and drift off. To stay awake, Stewart crooned the songs he had sung to his children when they were babies. Audrey would later roll her eyes in real embarrassment, but Stewart would never know.

Madeline was trying to talk herself down. She was clenching her fists so tightly; she had already drawn blood from her palms. She wasn't afraid of dying so much as she was of living forever in this tiny box. That couldn't happen. She was meant for more. Her parents always said so. They said God had a plan for Madeline. Madeline hoped this wasn't the whole of it. After a while, she prayed. *Please. I'm sorry. I never, ever worshiped Satan no matter what my parents thought. But you know. You know. Save me.*

Madeline didn't realize it, but it wasn't long before the wailing in her head started to flow from her lips.

"These people are whack jobs," Dylan said, his voice full of admiration. At his side, Joey wagged his tail. Dylan was sure the wag indicated agreement.

"Said the guy conversing with a cocker spaniel," Bekka said.

Dylan rolled his eyes at the dog who wagged again, this time demonstrating sympathy for his best friend with the pesky sister. Bekka didn't understand Joey's emotional range.

"Fine. Who's a whack job?" Bekka perched on the arm of the sofa since Dylan and Joey were taking up the rest.

"Everybody," Dylan said. He turned up the volume in an attempt to drown out his sister's voice then reached for the bag of chips she was holding. "Give me some of those."

"Who exactly are you talking about?" Bekka demanded. "The vampires?"

"No. The people in the coffins," Dylan explained. "It's a

challenge."

"Sounds really difficult," Bekka said. She was naturally inclined to be scornful of anything her little brother admired.

"Hey, it is for the claustrophobic guy," Dylan said. "And some girl was crying. Joey had to go outside, so I'm not sure why."

"Who's that guy?" Bekka said, nudging Dylan and Joey along the couch so she could make herself more comfortable. "He's totally fuckable."

"Gross. He's the host, and he's probably like a thousand years old."

"Hmmm. Well, he looks like he's twenty-two." Bekka considered. "Maybe being a vampire isn't completely stupid after all."

"And we're back," Chaz said. "It was a long night for the contestants and, I know, for some of you who stayed up all night watching them squirm."

"Squirm and scream and tear the flesh from their fingers in an attempt to escape," Nodin said.

"A big thank you to our esteemed judge, Nodin, for the recap," Chaz said.

"Always happy to assist," Nodin said, not recognizing the sarcasm.

"We have a very special surprise for you before we get started. Please give the best hello ever to special guest judge, Vlad the Impaler!"

It was a cheer to end all cheers. Everyone, even those who weren't heavily into vampire lore, had heard of Vlad. Nodin and Edmund looked a bit sour. Neither clapped, of course. A bat winged easily around above the stage. The lower it got, the bigger it looked. When it finally came to rest on the fourth throne, everyone could see it was the size of a raven. The throne was gold and adorned with blood diamonds as was required by Vlad's contract. Riley and Kiley had been forced to haul it out from backstage because the humans couldn't lift it and had broken two cranes in their various attempts.

Everyone was watching the gigantic fucking bat, and nobody was breathing much. Later, every human there would swear they blinked and opened their eyes to find Vlad sitting on the throne like he'd been there all night.

A fresh bout of cheers broke out; someone started chanting followed by someone else then all their neighbors until shortly the entire audience was chanting, *"Im–pa–ler! Im–pa–ler! Im–pa–ler!"*

"Let's get back to it!" Chaz bellowed. "About an hour ago, the contestants were released from their coffins and given the opportunity to freshen up. Those who damaged themselves received first aid. They will be rejoining us momentarily for the judge's recap." *As though they hadn't all had to live through it.* "In the meantime, we have questions and comments from viewers."

The questions were selected, by someone on the production staff, from the cyber storm of pleas for attention that accompanied each show. Chaz was given the questions cold to promote an authentic reaction. Someday, Chaz was going to drain the production staff. Or at least, a few key underlings.

"This is from Kayla, in Southampton, New York." Chaz read the question aloud as it appeared on the monitor beneath Kayla's selfie.

"I don't understand how you can use real human blood. Isn't that illegal?"

"Well, Kayla," Chaz said. "I won't say you asked a stupid question. However, it is a question to which you would know the answer if you'd ever once watched the news or checked Wikipedia. Since you, and I'm sure many other viewers, are too busy for reading, I'll explain. Thanks to the Supreme Court's decision in *Swadle vs. the Board of Mental Health and Supervision*, people have the right to do whatever they want with their bodies.

"For example, they can donate a bit of blood for the show or submit to being drained to death for the pleasure of a vampire. Humans have these rights regardless of their state of mental competence. Unrelated to our show, the *Swadle* ruling is also why you now have unrestricted access to any drug you desire and why doctor performed suicide is legal in all fifty-one states. Fun fact: all of the blood the contestants drank last night was donated by members of our studio audience."

"He already said that," Cyri said.

"Drink our blood! Drink our blood! Drink our blood!" Cyri's dad clapped and chanted along with the rest of the audience.

Please, Cyri thought. *Drink all of it.*

Before Chaz could quiet them down, there was a scream from the audience. Chaz saw Vlad was not on his throne because he had popped into the audience and sunk his fangs into a little redhead. He hadn't even had the decency to go for the neck. Vlad had picked the girl up, and his head was buried between her thighs. While she shrieked, her mother beat at Vlad's back with her purse. It looked like Vlad was doing something entirely different to the girl until you factored in her reaction. Chaz launched himself toward Vlad and arrived to find Delia already there, wrenching Vlad's head from beneath the girl's skirt. Chaz grabbed the mother's flailing purse arm and caught her around the waist.

Nodin had roused himself to take charge of the girl while Delia hauled Vlad back to the altar and deposited him on his throne.

"The taste from the thigh is so dark, so sweet," Vlad said. Chaz thought he was speaking only to Delia, but, of course, everyone could hear. "Neck, bah. She begged me to drink, did you not hear?"

"They were just participating in the show," Delia said. "Not volunteering to be dinner. Think of them like the chorus in the old plays. Part of the performance, not for eating."

"I always ate from the chorus," Vlad said. "They were the best part of the theater and easily replaceable. It is such a scandal when you eat Oedipus or Electra. No one ever misses one or two from the chorus."

Delia had taken Nodin's seat putting her next to Vlad. She was back to looking serene and fragile, but one hand rested on Vlad's arm, and Chaz had total faith in her ability to restrain him.

"Have you had enough for now?" Chaz said. There was no point in trying to explain the niceties of eating modern humans to a vampire of Vlad's age and condition.

Vlad waved a hand, acknowledging his current state of satiation. Nodin popped back to the altar.

"That was exciting, wasn't it?" Chaz said, and the crowd roared in agreement. The girl and her mother cheered along with everyone else. The girl even looked proud to have been chosen as a snack. "Let's take a look at what one more viewer had to say. His name is Cody, and he's calling from Indio, California."

"Love the show. But it needs some nudity."

Chaz sighed, a big exasperated one for the benefit of the audience. "Glad to hear you love the show, Cody, but we do have standards of decency. If nudity is what you're looking for, flip over to the Penthouse channel. After our show, of course. Contestants, come on out!

The twelve would be vampires filed out in various states ranging from exuberant to devastated and lined up facing the audience and judges.

The crowd whispered excitedly, and the judges sat. The contestants stood awaiting judgment. Eventually, the crowd abandoned their speculations and fidgeting and settled into silence.

Delia spoke. "Some of you did well, some of you behaved shamefully. And while the goal was to spend the night in a coffin without panicking, we do not feel that those of you who went to sleep earned the same respect as those who endured wakefully."

Ollie and Stewart looked abashed.

"However, those who slept were more impressive than those who pissed themselves with fear," Edmund said.

"Humans always piss themselves," Vlad said.

"I'm claustrophobic," Kannon said. "I was diagnosed as a child."

"No one cares about your acceptance of your infirmity," Edmund said. "And no one cares why little dancers are afraid of the dark."

"So unkind, Edmund," Delia said. "Although, not wrong."

"Right now, we're going to see which contestants you, our beloved audience, voted to eliminate from the competition. Girls, the envelope, please."

Riley and Kiley glided out bearing a silk envelope between them. Chaz nodded solemnly as they placed it in his hand, then he made sure to open it with proper panache.

"Okay. Because, by an overwhelming majority, the audience thinks you're a pussy, they have voted to eliminate you, Kannon."

"I'm—"

"Claustrophobic," Chaz interrupted. "We know. Sharing your shame, chosen for elimination by the audience for being 'a ginormous slut,'—which, by the way, is trending hashtag 'ginormous slut'— is Lola."

"The sisterhood at work," Delia said. "We are grateful for your input. Now for our conclusions. It was a disappointing showing by some of you, but we must make eliminations, and you have made it easy this time."

"It is always easy to eliminate," Edmund said.

"Stewart and Ollie," Chaz said. "We have addressed the fact you slept through the challenge, but neither of you panicked. Step back, you made it to round two."

Ollie grinned, bowed his head, and stepped back. Stewart waved to the camera, hoping his kids would understand he was waving to them, and joined Ollie behind the others.

"As for Lola," Delia said, "you have brought shame to the show and yourself."

"No more shame than any other human," Edmund said.

"Would you mind terribly not saying things like that aloud?" Delia asked.

"For you," Edmund said. *"I will make the attempt."* Of course, he couldn't.

"Do you have anything to say about your behavior, Lola?" Nodin said.

"Just that everybody does it, and it's perfectly natural," Lola said. "And I didn't know there was a camera in there."

Delia snickered. Nodin sighed.

"What a lucky thing you have no one who would be shamed by your behavior," Edmund said. "No children, for example."

Amen, Cyri thought.

Lola's pause was so brief it went almost unnoticed. "Nope. No children."

"Indeed," Edmund said.

"You may step back," Nodin said. "But please keep in mind some things are just not done on television."

Lola resumed her smile and thrust a triumphant fist into the air. She joined Stewart and Ollie behind the others.

"Emily, good job. You worked it out. You made all reasonable attempts to escape and then decided that your challenge was to make it through the night where you were. Because of that you are moving on to the next challenge."

The contestants still in the front row began to look worried.

"Donovan, you behaved like a—"

"Typical human?" Edmund suggested.

"Barbarian," Nodin finished. "We suggest you rethink how you comport yourself in the future. We will not have in our ranks one who behaves thus."

"However," Delia added, "you may step back. Brett, you accepted your confinement if not gracefully, then at least gleefully. You may step back."

"Thank you," Brett said. "And I just want to say, I completely agree. Humans are nothing compared to you guys. I want to be more. I'm going to do everything I can to be worthy."

"We are not getting stuck with that one," Nodin said.

CREATURE OF THE NIGHT

"We can't decide during the first challenge," Delia rebuked.

"But you agree?"

"Obviously."

"Portia, thank you for the entertainment," Delia said. "Although, your Eleanor was nothing like the friend I knew."

"I do not understand your fascination with pretending to be an old one," Nodin said.

"I like to play the part," Delia told him. *"I've missed so much."*

"There is much to come," Nodin said. *"It is true, you would have enjoyed Eleanor."*

"For what it's worth," Chaz said to Portia, "I thought your Ophelia was inspired."

"Yes," Delia said. "We must, at some point, rouse ourselves to watch some of your film."

Portia managed a smile. "I'd be honored."

"Step back," Nodin said.

"Celeste," Delia said. "We know your purpose, but your performance, while not special, was not an embarrassment. You may step back."

Vlad perked up. *"I would—"*

"You won't," Delia interjected.

"Two of you are safe," Chaz said. "The other two—"

"We are beginning to resemble the sound and the fury," Delia said. "Madeline and Jeff are eliminated."

"We have a process, Delia," Chaz said. "There's an envelope."

"Then get on with it."

"Cassie and Kannon," Chaz said. "You disgraced yourselves, but luck was with you. Others behaved far more unfortunately. Step back but be warned, we expect better." Kannon and Cassie scurried to take their places in the desirable line.

The front row now consisted of Madeline and Jeff. Madeline reached for Jeff's hand. Jeff took a half step to the side, putting himself beyond her reach.

"We were nearly finished," Delia said. "The process was

becoming excruciating and is not necessary for its own sake."

"They must be told why—"

"The male pissed himself, and the other one spent the entire night praying," Edmund said, indicating Jeff and Madeline respectively. "I would have thought even humans possessed that much reason. You should know we're going to have to throw your coffin away."

Jeff sank to his knees and started to cry. Madeline stared blankly at some point in the air. Chaz called the girls to wrest the losers off the stage.

The audience erupted with a nice mix of cheers for those moving on and abuse for Jeff and Madeline.

"The contestants are headed back to the Manor for a little down time before their next challenge, but there is one thing they're going to do before they rest."

"Now make them confess! Now they must confess! We want them to confess! Confess! Confess! Confess!"

"The chanting starts to grate sooner every season," Delia said.

"Exactly right," Chaz told the crowd. "After each challenge, the contestants will head back to the Manor where they are staying for the duration of the competition. There, they will have time to rest and get to know one another. They will also be participating in confessionals where they will share their thoughts and feelings as our journey progresses. So we all have a chance to check in, hear how they're doing, and judge them for whatever inner turmoil they choose to express."

The crowd screamed with excitement.

"We'll see you back here tomorrow night for the second challenge," Chaz said. "For those of you who are staying in the CreatureLand Hotel, the shuttles are standing by to whisk you to gothic paradise."

The judges disappeared the same way they had arrived, as one.

"We better run for the shuttle," Cyri's dad said. "We don't want to miss the first confessional." Cyri sighed and followed her father.

Behind her, she could hear Chaz calling goodnights to the departing crowd.

Mentally, Chaz was playing the vampire version of Fuck, Marry, Kill with the audience, which was obviously Fuck, Eat, Kill. Chaz found this version far more sophisticated; all the options could be easily accomplished at once.

Confessional: Lola

"What's up, world? That was some shit, right? I can't believe a bunch of vampires would be so uptight just because I let my fingers do the walking, but it just goes to show you never know how someone's going to react. Except it probably won't be good. For the kids watching, that finger-walking thing means I touched my pussy. And you know what, kids? Everybody does it. Touches their pussy, I mean, not mine. Or their dick, it's okay for boys too. The point is if something is natural and healthy, we shouldn't be ashamed to do it, even if other people can see. I knew they were leaving us in there until they let us the fuck out, you know?"

"But nothing has changed. I'm still here to win. You better believe I'm going to be the last bloodthirsty bitch standing. And, by the way, I liked drinking blood. It made me feel strong. I think I'm already halfway there. See you when I'm Creature of the Night, bitches!"

Confessional: Brett

"Holy fuck! The coffins were awesome. And the blood. We totally drank human blood. I couldn't believe it when that guy puked. He almost puked on me! Ha! But I kicked ass. And none of the judges said anything bad about me during the eliminations, which is good. It's got to be good. Unless it's bad. Maybe they're not interested in me. Shit. Maybe I have to be crazier. I should do something. Get their attention. That's it; that's the plan."

"So, be on the lookout America! It's getting hot in here! Woot! Woot! The rest of the world should be on the lookout too. I don't discriminate. And, oh yeah, I want to give a shout out to Jonah and all the lovely ladies. I am going to fuck this shit up!"

The contestants had been returned to the Manor and, for the first time, were not isolated in their rooms. After her session in the confessional, Lola roamed the Manor celebrating her quasi-freedom and searching for someone she could torment under the guise of social interaction. Unable to locate suitable prey, she swooped into the cavernous living room and flung herself across a black velvet sofa.

It was hideously uncomfortable.

It wasn't until she'd rearranged all the pillows and hung one leg over the sofa back that she spotted Jeff sunk into an armchair in the corner.

"What are you doing back here?" Lola said.

"I have no idea," Jeff told her. "They brought us both back and said we're staying."

"Who did?"

"Delia and Edmund," Jeff said. "Who the fuck do you think? It was some human lackey."

"After they eliminated you?" Lola sneered. "Fuck that." Let the losers go.

"He said we're still under contract," Jeff said.

"Under contract for what?"

Jeff shrugged and picked up the television remote. "Maybe we're backup in case one of you meets a tragic end."

"Sounds like bullshit," Lola said.

"What was the deal with the kid stuff?" Jeff said.

"What kid stuff is that?"

"I believe the exact words were 'My body, my choice' and 'Genetically speaking.'"

"So the fuck what?"

"So, you're the surrogate that decided not to be a surrogate."

"I got picked to be here," Lola said. "Which is better. They wouldn't have let me on the show in that condition. Where's what's-her-name? The other big loser."

"Sorry to see none of those death threats came through," Jeff said.

Lola blew him a kiss. "At least the check cleared."

Jeff had marched for many more causes than just vampire rights in his time. He turned a dead-eyed glare on Lola and turned up the volume on the television.

"Fuck you too," Lola said. She was not up for babysitting the little prick's feelings. It wasn't her fault he'd acted like a bitch. It wasn't her problem she'd done better. People had to take responsibility for their failings; Lola did. And whatever she fucked up, she found a way to fix. Or she found somebody willing to fix it for her. There was none of this fucking depressive shit for her.

"Hey, man," Ollie said. He walked over to shake Jeff's hand. "Too bad about today."

"They had to eliminate somebody," Jeff said. He nodded at Donovan, who had changed into sweats with the arms cut off.

"Somebody not fucking me," Lola told them. "And I think they should separate the losers from the rest of us who still have a chance. It's only decent."

"What do you know about decency? You tried to masturbate on live TV," Donovan told her.

"Yeah, and you wish you'd gotten to watch," Lola told him.

"You can show me later," Donovan said. She turned a scowl on him to cover the flare of lust and thought about what she would let him do if she had some time to kill. In Lola's book, there was nothing wrong with beefy and aggressive.

Donovan had made the mistake of marrying a nice girl. Lola

was a perfect change of pace. Donovan paused as he passed by, letting her feel his big presence at her back. Lola smirked.

Confessional: Stewart

"First thing I have to tell the world is, more than anything, I miss my kids. I love you guys. Sorry if that embarrasses you, but that's what dads are for, right? It's been intense, more than I expected to be perfectly honest. But I made a commitment, and I'm sticking to it. And I think I'm doing well so far. I knew I shouldn't have fallen asleep, but it doesn't matter now. I'm going to do my best to win this thing and come home to you guys. That's all I ever wanted. I can do this."

Confessional: Cassie

"Well, I'm still here. I thought they were going to eliminate me, but here I am. And you know what? The worst is over. My confession is I'm afraid of the dark. Edmund thinks that makes me weak, but I made it. I made it through to daylight. Not daylight, technically, but those studio lights feel like the sun after eight hours in a coffin. But I made it out of that coffin, and I have nothing else to fear. Except, well, I do worry a little about going to hell. I grew up Catholic, and the Church says vampires go to hell. But it might not be true. They can't know, I don't think, not for sure. But no worries, all I have to do is stay alive forever, and I won't have to worry about it. I just have to keep dancing."

"What are they saying?" Emily and Cassie were in the kitchen. Emily was slapping together a peanut butter sandwich, and Cassie was eating stuffed olives straight from the jar while the microwave irradiated some sausage links. Cassie thought it was almost criminal to be eating like drunken college kids while surrounded by yards of marble countertops and stainless steel, red knobbed appliances.

Cassie sighed. "I heard something about masturbating and then I tried to stop listening."

Emily smiled. "That girl is working hard to class up the joint."

"I hope she washed her hands," Cassie said, and Emily's snort of laughter sent peanut butter and jelly flying from her mouth.

"Are you going to clean that up?" Cassie turned to find Madeline and Brett had come into the kitchen. Apparently, they'd been just in time to see bits of Emily's sandwich spray the counter.

"Of course." Emily raised an eyebrow at Cassie, who turned away to hide a giggle. "How are you feeling?"

"I'm fine." Madeline turned her back to inspect the contents of the refrigerator. "Or I would be if we had any fucking liquor."

"There's a bar in the living room," Cassie said. In Cassie's opinion, it was smart to stay sharp, but if Madeline wanted to fog her abilities, Cassie wouldn't be the one to dissuade her. Either way, in Madeline's case, it was moot.

"I think I've earned a little oblivion," Madeline snapped and headed for the living room without another word.

"She's taking it hard, huh?" Cassie said.

Brett shrugged. "I don't know. I would."

"No reason to worry about that," Cassie said. There was something pathetic about Brett that made Cassie want to reassure him. She plated her food and dug in.

"We should all be worried about that," Emily said and popped the last bite of sandwich into her mouth.

"What is there to eat?" Brett said.

"All kinds of stuff," Cassie told him.

"They stocked up on themed foods," Emily said.

Cassie grinned as she pointed out to Brett the blood sausage, blood oranges, and blood pudding.

"Gross," Brett said. Emily laughed.

Cassie raised her eyebrows and managed not to follow Emily's lead. "You just drank actual human blood," she said. "Besides, it's pretty tasty." She forked in another bite and chewed. It would have been better if she hadn't mentioned drinking the blood. The thought that the sausage was made from humans jumped into her brain, and she was unable to banish it. She offered a bite to Brett so that, God forbid, she wouldn't be the only cannibal. Brett shook his head and stepped back.

"Want a bite?" Cassie said a bit desperately to Emily.

"I do not like them, Sam I Am," Emily said and sailed out of the kitchen.

"Can I have something else?" Brett asked.

Cassie was a firm believer in Nice, but she wasn't about to play mother to a needy twenty-something vampire groupie. She bestowed a patient smile on Brett and indicated the family size jar of Jif on the counter.

"I'm allergic," Brett said. Cassie couldn't think of anything Nice to say to that, so she smiled again, this time sans the patience, and left him.

"That's so mean," Penny said.

"What?"

"I said that's so mean. Really mean."

"I wasn't asking what you said," Penny's long-suffering daughter explained. "I was asking what's mean."

Penny cranked the volume on the TV down and repeated, "Really mean."

Allyson sighed. "Then why are you laughing?"

"Because it's funny," Penny said.

"What is it that's so mean and yet so amusing?"

"One of the girls tried to feed that guy peanut butter," Penny said with high outrage, "and he's allergic."

"Is it possible she didn't know he was allergic?" Allyson said. She was working through a practice test for bio.

"I don't know," her mother admitted. "Maybe. But I think she's just trying to kill off the competition. Come out here and watch."

"I have to study," Allyson said. "As my mother you should be encouraging my intellectual endeavors."

"I do, but you have to take a break sometime," Penny said.

"You made me take a break when they stuffed them into the coffins," Allyson said. "And I don't know why you're so surprised. I'd be willing to bet every one of them has killed one thing or another."

"Gawd, you're just like your father," Penny said.

Allyson rolled her eyes and refrained from saying "Thank you." Her father was deeply respected in the halls of academia and was the author of several authoritative and well-reviewed books which happened to be lay-friendly enough to be profitable. Her mother had been an overly accommodating waitress until Allyson had made her a fortuitously pregnant one.

Sometimes, Allyson wondered if there had been other pregnancies before her, courtesy of less well-heeled gentlemen, and if her mother had followed Lola's example and declined to have them to pursue greener pastures.

Confessional: Donovan

"One challenge down and already the saddest of the punk ass bitches have been revealed. These people are pathetic. On the other hand, I fucking rocked. I have to say I've never felt more confident. And that judge wants to call me a barbarian? I don't think so. What I am is I'm ready, and I'm focused, and I'm not a fucking pussy, you know?"

"I mean seriously, how the fuck do you end up competing on

this show if you're afraid of the dark? Vampires like the dark, right? Fucking people. Hey, Tara? When I win this thing, we're done. I want a divorce. You can keep the house and the fucking kids. I'm going to be balls deep in vamp-loving strange for the rest of my life. And if you see Judy from the office, do me a favor and tell her she's a lousy lay. And Sheila, don't wait for my call. I doubt the baby is even mine."

Confessional: Portia

"Okay. I can do this. Except I might be getting a zit, which is freaking me the fuck out because it's like a sign. But the host liked my Ophelia. He loved my Ophelia. And that's got to trump a zit, right? This is the break, the one they refer to as 'big.' My big break, and I'm so excited; I could die. And then come back to life. I'm just really proud of myself right now. The secret is I'm getting in character, and I'm committing. And my character? She's the one who wins. She's the one who gets to be an immortal star. No more waiting tables, no more children's theater. Not that I don't love the children, but anybody can entertain kids. I'm ready for more. I feel like this is my moment, this is where my real life starts. But if this fucking zit doesn't go away, I'm going to kill everyone I can get my hands on, and then myself."

Brett decided then and there Cassie would not be permitted to sleep with him once he was a badass rock star vampire. She could take her pert, muscular little dancer's body and, well, maybe he could let her do some girl on girl for his entertainment.

But, he would never let her make him breakfast.

"Hey." Brett almost dropped the jar of olives Cassie had left behind.

"Hi," he managed. Portia was not the kind of girl Brett would normally be courageous enough to talk to. She was the kind of girl he pictured in his vampire rock star stable. At least, she would be if she were more famous.

"What is there to eat around here?"

"Quite a bit if you cook," Brett said. He did not cook.

Portia brushed past him to rummage through the fridge, leaving Brett free to check out her ass. It was a high quality ass.

"Omelet?" Portia suggested. She pulled eggs, peppers, mushrooms, and an onion out of the fridge. Brett flushed and raised his eyes to her face.

"It's not the one I had when I was nineteen that's for sure," Portia said.

"Huh?"

"My ass," Portia said pulling more items out of the fridge. "You like?"

"I wasn't—" Brett fumbled the lid back on the jar and prepared to flee. Women could get pretty shitty if they thought you were too focused on particular parts of their anatomy.

"I'm not offended." She pulled a knife out of the block and started chopping. "It's part of my job, looking good and having a tight ass. I should probably thank you for the compliment."

"Thank me how?" *That was a bad thing to say.*

"How I just did." Portia laughed. "Did you think I was going to blow you? You're not a casting director. Hand me the salt and pepper."

"Do you think those two will get together?" Penny wondered.

"Still doing homework," Allyson said.

"What? I can't hear you. Come in here."

"Still. Doing. Homework."

"Don't scream at me. I know you're watching." Penny tossed a Gummi bear at her daughter's head.

Allyson thought of telling her mother she should be eating

something with a modicum of nutritional value, but she pictured being hit in the head with a salad and refrained. "She's married, right?" Allyson knew it was a mistake to engage, but it wouldn't be any better trying to ignore Penny. That was the beauty of her mother.

"Marriage doesn't mean anything," Penny said.

"Not to some people," Allyson muttered.

Confessional: Ollie

"Oh man, that felt like a close one. I can't believe I fell asleep. I didn't mean to. I was trying to take the time to think, you know, about my strategy and such. Next thing I knew, they popped my top, and it was all over. I was surprised how the sleeping pissed them off, but I guess I can see how it's not too exciting for the audience watching me catch zzz's. Sorry, audience. I'll do better next time. Right here and now, I vow to stay awake through the whole next challenge. The blood was something though. I guess I have to get used to it. Vampires can't live on pizza. Hey, dad, I hope everything is good back home. Miss you and mom tons!"

Confessional: Kannon

"So the cliché 'Money can't buy happiness' isn't just the anthem of the impoverished. Who knew? Not my father. I'm starting to get it though. This might be good for me. If I make it, I can be a kinder, gentler vampire. It would be funny if it weren't so terrifying. If it doesn't work out, I don't want anybody to feel bad. I wanted this too, at least, at some point. And it made sense. I don't want to sound like I'm counting myself out; I'm not. But the competition is stiff, as you've seen by now, which means, I'm going to have to make a real effort, and that's good. I haven't had to make a real effort in a long time. I always thought I liked having it easy. No, I *did* like having it easy. Just like the rest of you would. But if I'm going to die, I don't want to die a douche.

It was peaceful here in the billiards room and good to be alone. Stewart restrained a sigh of impatience when someone said, "That's not how you play."

Stewart sat up and swung his legs off the table.

"Want a game?" Kannon said.

"Sure." Stewart got off the table so Kannon could rack. The crack of the break filled the room, and they played in companionable silence.

"That was crazy, right?" Stewart said.

"Yes."

"Do you think it will get easier?"

"No."

Confessional: Celeste

"Considering the staggering number of releases we had to sign to be on this fucking fun-fest, you would think the amount of danger would exceed the perils of crossing the street. I know it was just the first challenge, something to get our feet wet, but I'm going to be super pissed if the next one isn't more intense. I mean, seriously, who do you have to fuck around here to get killed?"

Confessional: Emily

"That was a learning experience. Although, I don't believe any vampire, who's not an eccentric or a throwback, sleeps in a coffin. By that, I mean I don't believe it of any of them with the possible exception of Vlad. It is fascinating to see someone fly out of history as a giant bat. If you get the opportunity, I recommend it. I'm encouraged by my performance in the first challenge. In theory, I felt like I could do it, but it's a relief to have made it through unscathed. I would worry about acquiring a taste for blood, but I suspect once the transition happens, the appreciation will be there. Sorry, I can't seem to stop smiling. I'm never like this, but this is a whole new world. And I feel like it could be mine."

Celeste was skulking around the Manor catching bits and pieces of conversation wherever she went. She would call it exploring if anyone noticed her, but she didn't expect it to be an issue. The more she skulked, the more she felt at odds with humanity. She felt no kinship with any of these people, though, like Celeste, they had jumped through numerous hoops to be here and might be expected to have something in common with her.

Celeste was standing outside the billiards room listening to the crack and tumble of the pool balls. She hadn't managed to overhear a single snip of conversation since she'd been outside the door. She froze when Madeline came around the corner and walked toward her.

Celeste was casting around for a defense and considered ducking into the game room, but she wasn't sure who was in there.

Madeline approached without speaking and squeezed right by her as though she hadn't even noticed Celeste's presence. Celeste turned to watch Madeline continue down the corridor and hang a left that took her out of sight. Celeste shook her head at the degree of social awkwardness that allowed someone to pass within inches of a housemate and pretend not to notice.

"Crazy bitch," Celeste said to herself with what may have been affection.

Confessional: Jeff

"I'm not feeling great about this endeavor. Maybe because I'm officially not part of it anymore. It had to be someone, but why did it have to be me? I can't decide if I hate myself or the fucking vampires more. My mother always said they were no good. But maybe I was wrong about them. Maybe they're not just like us. They don't seem to think so. I'm starting to think they consider humans to be inferior. I thought marching for vampire rights might have won me a pass. I'm not saying that's why I did it. I did it because it was the right thing to do. At least I thought so at the time. But they couldn't grant me one tiny bit of forbearance while I found my stride in the competition. I mean, I know our lives before aren't supposed to matter, but I got maced while I was picketing the Supreme Court on their behalf. Mace hurts. And I have to say, if I knew they would eliminate me anyway, I wouldn't have licked the blood vomit off the table. I resent that."

Confessional: Madeline

"Here's the thing. You would pray too if you woke up in a fucking coffin. A little notice would have made a big difference, assholes. And now I'm stuck here? So I can ramble on for your entertainment with no hope of winning the prize. That's just great. No sadistic bastards here. But whatever. I have all the booze I can put away, and I don't have to be on set early. Sorry. I don't mean to have a bad attitude. But, I mean, it's not like I'm the one who threw up blood. That's a clear sign someone wouldn't make a good vampire. But the coffin thing? They don't even sleep in coffins, except probably that creepy fucker Vlad. It was comfy though. Everything here is comfy."

From the _ _ _ _ _ _ _ of Babes.

G ood evening all," Chaz said. "Welcome back. I hope you all had a lovely day's sleep. By now, you've all been able to observe the contestants in their off time and get to know them through their own words. What do you think?"

"Challenge them! Challenge them! Challenge them!" The audience rolled their eyes and gnashed their teeth and shook their fists, and it was all so terrible, Chaz wanted to banish the lot of them.

"Challenge them we shall," Chaz said. "In fact, the second challenge is coming up shortly, and this season, we've made the second challenge a special audience participation challenge. The audience, which is you guys, will be set up with accessories, and when I give the signal, you will become the biggest obstacle for the contestants. I'll give you a hint: the challenge involves a small pit of hot coals. But first, let's hear from the friends and family of Jeff and Lola."

There were some distracted cheers for the pre-recorded loved ones of Jeff and Lola, but most of the audience was speculating about what role they would play in the challenge. Cyri tried to ignore her father's excited musings.

"First up," Chaz said. "Jeff's mother."

"Hi, baby." Jeff's mother had dressed up for the filming of her segment. She was wearing a nice blue dress and looked like the kind of mom who made snacks for all the neighborhood kids. "I miss you, and I wish you were home, but I know you felt you had to do this. I want you to know I'm watching, and I'm thinking of you every minute. You make me proud with everything you do; it's just sometimes I wonder if you would be happier focused elsewhere. I just don't think vampires appreciate humans. And I don't want them judging my baby. All I want is for you to come home safe. I love you."

The crowd had quieted as the clip of Jeff's mom played. There was a brief silence when the screens went dark.

"Has her child not already met his end?" Vlad asked. Delia rolled her eyes.

"Jeff has been eliminated from the competition," Chaz said, "but he is very much alive. Let's hear from Lola's ex-boyfriend."

"What's up, sexy? I'm not going to wish you luck because I know you don't need it. You guys who are competing against her, I'll wish you luck though. Lola gets what she fucking goes after. The chick can't take no for an answer, seriously. If any of you find a knife in your back, Lola put it there. Fun girl, though. I've got to say sometimes I miss her. Lola, come look me up when you're Mistress of the Night or whatever. We'll have at it for old time's sake. Later, babe."

"Time for the second challenge," Chaz said. "We're going to take a quick break while I explain to the studio audience their part in all this; then, we'll be back to set it all in motion."

"Did they say what it is yet?" Dani said. She had just come back from grabbing a quick shower.

"No, but check it out."

Dani plopped herself on the floor beside Rose. "Is that an obstacle course?"

"Looks like."

CREATURE OF THE NIGHT

"Hmmm. That's boring, huh?" Dani tipped her head and thumped her ear with the heel of her hand. Cotton swabs had been on her theoretical shopping list for weeks.

Rose flinched away from whatever her roommate might be dislodging. "There are tightropes; tightropes are kind of exciting."

"They're only like five feet long," Dani said.

"I think it's more like fifteen feet. And they are strung over a pit of hot coals," Rose said.

"How thrilling," Dani said. "Someone may get scorched."

Rose laughed. "Would you rather see someone killed on the spot?"

Dani shrugged. "It's just more exciting if there's a little danger. Oh, my god. I so want to fuck him."

Chaz had appeared on the screen. He was riling the crowd, greeting the judges, calling the contestants out. The ten lined up along the edge of the stage, and Chaz explained the rules.

"Well, there's your danger," Rose said. "But he is hot. I still think Kannon is cuter."

"He cried," Dani said. "And he's claustrophobic. Soooooooooverysexy."

"He didn't cry. And claustrophobia is a recognized condition. Besides, men are allowed to cry. You're sexist."

"I'm a girl," Dani said. "So, I'm automatically not sexist. Hand me a pillow?"

Rose tossed a pillow at her head.

The girls watched intently as Chaz ran through the obstacles. The contestants would have to climb a pegboard to reach the first of two freestanding platforms. From there, they would swing on a rope to the next platform. Once they'd landed, the contestants had to mount their tightropes to reach the final platform, crossing thirty feet above a shallow bed of coals to victory.

"That library girl isn't buying it," Rose said. "I like her."

The pensive look Emily currently wore wasn't due to what would have been an entirely appropriate skepticism, but rather to the fact she was mentally reviewing her strategy.

"She's pretty," Dani said.

"She's smart," Rose countered "That's what matters."

"So that's it," Chaz said. "Once you reach the final platform, remain there until every contestant is, one way or another, finished with this challenge. You'll all be happy to hear we rethought having a pit of fire. The judges weren't comfortable with an open flame. And to make it easy, you don't even have to walk. You can straddle your rope, use your hands, whatever. Easy, right?"

Most of the contestants nodded and looked relieved, although a few of them seemed warier.

Who is the sick bastard that thinks these things up? Portia thought. *I am not getting fried over this.* Risking your life was one thing; risking your looks, however, was quite another.

"This isn't exactly a race," Chaz said, "but it's always good to be first. And although we probably won't eliminate you because of how you navigate the obstacles, you should do it with the most style possible. Climbing and tightropes might not seem like vampire activities, but we the undead have superb grace and athleticism, and we want to know the capabilities of our potentials."

That's good. Emily took a deep breath. *It doesn't matter if I'm first; it matters that I finish. Someone is bound to fall. Probably a couple someones.* To Emily's credit, she did not wish for any of the potentially fallen to land in the hot coal pit.

"Is everybody ready?" Chaz asked.

The studio audience was ready. Viewers around the world were ready. The contestants were making the best of it.

Donovan grunted and flexed his hands. *I'm leaving these pussy bastards in the dust.*

"Judges! Are you ready?"

"Get on with it," Edmund said.

"We are not only ready; we are also eager," Delia said.

"*You both understand that you do nothing to ease the misconceptions the humans hold about us,*" Nodin said.

"*Do you long for their understanding?*" Edmund asked.

"Contestants! On your mark, get set—" An earsplitting siren blasted from beneath the contestants, and they all jumped, most of them toward the peg wall.

Everyone scrambled to snatch pegs from the board. There was a flurry of arms and scrabbling feet as the contestants tried to make a strong start.

The more vigorous climbers jostled their fellow contestants as they fought for the lead. Donovan was in the front of the pack, and to the surprise of most, Portia was close behind. Her torturous workouts at the climbing gym had been, in hindsight, pure genius.

Ollie was near the rear of a small clump of climbers working to make up the ground they'd lost by startling away from the wall when the siren blasted. Ollie glared at all the heels above him and pressed upward.

Emily had started losing ground as soon as she hit the wall; Ollie passed her easily. Emily glanced back to see who was still behind her and swore.

"I don't think all the climbing is fair to the girls," Dani said.

"Well, they have to go up," Rose said, "to get to the tightrope. And most of the girls are doing okay. The librarian's the one that can't hang."

Emily was thinking along similar lines. Above her, Donovan had no such worries.

"Watch your heads, folks," Chaz said. "Donovan has made it to the first platform."

Donovan heaved himself onto his platform. There was a triumphant sneer on his face.

The platform was round and free standing with a two-foot diameter. From here, Donovan had to grab the rope hanging a couple feet out and swing to the second platform.

Donovan could feel the heat wafting up from the bed of coals on the stage below and risked a look down. He found no comfort in Chaz's assurance that the pit wasn't deep.

Ha! Brett thought as he scrambled from the peg wall to his platform. Brett felt himself grin at Donovan's start of surprise. *That's right; I'm here. About to beat your ass, muscle man.* Then he too looked down.

Donovan's platform started to spin. Before Brett could articulate to himself what was happening, his platform followed suit.

"I didn't mention that, did I?" Chaz said to the audience.

"Spin them off! Spin them off! Spin them off!"

Spin? Emily grimaced.

Kannon and Stewart gained their platforms simultaneously; Brett and Donovan didn't notice.

When the spinning started, Donovan had one hand on his rope. He instinctively tightened his grip and twisted to grab on with his other hand. As the speed of the spin increased, he lost his footing. Donovan let his feet leave the platform and clung to his rope.

Brett had been reaching for the rope when he started to spin. He pulled his arm back and dropped to a crouch.

I can't. Kannon looked down into the pit and felt his stomach lurch in cold terror. *This is not a good place for people with phobias.* And why was all this self-awareness hitting him now, thirty feet in the air with nowhere to go but into a fiery pit? Just as he gathered the composure to glance to his left at Donovan and Brett, he began turning.

Brett managed to grab his rope on his third rotation. He'd caught it and sprung, hoping to generate enough momentum to carry him across.

Stewart grabbed his rope and pulled it close enough to wrap a leg around. When his platform started to rotate, he picked up his other foot and sent himself swinging slowly over the coals. *There are people who live perfectly happy lives with no family,* Stewart thought as he pendulumed back and forth.

Lola scrambled over the top of the pegboard. *Idiot,* she thought when she saw Donovan gyrating desperately at the end of his rope trying to build up enough of a swing to reach the second platform.

Donovan redoubled his efforts when Lola swung past him and yelled, "Loser!" He managed to pull himself higher on his rope and got the swinging of his legs synced up with the swing of his rope, so he wasn't sabotaging his progress. He was going to kill the bitch.

Ollie swung onto the platform. "Fucking peg broke." *Fucking lava. Somebody's going to get killed. Nah. There's got to be some safety feature. Maybe an invisible net. Okay, maybe an invisible net is hokey. But no one wants to see us die. That would ruin ratings for sure.* Ollie grasped his rope with both hands, leaned back, and leaped.

Behind him, his platform started to spin.

Cassie crested the peg wall, and a graceful bound later was swinging over the pit, hands tight on her rope, legs scissored around it. She dropped lightly onto the middle platform as if she'd been rehearsing it for days and grinned. *That was fun.*

Cassie had landed just after Stewart, who had finally managed to swing far enough to gain his platform.

Portia scrambled onto her circle and grabbed for her rope. The contestants in the rear had observed that lingering on the platform was not advisable.

On the other side of the rope swing, Brett landed on his second platform. He immediately dropped to his knees. *Please don't spin.* Brett was imploring the platform, not God because, as Madeline had learned, soon to be vampires should not ask the Almighty for favors.

"What?" Lola taunted. "Afraid the ground is going to move?"

"Yeah," Brett said. "But it looks like you're afraid of falling off the tightrope." *Bitch.*

"It's not a race," Lola snapped.

Emily gained the platform just behind Celeste. She scraped together every ounce of will she had and kept her focus on the far platform.

Celeste and Emily swung towards the second set of platforms as one, their feet hitting first and scrambling for purchase.

Are we supposed to wait here? Celeste wondered. Everyone had made it through the rope swing; everyone was staring down at the coals and staying put.

Stewart had decided walking the rope was not his best option. Sure, he'd come here to be a hero to his kids, but suddenly he found he was a fan of the live coward school of thought.

Stong core, Portia told herself. *And stop looking down.*

Cassie thought the tightrope looked far easier than hauling her weight up the wall. She took a deep breath and choked on the smoke rising from below.

"*Do they plan to stand there gaping for the rest of the competition?*" Delia said.

"*They're afraid,*" Chaz said. "*And some of them are dizzy.*"

"*They are meant to overcome their fear,*" Edmund said. "*That is the challenge.*"

"*They'll cross,*" Chaz said.

While the other nine contestants were working themselves up to step into nearly nothing, Celeste thought, *Finally,* and put a foot on her rope.

Everyone else snapped to, realized they were still mid-challenge, and started to follow suit. The contestants extended their feet with precision, some stepping, others sliding. Scores of toes did their best to cling to ropes, and arms extended for balance.

Emily made a good start, placing one foot in front of the other with precision. She held her arms away from her sides without fully extending them. Emily was channeling the tortoise.

Kannon crouched down and grabbed the rope with his hands. He swung down, so he was hanging beneath the rope and started moving across it, hand over hand like a kid on a jungle gym.

"See?" Rose said. "He's awesome."

"Those are some nice arms," Dani admitted. "And he's pretty fast. Chaz is still hotter."

"Chaz is a monster," Rose said. "He would eat you."

"I'm okay with that," Dani said.

Lola had also chosen to travel under the rope. She hung by her hands and ankles, contracting and expanding like a caterpillar, progressing foot by foot. She was yards ahead of Celeste, who had crouched down and was moving in a squat along her rope. Celeste had her knees spread wide, and with both her hands and feet on the rope, she looked quite like a frog out of its element. She was traveling headfirst so she could keep an eye on those behind her.

Brett hadn't moved from his platform. He seemed to be talking to himself.

"What's the crazy weirdo doing?" Rose said.

"Shut up. Chaz is talking."

"What the contestants don't know," Chaz was saying, "is we have another surprise in store for them."

Thirty feet above the stage, Emily paused for a brief second then resumed her journey with newfound haste. None of the other contestants seemed to notice the commentary beneath them.

"Members of the audience, your time has come! As I said before, this challenge is about physical prowess, but it is also about being ready for anything."

"Are those guns?" Rose sat up and thrust her face nearly into the screen.

"No way, that would be crazy," Dani said. "Move your head. Fuck, you're right. Those are totally guns."

Chaz was reiterating key instructions for the audience. "Remember, it's not your job to kill the contestants. Our only aim is to make the tightrope portion more challenging."

The audience chortled. Many of them were already sighting along the barrels of their guns.

"Our aim." Cyri's dad snickered and poked her in the side. "Get it?"

Cyri sunk in her seat.

"Those that are marksmen or women, please, do not shoot to kill. Your **bullets** are micro-chipped, so we will know who made any successful shot. You will have bragging rights if you hit a contestant, not to mention a very small prize. Since you only have one bullet each, make your shot count. Once a contestant reaches the platform at the end of their tightrope, they are off limits."

"They really went above and beyond on those safety precautions," Cyri said.

Her dad beamed. He wasn't sure if he was prouder of Cyri or himself for raising her. He gave her a quick pat on the head and then raised his gun and sighted.

"So that's it," Chaz announced. "Fire when ready!"

Brett chose that moment to launch himself onto his tightrope. He was taking long, quick strides and made it halfway across by the time someone got a shot off. Some of the audience considered how best to spend their precious bullet while the rest realized they were late to the party and fired indiscriminately. The studio sounded briefly like the Fourth of July. Chaz did his best to keep up with the action, but a lot happened at once.

In the brief seconds of calm following the first shot, Brett had reached the middle of his rope and was closer than anyone else to the far platform. "Brett is past the halfway mark," Chaz said. "And Emily is right behind. It looks like they're going to make it folks!"

Some members of the audience sensed subtext and took aim at the leading duo. By now, Brett was moving so fast most of the audience couldn't hope to hit him, and none of them managed to hit the librarian shaped bull's—eye either. So it was all the more galling for Emily when a bullet whizzed by her face, and she shrieked and lost her balance.

Cassie had been halfway across her tightrope when the audience opened fire. She was looking confident and wearing a look of concentration touched by a slight smile. So, it was a shock to everybody watching when she toppled off the rope and plummeted. Brett gained the platform in time to see Cassie hit the coals. He threw his arms up in triumph and yelled, "Fuck yeah!" No one heard him over the screams and gunfire.

"Look at that shot!" Chaz shouted. "Cassie is down thanks to a shot in the ankle. She's done dancing now! And look at the shooter; he's adorable. Look at those cheeks." The shooter did indeed have adorable and plump little cheeks, the kind of cheeks that get fondled and pinched by strangers.

Emily had managed to grab her rope as she fell. She was hanging by an elbow trying not to imagine landing in the coals. Cassie was a few feet back and to the right, but Emily could see her trying to fight her way out of the pit. Cassie's original scream had morphed into a high keen that was giving Emily chills in spite of the rising heat.

From where she hung, Emily could see the lining of the pit wherever Cassie's struggles shoved coals aside.

At least they hadn't lied about it being shallow, Celeste thought. "Just stand up," she said, but, of course, Cassie didn't hear her.

Cassie was scrambling. If she had been in prime condition, she could have escaped with a couple quick leaps, but the ankle that had taken the bullet was useless. Realistically, no one would be in prime shape after a thirty-foot drop ending in a good scorching. By the time she realized the coals were quite shallow, she was burned from the knees down and both her hands had sustained damage.

Ollie had abandoned the uncertain footing to follow Kannon's example and was making good progress, his long-armed swings eating up yards of rope.

Two ropes to Ollie's right, Portia was trying to recover from a nearly disastrous wobble.

"Look at that!" Chaz shouted. "Kannon is down now. It looks like he could be missing an eye! Yes! Yes! He is missing an eye! What an incredible shot, folks! This is one for the books! He's in the pit, but he's still moving. Kannon is crawling out of the coals. Looks like he and Cassie have both made it to the edge of the pit."

By now, most members of the audience had taken their shot. Only an occasional bullet sprang from its chamber.

The contestants traveled grimly onward.

"And look, Lola made it. Lola is across. She would only have been third, if not for our sharpshooter audience." Lola clambered onto the platform and waved to the audience. She then leaned over the platform's edge to blow kisses at Kannon and Cassie, who were pushing and pulling each other out of the pit.

Ollie swung to the end of his rope, threw a leg onto the platform, and pulled himself up easily. The final platform was large enough to hold all the contestants. Ollie joined Brett near the back edge in case anyone who hadn't spent their bullet decided to violate the safe zone of the platform.

"Firearms, bah," Vlad said. "If you have fangs, there is no need for silly toys."

"Thanks, Vlad!" Chaz checked the crowd for anyone still aiming. "Is everybody out of ammunition?"

"Give us more! Give us more! Give us more!"

Emily had made it to the end of her rope by pulling herself

along hooking one elbow then the other over the rope.

"Nope." Chaz shook his head at them. "And they call us bloodthirsty. To recap, we have Brett, Lola, and Ollie safe on the platform. Okay, Stewart, good job. And he's been shot as well, ladies and gentlemen. Right in the ass. Way to keep going, Stewart. And here comes Donovan, also doing it monkey style. Emily is hanging from her tightrope. Did someone shoot Emily?"

"She slipped," Nodin said.

I didn't fucking slip, Emily thought. There was a painful thud on her back.

"Was that a shoe?" Delia smiled.

"No throwing shoes," Chaz told the audience. The audience groaned in protest.

Portia stepped onto the platform and dropped gratefully to her knees. Celeste edged up next to her.

Kannon and Cassie were slumped together downstage from the coal pit.

"Emily, you're last to make it, *but* you made it. Let's give these guys a round of applause, shall we?"

The crowd cheered so loud and so long Edmund disappeared in another snit.

"Okay, people. Kannon and Cassie are going to get patched up and then we'll meet the folks who did the shooting."

Riley and Kiley appeared to help Kannon and Cassie offstage.

"You forgot a bullet," Nodin said.

Chaz did a fake smack on his forehead. "Stewart! Take your wounded ass and follow Cassie and Kannon, and we'll get that looked at too." *Such a waste of blood.*

"Do we get to drink that blood?" Vlad said.

If Vlad's insane commentary didn't make you reexamine yourself as a vampire, nothing would, Chaz thought. Delia broke the news to Vlad that the bleeding contestants were not to be considered a buffet.

Cyri wished they would just let Vlad eat everybody so she could go home.

"That was way too intense," Rose said. The pizza they'd ordered had arrived just before the crowd had opened fire and Rose's half, pepperoni and pineapple, sat untouched. Dani's half, extra cheese and mushroom, had been demolished.

"Sorry about your boyfriend," Dani said.

"It's not that," Rose said. "It just made me sad for some reason. It's probably stupid."

Dani shrugged. It was a little stupid. You couldn't go around getting upset over some lame TV show. Dani eyed Rose's half of the pizza. "Are you going to eat that?"

"Is everybody paying attention?" Chaz said. The crowd assured him of their focus. The unlucky gentleman seated in front of Cyri's father took some projectile saliva to the back of the head. "Okay, time to meet the lucky audience members who managed to land a shot on one of our contestants. We have with us onstage Melvin, Bob, and Jake. Jake's mom is here, but she didn't win a prize, did she, Jake?"

Jake shook his head and giggled. The audience *aaawed*.

"Melvin is the one who shot our favorite dad, Stewart." Chaz slung a friendly arm around Melvin's shoulders. Melvin cringed and tried to cover it. "Popped him right in the hiney. So Melvin, do you hunt? Are you a sharpshooter of some kind? Tell us."

Melvin laughed. "No, Chaz. I haven't picked up a gun since I was in the Marines. That was twenty years ago. Muscle memory, I guess. Like riding a bike."

"Well, consider us impressed," Chaz said. "You were promised a prize, so we're setting you up for three days and two nights, all expenses paid at Villa Del Sol. Have you heard of it?"

"That's the place where they give you massages on the beach

and make you drink things with little umbrellas. Yep, I've heard of it. And then I heard again. I heard a couple more times after that, know what I mean? My wife has wanted to go there for I don't know how long."

"Luckily for you, the prize is for two," Chaz said. "Or not luckily, I have no idea."

"I love my wife," Melvin said. "Hi, honey." The vampire twins answered Chaz's frantic signaling and came to escort Melvin offstage. "Bye, honey."

"Why must we meet them?" Edmund said. "Just give them their prizes and let us move on."

"I want to see the little one," Delia said.

"I want—" Delia slapped a hand over Vlad's mouth.

"We're saving him for the last," Chaz told her. "Let's meet Bob, the man responsible for relieving Kannon of his left eye. You're here with your family, aren't you, Bob?"

"That I am, Chet."

"Chaz."

"Chaz," Bob said. "You can call me Bobby."

"Fantastic," Chaz said. "Do you handle a gun often?"

"Often enough, but anything can happen. Every time I make a shot, I like to thank the Big Guy for helping me out."

"The Hulk?" Chaz wondered.

"The Hulk is not real," Delia said, "but perhaps that is not a deal breaker."

"We do not fear your god," Vlad said.

"Sorry sir, Vlad, Impaler," Bob said. "Sorry, Chaz and ma'am. No offense meant. It just felt a bit uncomfortable to be talking about, you know…"

"God?" Chaz said.

"Yeah." Bob nodded. "With you know…"

"Bloodsucking fiends? It's okay, Bob. We know we're vampires. You don't believe all that 'damned to hell' nonsense do you, Bob?"

"No. I don't. No way. My pastor does, is all. But you would

probably know better than he does about vampires and their souls, what with you being one and all. Wow. So you can say His name? Wow."

"Isn't it technically more of a title?" Delia said.

"Let us stay on point," Chaz said. "To clarify, you regularly thank the 'big guy' for helping you visit death upon his other creatures?"

"Well, He did make those creatures for us," Bob said.

"Us?" Chaz raised one eyebrow and regarded Bob until the latter began to squirm.

"I meant humans, no offense," Bob said. "You know, because we're His children created in His image."

"Is our image not indistinguishable from your own?" Vlad said.

"I'm not sure what you mean," Bob said.

"Indeed," Vlad said.

"Is that your family?" Chaz considered eating Bob's family as retaliation for this excruciating interview.

"Yes, that's my family. My wife Dora and the three boys, little Robert, Joey, and Carson. Their mom likes Carson Daily. Maybe the next one we'll call Chet." Bob laughed. His family beamed.

"What is wrong with that one?" Vlad said.

"The same thing that is wrong with them all," Edmund shot back.

"I can only dream," Chaz said. "You win a new golf cart. I think it's a Mercedes. Thanks for being here. Girls."

The girls obliged and swept Bobby from the stage.

"And last but not least, as long as we refrain from factoring in his size, meet Jake!"

Jake had huge eyes, and fat, pink cheeks. He was wearing a cowboy hat and a cape; clearly, he had dressed himself. The audience showered him with cheers, coos, and blown kisses.

"How old are you, Jake?"

Jake held up a hand with all his fingers splayed open. He then tried to work his little index finger down. He wasn't having much luck.

"He just turned three," Jake's mom said. "He's not a big talker."

"I phwee," Jake agreed, finally managing to display four fingers.

"I could just eat him," Delia said.

"I thought you said no eating," Vlad complained.

"He is almost certainly a virgin," Nodin observed.

Vlad nodded agreement and crooned, "Virgin. Yes." He smiled dreamily, and his fangs slipped out. Jake's mother pulled him closer.

"Vwergn," Jake said.

"What did you say, honey?" Jake's mother asked.

"I think it was just a happy sound." Chaz shook his head at the judges and crouched down to be nearer the kid's eye level. "So, Jake, do you have toy guns at home?"

Jake nodded. "Bang, bang!" He managed to work his tiny fingers into the shape of a gun.

"That's right," Chaz said. "Bang, bang. Do you know you shot a girl in the leg?"

Jake nodded and smiled. His grin made his fat cheeks fatter, and the audience melted.

"He pulled the trigger all by himself," Jake's mom said. "I only helped hold it up."

"That's fantastic, Jake," Chaz said. "Do you know you won a prize?" Jake looked up at his mom, his eyes wide at the word prize.

"Pwize?"

"A prize is like a present you get for doing something well," Chaz said.

"Pwesnt! Prwesnt!" Jake clapped his hands.

"This is fucking ridiculous," Edmund said. The audience gasped. Jake's mother belatedly clapped her hands over his ears.

"Phuckndiclus," Jake said.

The crowd howled with laughter as did Chaz. Jake's mother flushed with mortification. "We don't say those words, Jake." She gave him a good shake. "Those words are very bad. It is very bad to say them. Do you understand?"

Jake nodded. His big eyes were wet with tears. "I sowwie," he said.

Jake's mother leaned down and whispered in his ear. "You are getting a spanking when we get home."

Jake started to cry in earnest. The audience booed.

Cyri was now the proud possessor of the only gun that still contained a bullet. She briefly considered the justice of shooting Jake's mother.

"It's okay, Jake." Chaz patted the kid on the head. "We had a different prize planned, but we switched it to one we thought you'd like better. Guess where you and your family are going?"

Jake didn't answer, but he did let the waterworks die out and looked at Chaz with his big eyes.

"Wrap it the fuck up," The Voice said in Chaz's ear.

"You're going to Disneyland," Chaz said and signaled for the twins. "Yay."

Rylie and Kylie swept out to escort Jake and his mother away. Kylie picked the little boy up and hugged him close, smelling his neck. Jake's mother smiled at the sight of what appeared to be a wholesome, if somewhat overdressed, coed adoring her child and took a moment to address the audience. Rylie shrugged and followed Kylie and the boy.

"Thank you all so much, I'm just so proud of my little guy. My life began when I went through twenty-seven hours of labor to bring my little love into the world, and when I came out the other side, I found I finally knew what it meant to love."

Jake had disappeared from the stage still wrapped in Kylie's arms.

"*Kylie and Rylie are often hungry being so new,*" Nodin said.

"*It would serve her right.*" Edmund scowled at Jake's mother.

"Do you think the girls are enjoying the child?" Vlad said.

"It's impossible not to enjoy him," Jake's mother said. "It's what I do all day, every day. The selfless pride I felt when Jake shot that contestant—moments like that are just the icing on the mommy cake. For those of you who aren't parents, I could never explain the pride I feel in his accomplishments. I'm sure there are nice things about being vampires, but if you can't make life. You can't ever really be complete. You can think you're happy, but you're not. You can't be because what you're missing is everything pure and good about the world."

"*For fuck's sake, Chaz,*" Delia said. "*Get rid of her.*"

"That's—" Chaz started.

"Are they going to eat the kid?" The Voice demanded. "Because if they are, it needs to happen on camera."

"Children," Jake's mother said. "Children are the only point."

"Actually," Chaz said. "We do produce children. And your son? He just left the stage with two of our newest. You probably should go get him."

"While you seek to extol your questionable virtues, your child may be consumed." Nodin sounded, more than anything else, hopeful. "And you will have no one but yourself to blame."

Chaz knew she would find someone who wasn't herself to blame. The twins for eating the boy perhaps, although it was like leaving a hungry dog to guard dinner. You were the fool for expecting your plate to be untouched when you returned.

Jake's mother finally showed some comprehension and moved her ass when Vlad said, "I wonder if there's any left," and disappeared from his throne. Her low, square heels made an abominable racket as she sped across the stage shrieking Jake's name.

Everyone listened for additional screams from backstage. When none came, Chaz went on with the show.

"That little boy is darling," Mandy said.

Seth was unimpressed. "I can't believe they give kids guns over there."

"Well, I'm sure he doesn't always have a gun." Mandy peeked at her husband. "Wouldn't it be fun if, someday, we took Mason?"

"It's time to hear from some more viewers," Chaz said. "Let's start with Jessyca, from Raleigh, North Carolina."

"I just wanted to say, I love the show so much! I tried to buy a ticket to be in the audience but they sold out in like thirty seconds. Do you think there might be more seats available next season?"

"We can hope, Jessyca," Chaz said. "I'll be looking for you right here in the front row next time! Spend anything! Trust me, you'll have the time of your life. Now we have a comment from Glen in Medford, Oregon."

"That was the most exciting thing I've ever seen. And I want to say that Lola is fucking hot! I hope you win it, Lola. And then I hope you come look me up."

"I'm sure she'll get right on that," Chaz said. "But first, Lola and the other contestants are coming out to see what the judges have to say about the second challenge and to find out who they are eliminating from the competition. Contestants, let's see you!"

The ten remaining contestants filed out. Cassie was on crutches, and half of Kannon's head had been bandaged over. There were few smiles. With two challenges down and three to go, the competitors had abandoned mindless optimism in favor of grim determination.

"Audience!" Chaz paused for them to scream their acknowledgment. "Want to hear who you voted to eliminate?"

"Eliminate! Eliminate! Eliminate!"

"I'll take that as a yes," Chaz said. "You, my human lovelies, want to send home a guy for being a douche and a gal for being stuck up. In short, you voted to be rid of Donovan and Emily."

The crowd cheered. The crowd booed. The crowd hissed.

"Taking your vote under advisement," Chaz continued, "the

judges will make their decision."

"Brett, step forward." Brett fidgeted under Delia's gaze.

"Brett, your hesitation when you reached the tightrope gave me pause, but perhaps it was strategic."

Brett nodded. "Totally strategic."

"His reek of desperation disgusts me," Edmund said.

"Let it go," Nodin said.

"Inform the contestant he may step back," Edmund decreed. Chaz rolled his eyes and gestured for Brett to return to his place in line.

"Lola." In response to the command of her name, Lola stepped forward.

"You finished second," Nodin continued. "Tell us why you chose to taunt those in the pit."

"I don't think I taunted them," Lola argued.

"She speaks as though what she thinks could matter," Edmund said.

Lola's face was a mix of emotions one of which looked like rage. It was impossible to tell whether she was trying to muster the courage to talk back to Edmund or the sense not to.

"I eliminate that one," Vlad said. He pointed at Stewart before he popped from his throne to Stewart's side.

"The one who thought of inviting the madman to sit with us will be dealt with," Edmund said.

"You know who invited him," Delia said. *"Leave it. I happen to enjoy the perks here. Besides, if you eat him, you'll never work in this town again."*

"Burbank?"

Stewart looked wildly at the other judges then turned to Chaz for reassurance as he stepped forward and to the side, trying to get an eye on Vlad. He nearly screamed when he felt Vlad's tongue sweep over the nape of his neck. Chaz raised an eyebrow in Delia's direction.

"Sweetie, we have to talk to each contestant before we eliminate,"

Delia said. *"And stop licking."*

"But I will get to eat the elim —"

"No! Just say something about Stewart's performance in the challenge," Delia said. *"Stewart is the one standing in front of the others."*

"I do not believe, Stewart," Vlad said, "that you fell. At this time, I am not to eat you."

Stewart shuddered. He felt sick at the remembrance of Vlad's touch.

"You are never to eat a contestant," Nodin said.

"Never cannot be promised but perhaps not today," Vlad conceded.

Vlad moved away from Stewart and began making his way down the line of contestants. He ran a finger down Lola's cheek, inhaled the length of Celeste's collarbone. The audience found itself enthralled. The contestants didn't move.

Vlad continued his survey. He stroked, he pinched, he looked deeply into several sets of terrified eyes and then into Kannon's one. The contestants elevated stillness to an art form. Their thoughts ranged from *Please God, please* to *Come on, already.*

"Vlad! No biting." Delia patted the arm of Vlad's empty throne. Vlad blinked off the stage and reappeared beside her.

Stewart stepped back, his hands thrust deep in his pockets to hide their trembling.

Ollie was next to be ordered forward.

"Your start was unimpressive," Nodin said, "but you finished acceptably."

"Yet you are damned with faint praise," Edmund said. "Begone."

"Returning to your place in line will suffice," Delia said as Ollie started to head offstage. He blinked away the onslaught of tears and about-faced back into line.

"You take your role too seriously," Delia said to Edmund.

"Bah."

"That one," Vlad said.

"Emily, step forward," Chaz clarified. Emily stood without moving, hands clasped in front of her. Chaz could tell she was nervous, but she managed to hide it, at least from the other humans.

"Please don't ask if you can eat her," Delia said.

Vlad huffed. He might have been frustrated or offended.

"Is a semblance of order so much to ask?" Nodin said.

"You can see it is," Delia said.

"She fell," Edmund said.

"I caught myself," Emily told him. "I finished the challenge."

"I was not speaking to you."

Emily debated a second too long over whether to object to Edmund's attempt to shame her.

"Emily, you reacted with poise and grace to the unexpected," Delia said. "However, your overall performance was not what we would hope to see from our new Creature of the Night. You are here to become a vampire, not to study them. Choosing action over observation would serve you well. Step back."

"Donovan, you may step forward," Delia said.

Donovan swaggered a few steps, winked at the audience, and turned a grin on Delia.

"Creepiest dimple that ever was," Cyri said.

"What, honey?" Cyri's dad didn't bother looking at her, so she didn't bother to elaborate on the sleezy vibe Donovan was putting out.

"Ape," Edmund said.

"There's always one," Delia observed.

"You are a man in his prime," Delia said.

Donovan smirked. He could envision getting a piece of Delia before this was over.

"So, please explain how you justify your middle of the pack finish," Delia continued.

"I was pacing myself," Donovan said.

"Step back," Edmund said, "or I will allow The Impaler an indulgence."

"I don't want that one," Vlad said.

"I long to eliminate you," Edmund said. "I long to eliminate you all."

"Step back," Nodin said.

"Portia," Chaz said. "Step forward."

Donovan grinned and tried to high-five Portia as they exchanged places. Portia ignored him.

"You did well," Nodin said. "You were the second of the weaker sex to complete the course." Portia let out the breath she'd been holding but didn't fail to notice the sexism.

"Climbing gym," she said.

"How utterly fascinating," Edmund said.

"Seriously," Cyri muttered.

"Really?" Cyri's dad said. "We could totally go rock climbing."

"What brought you here?" Delia asked.

"I've always adored the show and the majesty of vampires," Portia said as smoothly as if she'd rehearsed her answer a hundred times.

"As long as we are not marrying your kind, yes?" Delia said.

"Hollywood has always been quite liberal," Nodin said. "It must be hard for you."

"Perhaps even the reason for your limited success," Delia said.

"I think it's important to give back," Portia said, sticking firmly with her PC catch phrases. She uncurled her fingers when she realized her hands had clenched into fists.

"You may step back."

Portia scampered back before more could be said. Chaz indicated that Celeste should step forward.

"*Eternal life has never felt so eternal,*" Nodin said.

"*Shut it,*" Delia told him.

"Step back," Edmund snapped at Celeste. "This process tests my control. I find myself exhausted by the sea of humanity in which I am adrift. However for now, here we will remain."

Celeste looked to Chaz for direction. Chaz flashed his hostiest smile and gestured for her to rejoin the others.

"There are two exceptions to Edmund's disturbing sea metaphor," Nodin said. "It is clear Kannon and Cassie have failed this challenge. Know that it is not entirely because you were shot down by our esteemed audience participants. It is also because each of you thought your wound was a reason to give up. More fortitude is required. Neither of you so much as attempted to drag your broken body to the finish. Therefore, we dismiss you both from the competition."

Cassie let out a burst of dismay but clamped down on it immediately. Kannon bowed his head but made no sound.

Rylie and Kylie appeared and began to herd both the current and former contestants away. The crowd began to chant without Chaz prompting them.

"Confess! Confess! Confess!"

"Is this the best audience ever?" Chaz said. "I think they're trying to steal my gig. But for now, it's time to say goodnight! I expect everybody to have a look at the next round of confessionals and take in some Manor action!"

Chaz was doing research.

He had let himself be distracted by the motion of his assistant's head, but almost immediately, his attention came home.

He looked good with a blond going down on him. Although, he felt he looked better with a redhead. The frustrating thing was he couldn't put a finger on why.

"Switch with Bella," he said. Ana drew back and wiped her mouth.

Bella obediently ceased rubbing his shoulders and came around to take Ana's place. She put her mouth over him where he was still wet with Bella's saliva and commenced her new task with becoming enthusiasm.

Chaz nodded. He definitely looked better with Bella kneeling before him. He had just signed a three-film deal with SuperFetish Films, and he had never been happier that he had clung to some creative control.

Chaz let thoughts of career growth drift from his mind and focused on the sensations being teased to life throughout his body. His eyes closed, and he lost track of which touches came from Bella and which from Ana, but it didn't matter. Chaz chose to think of them as one extremely talented girl.

Confessional: Celeste

"I can't take this. Who do you have to fuck around here to get burned or shot to death? I did manage to get fondled by the crazy freaking vampire judge. That part was horrible. I don't think this is fair. I don't know why I thought this was a good idea. I can't believe I thought this would be a simple way to deal with my life. I have to do better. I'm not going to let myself freak out, but it's hard not to dwell on all the possible bad outcomes. The most obvious being I end up going home to my crappy job and my shitty apartment with only one eye."

Confessional: Donovan

"I'd like to shoot that fucking judge—the asshole—but whatever. Fuck him. I'm still here, and I'm kicking ass. But it's getting fucked up. That Kannon guy seemed okay, and now he's missing a fucking eye. How the fuck are you supposed to get laid with only one eye? I can't even think about it. I didn't think I'd see that when I signed up. I almost miss my fucking wife. That ought to tell you how fucked up this shit is getting. Don't get me wrong.

I'm still planning to win this bitch, but anybody would be disturbed by the shit that just went down. And if you think you wouldn't, you can come say it to my fucking face after I win. I'm going to show these assholes. I'm going to show *you* assholes. I'm going strong because that's just me. Fucking 'ape,' my ass."

"Did you kids have fun?" Jeff was lying on the couch, eating a pizza he'd managed to burn around the edges yet keep nearly frozen in the middle, when the others trooped back into the Manor.

"No," Stewart said, passing through the living room without pause.

Jeff sat up. A couple black olives and a piece of pepperoni fell onto the floor. "What's his problem?"

"I can't say definitively," Emily said, "but it's possible he's still agitated because the audience shot at us."

"Didn't you watch?" Celeste said.

"I got eliminated." Jeff glared. "Why would I give a shit what happens to the rest of you?"

"I don't know," Celeste said. "Because that's what a decent human being would do? How did you go from pie in the sky vamp lover to creepy, bitter cynic so fast?"

"Funny you should ask. I've been doing some self-examination, and I think the answer has something to do with my humiliating elimination after I was forced to lick up bloody vomit. I suppose I should go back to embracing humanity now that it's my only option," Jeff said. "Please tell me, is everyone okay? Should I open my free hugs booth?"

"You're a dick," Celeste said. She collided with Madeline on her way out of the room, sending the self-proclaimed dark mistress sprawling into the doorjamb.

Madeline shrugged at Celeste's back, crossed the room, and snagged a piece of Jeff's pizza "Did you cook this?"

Jeff shrugged. "For a while."

Madeline blew him a kiss and departed with her slice. Jeff wished the others would leave too. He wished they hadn't come back. It had been nice having the house essentially to himself.

"So, how was your day, dear?" Emily said.

Jeff rolled his eyes and ignored her. He couldn't evict the others from the room, but he didn't have to interact either. When you had all the frozen pizza you could eat and a big TV to watch, who needed other people?

Confessional: Emily

"I walked a tightrope today, and that was amazing. However, the flying bullets were an unpleasant touch, which brings me to luck is a bitch. You can plan to the point of insanity, research every fact, memorize every precedent, and know the judges better than they know themselves, but you can't undo luck. Or maybe I mean chance. It doesn't matter; I don't believe in any of it although, right now, I wish I could.

"I'm still in the running so I shouldn't complain, but what about next time? Reinhold Niebuhr said we're supposed to accept the things we cannot change, and that essentially covers everything in the competition. I'm neither religious nor serene so it's best to dwell on the near future as little as possible. The challenges are bound to get worse, and backing out isn't an option. On the bright side, I think a couple of people are ready to lose their shit, and I don't plan on being one of them. Of course, this is one of those situations where it's easy to surprise yourself, for better or for worse. Maybe even both."

Confessional: Stewart

"Hi, kids. Three challenges to go, and I'm still here. Winning didn't seem so hard before I got here; now I'm happy I only got shot in the ass. Those kids who got eliminated today, I feel for them. They're not much older than you guys. I want to tell you I was wrong to do this. I wanted a grand gesture to show you how much you mean to me. I wanted to win you guys back, and that was a mistake. I should have done it by being there every day even when you hated me. I shouldn't have listened when you wanted to skip a weekend here and there. Those missed weekends eventually became months of not seeing you, and then it was six months and we'd had dinner maybe three times.

"You guys are my life, and what I'm trying to say is don't try to prove yourselves with some stupid gesture, not ever. You prove yourselves by doing your best every day. Every day. Do your best to love your mother; do your best to be good friends; do your best in school. You can't slack off on things that matter and expect to make it up all at once. Remember, you can't ever make up for absence. I wish I had realized that years ago. Or at least months ago. If I had, I'd be there, knocking on your mother's door, asking for an unscheduled weekend even though I know you guys are busy. Because there is nothing I'd rather do with my time than give it to you. I hope you're watching. And I hope you're not. Love you guys."

Donovan burst through the front door, took in the librarian and the loser, and went through without bothering to acknowledge them. He had plans to hit the gym. Donovan was two steps closer to paradise, and to celebrate, he was going to admire the way his muscles bunched while he lifted. Maybe Lola would want to watch.

Except Lola was nowhere to be found, so Donovan made his way to the gym without an adoring audience. He stopped in the doorway when he found the room already occupied.

Ollie released the curl bar to the floor with a clang and a thump. "How are you feeling?"

Donovan let his lip curl. "I'm good."

"Can you spot me?"

Donovan shrugged and followed Ollie to the bench press. He watched Ollie add another twenty pounds and then stood with his hands under the bar while Ollie strained and grunted through ten reps.

Donovan wondered what it would sound like if he pushed the bar all the way down to Ollie's neck. There was a chance no one would even care, and Donovan would be one step closer to his goal. "So, that was something," Donovan said.

"It was horrible," Ollie said once he'd gotten the bar onto the rests. "It's amazing none of us was killed."

"A couple of people probably wish they had been," Donovan said. He should never have brought it up. When he thought of Kannon's ruined eye, he wanted to scream. But he wouldn't.

Confessional: Jeff

"I'm so over being stuck in a house with this bunch of self-obsessed sharks. I don't think any of these assholes deserve to win, but if I had to bet on one, I guess it would be Portia. It would have been the rich kid, but I just found out from the librarian some kid shot out his eye. Shot out his *fucking eye*. If that doesn't make you feel better about being out of the whole thing, nothing will. I don't mean that in an insensitive way. I mean, it sucks for him, but you know, what matters is it didn't happen to me. I feel now like I've been a dick, but that is going to change. I'm a nice guy. And the world is going to see it."

Confessional: Lola

"Some asshole almost shot me. I felt it go through my fucking hair. Stupid fucking— You know what? It doesn't matter. Whoever you are, you don't matter. I matter. I'm going to win. Two more down, seven to go. I'm ready for the next challenge right fucking now. The faster we get through this shit, the faster I'm sinking my shiny new fangs into the neck of some hot twenty-year-old. Seriously, the suspense is killing me. As long as nothing else does, I guess. I just want to know what's coming. Maybe we'll have to kill an endangered animal or something."

Little P was in the hall conferring with the doctor. Kannon and Cassie were alone in the infirmary.

"How are you feeling?" Kannon said.

"Like I want to die," Cassie told him. "But I'll probably get over it. Someday."

"I'm relieved," Kannon told her.

"That I'll probably get over wanting to die?"

"That it's over," Kannon said.

"Really?" Cassie abandoned her examination of the ceiling to look at him. Kannon thought she was beautiful. He, on the other hand, was looking forward to a new glass eye and a lifetime of stares. A newly made beast.

"Okay. A part of me is relieved," Kannon said. "Most of me is pissed. Then there's the shock. I'm sorry I came here."

"Well, I'm sorry to hear that." Little P had slipped in to stand between their beds. "I know it's easy to feel upset right now, but plenty of people do just fine with only one eye or a permanent limp. The important thing is not to make this the focus of your entire experience here."

"Fuck off," Kannon said.

"He's right." Cassie turned her face to the far wall to hide the tears that had started to trickle out of her unmaimed eyes. She didn't want to make Kannon feel inadequate. "Besides, what doesn't kill us makes us stronger."

"The doctor mentioned amputation," Kannon said. "Cutting off part of your leg. Is that going to make you stronger?"

"He said it wouldn't be necessary," Cassie said.

"Which means he considered it." Kannon pushed himself to a more upright position so he could give half a glare to the producer. "You destroyed us. How can you stand there and give us a goddamn pep talk?"

"Everyone was informed of the risks," Little P told them. "You did read the contract, didn't you?"

"So what?" Kannon demanded. He hadn't read the contract; one of his father's lawyers had. "Do you know how many waivers I've signed in my life? Whitewater rafting, bungee jumping, skydiving, and, and plenty of others. I've never had so much as a scratch."

Under the heading *plenty of others* lurked Kannon's safari, during which he'd managed to take out a lion dozing in the sun. As he bragged, it had occurred to Kannon that Cassie might be the sensitive type who frowned upon shooting wild animals from a jeep as they napped.

"It could have just as easily been two of the others, or no one, or even all of you." This wasn't Little P's favorite part of the job. He'd been with the show from day one, and he still couldn't comprehend why every contestant on the receiving end of a catastrophic injury was shocked. "Fate takes a hand in everything. Or nothing. Basically, I just wanted to touch base and wish you a speedy recovery while in no way admitting any liability beyond that for which you already signed a waiver. A waiver which covers everything."

"Go fucking die," Kannon said.

You first, Little P thought.

"I think we need to rest," Cassie said. She couldn't stop herself from adding, "Thank you for stopping by."

"Of course, of course." Little P did his best not to look relieved. "Rest is certainly what you need. I'll leave you to it. The television will respond to voice commands if you want to turn on the show. We'll talk soon."

Confessional: Ollie

"Nothing prepares you for that. At this point, I don't know whether I should be more worried about the challenges or the judges. I walk a tightrope of all things, somehow avoid a bullet from the crowd, and then go through thinking the damn crazy judge is going to lose it and eat all of us. Sorry about the language, Mom, Dad. I'm doing my best, and I hope you're out there rooting for me. I want you both to know I'm dealing with this as well as I am because you guys are great parents. And, believe it or not, this is the adventure of my life. But I have to admit—a big part of me is missing the farm."

Confessional: Portia

"Poise under pressure, that's my middle name. Of course, that makes no sense. I'm babbling. Don't babble. Note to self. My hands are still shaking. Look. Like a leaf. I've never felt like I was about to die until today. For the record, it's worse than stage fright. Not that it's something that needs to be on the record. Pretty obvious, right? The judge. Wow. I don't think it's safe for him to be around people. Of course, I won't be pointing it out. I'm exhausted. I feel like I could sleep for a week. I feel like I'll never sleep again."

"But this too shall pass, just like the last challenge did. And in case anyone is wondering, when I was on the tightrope, I made myself think about my role as the one who wins it. And I'm still here, so I think that says it all. Also, having my personal and political views hinted at out there shouldn't matter. Just because I have traditional values about marriage doesn't mean I shouldn't be Creature of the Night."

"There should have been a 'no faces' rule," Lola said.

"What good would that have done?" Emily rolled her eyes. "Do you think any of those people are capable of putting a perfect triangle in someone's shoulder?"

"How should I know?" Lola snapped. "It just sucks they disfigured the hottest guy here." *The richest guy here,* she added to herself.

"At least you're focused," Emily said. She was face down in her yoga mat, also trying to focus. The room had been empty when she started. Circumstances weren't ideal, but that probably meant it was even more important not to let her practice slide.

"Does anyone know how they're doing?" Brett hadn't stopped moving since their return to the Manor. More than one of the other contestants had wished Brett was locked away in the makeshift hospital room. Emily breathed in and out of downward dog and tried not to listen.

"We didn't know five minutes ago," Jeff said. "How would we know now?"

"I don't know why everybody is in such a shitty mood." Donovan came in from the kitchen with a plate of sandwiches. "That's two more down, which means we're two closer to having a winner. And I do mean me."

"I was just thinking that," Lola said. "About the two down. But I'll be the one to win this bitch."

"If you win, it's because you are a bitch," Jeff said.

"We all plan to win," Portia said. "Which doesn't mean we can't have compassion for Kannon and Cassie."

"What's wrong with Kannon and Cassie?" Madeline snagged a sandwich off Donovan's plate and chased a bite with a swig of scotch. When no one managed a prompt answer, she left.

"Jesus, people," Donovan spat pieces of half chewed ham and bread as he spoke. Emily's warrior pose lost some integrity as she tried to avoid the crumbs. "It's not like they're dead."

"What about Stewart?" Brett said. "They took him too."

Lola snickered. "I can't believe he got shot in the ass. I'd rather be shot right through the heart. It would be way more dignified."

"I'm sure most of us would prefer that option," Emily said. Portia laughed.

Confessional: Cassie

"So, you guys aren't going to believe this, but getting shot does not excuse you from confessionals. Fine. I never believed in karma. I was raised Catholic, and sinning and being forgiven is our thing, the opposite of karma. And I always believed everyone was doing their best, so the woo-woo idea of being sentenced to life as a dung beetle didn't make sense. But since I'm a person who let her brother die because saving him would have interfered with my career, believing in karma isn't in my best interests. I was wrong to give up the time I had left for the slim chance of extending it forever. I'm not my best right now, so take it with a grain of salt, but my advice is don't hate yourself for being human. Turns out that can end badly. From my new perspective, aging gracefully doesn't look so bad."

Confessional: Madeline

"This place is awesome. They're going to have to pry me out of here with a crowbar. I'm going to find out how to apply to be the housemother like they have in a sorority. This will be better though because I won't have to deal with all those little sorority cunts. I can just live here and check on everyone. I was a little disappointed at first, but this is safer. That eye business was unfortunate. And besides, isn't the point of being immortal and powerful to get to live in a place like this? I mean, good grief, there's a movie theater. And I ordered some cookbooks today. I'm going to learn how to make ziti. The kitchen is too good to waste. Plus, it would be nice if we ate together more. That's why I'm not participating too much in the drama. I want to show the producers I can be neutral and not take sides when they get new contestants."

Portia let out a private sigh of relief when Emily took her ass out of the air and exited the living room. It was completely unnatural for a librarian to be the proud owner of such tight a body. Portia had been clenching and unclenching her own cheeks, unobtrusively she hoped, as she sat on the couch and seethed over Emily bending and flexing.

"I don't like her either," Lola said.

Portia considered denial, but the effort was beyond her. "She hasn't done anything," she offered.

"She's annoying," Lola said.

"She's got a great ass," Donovan said, and Brett nodded.

"Mine's better," Lola said.

Portia transferred some of her annoyance Lola's way. It would be nice if she weren't the only woman here who had the decency to be over thirty. Albeit, not on her resume.

"Prove it," Donovan said to Lola.

"What if we don't act like a bunch of horny teenagers?" Portia said.

"What?" Donovan had moved up behind Lola and slung an arm

around her neck. Lola smacked his arm away then butted up against his chest with her own, smirking and telling him he better not fucking touch her again.

Portia wanted to wipe that ever-present smirk right off Lola's face. Instead, she left. Before the first challenge, her nerves had been screaming for freedom. Somewhere in her warped brain, she had harbored fantasies of bonding with the other competitors. She had envisioned something akin to the fleeting bonds that often formed between castmates in more traditional productions of stage or screen.

This wasn't some experimental production of Hamlet; this was big. And she hated these people. But this mattered on a primal level. As she made a beeline for her room, she clung to the thought that despising her fellow contestants was the only sensible option.

She barreled around a corner straight into Madeline.

"What the fuck are you doing?" Portia struggled to hold back a scream of frustration.

"Nothing," Madeline said. "What's your issue? I mean, are you okay? Is there anything I can help you with?"

"You could find me a pair of ruby slippers so I can wish myself the fuck out of this disaster."

"It's going to be okay." Madeline took a step forward and extended her arms as though she were going to wrap them around Portia. Portia pushed past her and ran the rest of the way to her room.

Confessional: Kannon

"My confession. If I could manage to get up and set off a bomb in the studio, I would. Confessional is just a self-cheering session with a moment of insecurity thrown in for human interest. Since there's no point in rooting for a useless bastard with one eye, I'm going to root for Jeff. Wait. Nope. Jeff got eliminated even before I did. Still, he does have two eyes. Donovan seems like a prick, but who am I to judge. They say Justice is blind. Technically, I don't qualify. By the way, about that bastard comment, I was the reason my parents got married. I guess by convincing me to come here, they've finally gotten their revenge.

"Perhaps I should root for one of the fairer sex. Lola reminds me of the prostitute my father procured for me on my sixteenth birthday. I wasn't a virgin, but he didn't know. The prostitute was a nice girl, though. So on second thought, she was nothing like Lola. You know, suddenly I cease to amuse myself. I'll just say to anyone who's been entertained by my misery, please fuck off."

Confessional: Brett

"First fucking one across a goddamn tightrope. And I've never even seen a tightrope. Oh, and giving the audience guns? Fuck. Shit. Vampires are dark. I mean I know they eat people, but that was unbelievable. I still love 'em though. I can see myself drinking blood and hanging out, and maybe someday I'll be a judge on the show. After I become a rock star. Rock star judge would be cool. I wonder if Vlad gets chicks. On the one hand, famous fucking vampire, which is cool; on the other hand, creepy as hell. I wonder what he looks like naked. Not that I want to see him naked. That would be weird. It's more like scientific curiosity. I wonder what Delia looks like naked. That's what I want to see."

Run, _ _ _ _ _ _ _, Run!

As do we all," Chaz said as the clip from Brett's confessional ended. The audience cheered. Delia flashed some fang and struck a femme fatale pose. "I'm sure most of you had already seen Brett's confessional, but now you've seen Delia see it. Glad to see you all back. A bit later tonight, the contestants will be going through their third challenge."

Cyri hoped she wasn't going to have to watch her father participate in any other morally dubious activities.

"But for now, we'll have to content ourselves with hearing from some more friends and family," Chaz said. "We're going to hear from Stewart's kids first. And in their defense, this was recorded long before Stewart delivered his heartfelt confessional. Take a look at what Audrey and Logan had to say to their dad."

On the monitors, Stewart's much-loved children appeared.

"Hey, Dad," Audrey said. "Hey, Dad," her brother Logan echoed.

"Oh my God, Dad. You better win. Don't puss out, or I'll die of embarrassment. It's bad enough you're even on a reality show. They're lame."

"I think it's cool," Logan said. "We hope you win. Can you make me a vampire too?"

"No, me first," Audrey said.

"Neither of you is going to be a goddamn vampire," a voice shouted from off-screen.

"That was Mom," Logan said. "Guess what, Dad? My soccer team made it to the semifinals."

"It's supposed to be about Dad, dumbass."

"*I thought these were pre-recorded,*" Delia said. "*Do they have no sentiment for their father?*"

"*They were pre-recorded,*" Chaz assured her.

"*I think the world might be a better place if we ate more children,*" Delia said.

"*Agreed,*" Edmund and Nodin answered in unison.

"*I have always been a lover of children,*" Vlad said.

"*A lover of eating them, you mean?*" Delia said.

"*Yes,*" Vlad said after an uncomfortable moment.

"Love you, Dad." Stewart's kids were still onscreen. "Sorry, we couldn't come over before you left for the show. Coach called an extra practice, and there's more homework this year than in second grade, so you know."

"Okay, Dad. Don't embarrass me. See ya." Stewart's children disappeared from the screens and were replaced by Emily. The crowd erupted in murmurs of surprise. Edmund sneered.

"How incredibly touching," Chaz said. "And the young lady you see onscreen is not Emily, but her twin sister, Evelyn."

"If there are two, I can surely have one?" Vlad said.

"Let's listen," Chaz said.

"Emily. First, I need to say, in spite of what has passed between us recently, I pray you are well. And because I fear the sister I have known is lost to me in this world, I want to tell you I forgive you. You should also know God will forgive you even now. All you have to do is ask. But make no mistake. You must ask, or you will have an eternity to regret it. Not the eternity you so desire, the one that doesn't exist, but an eternity of flame and anguish. It pains me to have to say these things to my sister as much as it shames me to know you are a willing participant in this abomination. Repent, my sister, else my sister in the flesh you will be only. Never my sister in spirit. Never my sister in Christ. Repent!"

"We tried for a less judgmental take," Chaz said, "but she started trying to bless the cameraman, and he wanted to get out of there. As you can imagine, the contestants are a bit worn out. Since that's their problem, we'll have the third challenge coming up after this short break! Don't miss it!"

"Really? I want to see it." Kip had answered his door to a tearful Gina. It had been hard to muster interest in yet another spat between Gina and her pretty (but insufferable) boyfriend. However, the idea of a bunch of psychos fighting it out to see who got to be a vampire was fascinating.

"No, it's awful," Gina said. "And Brad was being a dick. The whole thing was pissing me off."

"I can't believe I've never heard of it," Kip said.

"You're not missing anything." Gina had hoped to find stauncher support. What good was a gay best friend if he was just going to act like a regular guy?

"Well, I'm not going to miss anything else. I'm putting it on right now." Kip fiddled with the remote while Gina sulked. "You did *not* say the host was beautiful," Kip added when he found the show.

"Yeah, he's cute," Gina said. "But that's not the point. The whole thing is barbaric and disgusting."

"There is nothing disgusting about him," Kip said. Chaz was laughing at something Delia said. "The things I would do to that man."

"He's not a man," Gina said. Although she wouldn't admit it, she would have jumped on the opportunity to do some of those same things to Chaz. "And he'd do much worse to you. What happened to the sound?" Gina asked.

"You kicked the speaker cord. Move your foot. Okay, got it. So, who should I root for?"

Edmund wondered what the consequence would be for eating Little P. The Voice's dominant hand man was nattering on about the virtues of this latest adjustment.

As Little P talked, he wondered if Edmund was thinking of eating him. "You're great like I said. Everything is great. It's so great we want to take it further, you understand?"

"I am far too lofty and magnificent a creature to speak to humans," Edmund said. "What do you imagine I will misconstrue?"

Little P sighed and pressed on. "We know," he said, "about your proclivities."

Edmund snarled, and Little P quavered. "We, that is He, doesn't care. As long as you remain discreet. And as long as you continue to play your part with the enthusiasm we've come to expect."

"What else would I do?" Edmund said, clinging to the thought that Little P was doing his human best to be valuable in a big, scary world.

"All right, people. The contestants have rested as much as we're going to let them, and they are raring to go. Who's ready to watch them meet their third challenge?"

"We are! We are! WE ARE READY!"

"Have you guys been rehearsing that?" Chaz said. The crowd cackled at his wit. Chaz thought they were morons. "As you may remember, two short challenges ago, our contestants kicked off the competition by downing chalices of blood."

"Why blood in a chalice?" Vlad said. "Blood should be warm from the flesh."

"Everyone, welcome back our special guest judge, Vlad the Impaler, and don't forget about Delia, Nodin, and Edmund!"

"Back to tonight's challenge," Chaz said when the applause had died down. "Although the contestants are long past their first sip of human blood, they have yet to enjoy it as it's meant to be enjoyed. That is, straight from the tap. Tonight's challenge is to drink from a human. Which means piercing a vein with nothing more than teeth, and drinking for a full minute. The contestants will be drinking from volunteers; many of whom auditioned to be on Creature of the Night but didn't make the final cut. No one will be drained to death for this challenge, not intentionally at any rate. So parents watching with small children, listen up: we are still suitable for the kiddies."

"Hear that, honey?" Cyri's dad chuckled.

Cyri wasn't convinced it was suitable for *her*, but the thought of some dad out there watching with his three-year-old made her think a shade more kindly of her own father.

"We paired each contestant with a volunteer, and the pairs are waiting to come out. Because we need to know how long each contestant has been drinking, they will stop to show us when they pierce the skin and draw their first mouthful of blood. It is then their minute will commence. If your donor passes out, we will consider your challenge completed."

"Are there extras?" Vlad said.

"Is he not eating?" Nodin snapped. "Someone order a prostitute or a pizza boy."

"I think food is an excellent idea," Chaz said. "We all know a hungry vampire is a massacre waiting to happen."

"He fed recently," Delia said. "Meals on Heels sent a snack over during the last break."

"*They might have ordered enough for everyone,*" Edmund said.

"If I am ever in such a state," Nodin said, "you must slay me."

"You should have more respect," Delia said.

"I have respect," Nodin said. "If I didn't, I would have—"

Vlad had flipped Nodin out of his throne and pinned him down on the altar before anyone else could move. Delia went to Nodin's assistance, and Chaz hovered slightly behind. "It's almost as if he can still sense a threat, even in his present state," Delia said. "Perhaps an apology would appease him."

Nodin managed to utter an apology, and Vlad consented to releasing his throat. Nodin set his throne upright and slunk onto it.

"Well, that threw our timing a bit," Chaz said. "Contestants, come on out, and bring your dinners!"

There were eight chairs onstage. Simple and armless, they nevertheless appeared sturdy. The donors took the chairs, and each contestant stood behind their donor.

This is getting to be too much, Stewart thought. He shifted uncomfortably. His ass was sore, but there was something embarrassing about making a big deal out of a modest furrow when the others had been wounded more severely. Stewart looked down at his donor and grimaced at the flakes in his donor's hair. He wasn't looking forward to putting his lips to the matching neck.

Don't rush and you'll be fine, Emily told herself. She had Googled the best place to bite and had spent the night mentally rehearsing. That hadn't felt like enough, so this morning, she'd bitten into her own wrist until she'd drawn blood. As long as no one started raining acid on them, this should be a piece of cake compared to the last challenge. Bloody, human cake.

I'm going to kill him, Portia thought. Her donor had asked her to dinner while they were lining up to walk onstage. In spite of her vehement rejection, he was now leaning back in his chair trying to brush her breasts with the back of his head.

Ollie liked the look of his donor. The contestants weren't supposed to chat with their assigned victims or even introduce themselves, but Ollie and his donor had exchanged a handshake and a friendly nod. There was no reason Ollie could see for not being on good terms with someone nice enough to donate some vital fluid so Ollie could advance in the competition. Ollie had been feeling a little down thanks to the cutthroat attitudes of some of his competitors; it was nice to see a little selflessness.

Lola planned to take full advantage of the simplicity of this challenge to put on a memorable show. *Good thing this guy isn't completely revolting.* To Lola, vampires were all about power and sex, and the competition thus far had been missing any element that could be deemed sexy. *Not for long.* Lola twisted her fingers in her donor's hair and waited for the signal to begin.

This guy needs to hold the fuck still, Donovan thought. His donor was a sweaty, hairy little guy who was letting his anxiety get the better of him. *Guess you should have thought this through, pal.* Not that Donovan was wasting sympathy on some loser and his second thoughts. It wasn't like the donors weren't going to walk away from this, and it wasn't like Donovan was going to go easy on some little pussy in his mission to dominate this competition.

Just like the first time, Celeste thought. *No big deal.* The gridlock in her intestines argued otherwise. She tried and failed to banish thoughts of what might happen when she sent blood flowing through her digestive tract. True, she had managed the first time but now, there was also the biting to consider. *There's nowhere to go but through.*

Mainly, she was disgusted by the fact that death would be hard to come by in this challenge. A quick death at any rate.

Come on, man; let's get started. Brett was bouncing on his toes, much to the alarm of his donor, who wished anyone else had drawn him. Emily or Portia would have been ideal. Unbeknownst to both Brett and his donor, they had a lot in common. All Brett knew was this was an undeniably vampiric undertaking, one that would truly put him one step closer to being one of the magnificent undead. He wished Chaz would wrap up the foreplay and start the challenge.

"This is some sick shit," Tim said. "Move the fuck over, would you?"

"I was here first," his sister said, stretching out in an attempt to oust Tim from the sofa. "You move the fuck over."

"Knock it off, both of you." Their mother couldn't wait for the damn vampire show to conclude. "One more argument, and I'll turn it off and you can go to your rooms and watch on your iPads."

"Mom," Kristen protested. "Tim started it."

"I don't care who started it." Tim and Kristen's mother was trying to put dinner together after a long day of teaching, and she was wondering what had possessed her to believe she wanted so many children in her life.

"Fine," Kristen said. She aimed a final kick at her brother's leg. "They're getting ready to start."

"I'm amazed people volunteer to have their necks sucked on," their mother said. She hovered between the kitchen and living room shaping a wad of raw ground beef into a patty. "It seems gross."

"How is it gross?" Tim said. "You don't think it's gross when vampires do it."

"They're vampires; drinking blood is normal for them."

"Yeah, but these guys are *going* to be vampires," Tim said.

"No. One of them is going to be," Kristen said. "It's called *Creature of the Night*. Singular. They don't all get to be vampires. Idiot."

"Fuck you, Kristen."

"Tim?" Their mother stuck her head back into the living room to dispense a threatening look. "That's your last warning."

"Oh my god," Tim said. "Look at Lola."

"Yeah, she's seriously trampy," his sister said.

"They're making the big guy suck blood out of another guy."

"So? Lots of the guys have guy donors."

"Yeah, but, I bet this guy's pissed."

In the eight chairs, the eight donors waited. The contestants hovered behind their human meals poised to sink their teeth in.

"The contestants are ready," Chaz said. "I do believe our audience is also ready, am I right?" He was right. "Remember to show your first blood. After which, your minute of drinking will commence. Audience, count it down for them."

"Three, two, one, drink!" The crowd screamed.

And drink the contestants did.

Or at least, attempt to drink. Donovan proceeded to confound Tim's expectations by digging into his donor, not sparing a single thought for that donor's possession of a penis. He beat Lola to the punch thanks to said contestant being rather consumed with the theatrics of it all.

Shit, that hurts like a motherfucker, Donovan's donor thought as Donovan gnawed at his neck. *I can't fucking do this.* But he was doing it. Or more precisely, it was being done to him, and he couldn't see a way to stop it.

Lola took a more sensual approach. At the crowd's signal, she swung around the chair and plopped down on her donor, straddling him with her fingers in his hair, using it to pull his head aside and expose his neck.

Awesome! Lola's donor thought when she climbed aboard.

Down the line, Emily was holding her donor's head to the side examining the neck for the optimum chomping zone. Satisfied, she leaned down and caught the precise vein she wanted between her upper and lower canines. It took a bit of grinding and more pressure than she had anticipated, but she was rewarded a second later by a spurt of blood in her mouth.

As rewards went, she'd had better.

"First blood, Emily!" Chaz shouted when she raised her head to display her bloody lips. "Start your minute Emily."

Emily's donor craned her head further to the side. She was a big believer in the sisterhood. She wanted her contestant to win.

Lola realized she was wasting time vamping it up and gave her donor's head another good yank until she had exposed a satisfactory stretch of neck. She sunk her teeth in somewhere between his ear and his shoulder, taking the biggest, most vicious bite she could manage. Human teeth are dull and almost useless compared to fangs, so Lola ended up with a mouthful of neck, which tasted sickeningly of Drakkar Noir and no blood.

Being a determined girl, Lola pushed past the taste of the once popular cologne and continued chomping with all her might, but there was just too much flesh in her mouth. Her victim wasn't being pierced or even ripped, only bruised. Beneath her, the enthusiasm of Lola's donor began to wane.

"First blood for Brett! Brett start your minute," Chaz said. Brett offered the audience a bloody grin, threw a thumbs up, and dove back in.

On the next chair, Donovan's donor was starting to freak the fuck out. He considered himself a liberal guy; he voted for equality every time whether the oppressed were gays, vamps, or women. But having your neck sucked by some middle aged guy who sure as shit had done a bunch of steroids in high school was taking open mindedness one step too far. It was, perhaps, taking it several steps too far.

When a chair down the line tipped over and the guy sitting in it sprawled onto the floor with one of the wannabe vampire chicks riding him down the whole way, Donovan stopped gnawing to take in the commotion. Donovan's donor (whose name was **Francis**) seized his chance like he hadn't done since Suzie Kingsman, the sluttiest girl in school, caught her boyfriend with his tongue down another cheerleader's throat and looked around for a tool with which to achieve revenge. He rammed the palm of his hand into the bottom of Donovan's jaw with enough force to send Donovan staggering back, and then Francis took off running.

Francis was within three feet of Chaz (who had spent the duration of the un-choreographed sprint debating whether or not to intervene and was leaning heavily toward not bothering) when

Donovan tackled him.

The donors gawked at the spectacle, and half the contestants had paused to see the outcome. Emily was not one of those. She had been sucking as slowly as she reasonably could and counting down to *five—four—three—*

Brett's donor fell off his chair, unconscious.

"Brett wins the challenge!" Chaz said and sidestepped to avoid the squirming, clawing mass made up of Donovan and Francis that was sliding across the floor toward his feet.

—one.

"And Emily has completed her minute," Chaz said.

Emily let the neck go and stood up trying to figure out how someone had gotten through their minute ahead of her. She finally caught sight of Brett's guy sprawled on the floor and had to resist the urge to walk over and kick him.

Donovan and Francis came to a stop where Chaz had been standing. Donovan had caught Francis around the ankles. The kick he took in the face when Francis yanked a foot free surprised only Donovan.

"This is good," Vlad said as Donovan released Francis to clamp a hand over his suddenly gushing nose. Delia moved to restrain Vlad when the blood started to flow. Francis scrambled to his feet and jumped off the stage. He sprinted down the aisle taking every eye in the theater with him.

"Stop him!" Donovan was talking through a mouthful of his own blood, but the gist was clear.

"Muskrats have more nobility," Edmund said.

"Muskrats are the royalty of the vermin world," Chaz countered. Edmund hissed.

"Ollie has drawn blood," Chaz said, magnificently (if he did say so himself) keeping track of the proceedings, both scheduled and not. "His minute starts now."

"Why the muskrat?" Delia wondered. "Why not the capybara? It is the largest."

"Because size doesn't matter?" Chaz said.

"Dearest Chaz," Delia said. "It matters."

Ollie was caught up in what he was doing, but several of the others were still staring at Donovan. "The challenge is not complete," Nodin said. The contestants gaped at him for a moment and resumed their attempts.

"They eat like zombies," Vlad said. "Look at that useless gnawing. I can show them how it should be done."

"That is the point of the challenge," Nodin told him. "For them to learn. And let us not speak of z-o-m-b-i-e-s in front of the h-u-m-a-n-s."

"We can spell," Cyri said to her father with some indignation then instantly regretted it. Even from fifty yards, Cyri could feel the weight of Nodin's regard.

"All of you?" Nodin asked, judgment and a hint of disbelief mixing in his voice.

"She only got ninety-eight percent on her last English test," Cyri's father said. "There are lots of words she can't spell."

"It's going to serve you right if they eat me," Cyri said.

"Don't worry," Chaz said. "I'll protect you." From the others. He would obviously savage the girl himself. He flashed his breathtaking smile Cyri's way. She ignored him.

"Earth to Chaz," Delia said.

Chaz stopped trying to make the audience girl swoon.

"So, this is the one we get to eat?" Vlad was pleased.

"No," Edmund said.

"He's getting away." Donovan slammed a foot into his donor's overturned chair. "Is someone going to stop him?"

"It is your donor. Your responsibility." Edmund looked as if he would as soon eviscerate Donovan as instruct him.

"Yes, you should retrieve him," Nodin said, releasing Cyri from his gaze. "If you wish not to be eliminated."

Donovan left the stage in a hurry, still unsuccessfully trying to contain the blood.

"We should eliminate him regardless," Edmund said. "I hate that one more than most. And what is the problem with the female?"

The vampires all looked at Celeste, who had briefly gone back to the neck of her donor but was now rooting around her mouth with a finger.

"Looks like Celeste has some skin stuck between her teeth," Chaz said. "And look, Lola has drawn blood." Lola was lying on top of her donor, sucking away. Her donor had his hands on her ass, and she was grinding herself against him. Both of them were enjoying themselves immensely.

"Start your minute, Lola." Lola's donor was gyrating beneath her, and as she again buried her face in his neck, his tempo increased. Lola was pushing down on his shoulders, but clearly her donor was not offering resistance.

Portia stepped back from her donor and raised her hand.

"It's okay," Celeste said. "Got it. Oh fucking shit, it's a mole."

"And Celeste has eaten a mole."

The audience jeered.

"I didn't eat it," Celeste said. "It's here."

"Celeste has saved the mole," Chaz corrected.

Portia waved her hand back and forth.

"But does this count as blood?" Celeste wanted to know. "I think there's a little on the mole."

Donovan ran up the aisle toward the stage. "I couldn't catch him." He was breathing hard and had acquired scratches that ran from his left eye all the way down his face. The blood from his nose had slowed to a trickle. "He's gone."

"No," Delia ruled. "The blood must come from a vein, not a growth."

Technically, they didn't specify, Cyri thought.

"Now we may eliminate him," Nodin said with deep pleasure.

"Not yet," Delia said.

Chaz raised an eyebrow at Delia. "We will confer," Delia said.

"Attend the actress."

"Is there a problem, Portia?" Chaz asked, sounding, to all the world, concerned. Her mouth was bloody. "You have to drink for one minute to complete the challenge."

"He has a..." Portia pointed to her donor's crotch. It seemed to have a life of its own. "It's popping up at me. I can see it wiggling in his pants while I'm trying to suck."

"Prude," Delia commented.

"Any actress worth her salt knows how to deal with wiggly pants." Vlad cackled and mimed a method of relief that involved poking his cheek out with his tongue.

"Suck it! Suck it! Suck it!"

Cyri hoped none of her friends would see her dad chanting along.

"I'm assuming you mean his neck," Chaz told the audience, "because *Creature of the Night* is strictly PG."

Celeste raised her head to show she'd drawn proper vein blood. "Start your minute, Celeste," Chaz said.

"Hold." Delia held up a hand. Everyone froze. "We have conferred. The majority of us wish to expel from the competition the one who lost his donor, but we are also enjoying the freshness of this event. Donovan may find a way to complete the challenge."

"What am I supposed to—"

"Drink from me! Drink from me! Drink fro–"

"We said Donovan may find a way," Delia chided. "Quiet, or I release Vlad to drink his fill." The audience didn't peep.

"First blood for Stewart," Chaz said. "Start your minute." Stewart grimaced but dutifully returned to his donor's neck, which he had been devastated to find no cleaner than his donor's hair. Unbeknownst to Stewart, his scheduled donor had been pre-selected from the contestant applicants like the others. Alas, the man sitting in front of him had been plucked from a nearby park about an hour before the challenge began to replace the no-show.

Stewart's donor was thinking of the hundred bucks and the hot meal. He had also been granted five minutes to shower before the challenge, although both he and Stewart would have been better served by thirty. The industrious part of him thought if his guy won, he could stay on as a permanent food source. He would have been heartbroken to learn he had missed some key areas when cleaning up and that Stewart had noticed every one of them. Stewart's donor sat up straighter so Stewart wouldn't have to bend down so far.

"Lola has completed the challenge," Chaz said. Lola remained in position, sucking away and dry humping her donor.

Donovan was trying to chat up a cute redhead in the front row. She leaned away and rolled her eyes.

"Aim lower, barbarian," Edmund said.

"Lola, dismount your donor," Chaz said. Lola unclamped from his neck. Her donor grabbed her head and guided her lips to his.

Portia had given up on gaining assistance and had gone back to half-heartedly chewing on her randy donor who shortly began touching himself. This inspired such a flare of rage in Portia that her bite changed from reluctant to savage, and she finally managed to tear open a vein.

"Portia, start your minute," Chaz said. Portia spit out the chunk of neck and proceeded to drink while periodically slapping the hand of her donor away from his raging penis. Her donor moaned each time she hit him.

Miranda Sanders, a portly woman in her fifties, was making her way down the row toward Donovan. People leaned back and turned their knees aside to facilitate her progress.

"Ollie has completed the challenge!" Chaz announced.

Miranda tapped Donovan on the shoulder. Donovan turned away from the fifth cute young thing in a row to reject him and found a stout woman who would have reminded him of his wife if her eyes hadn't sparkled. Tara's eyes had lost their sparkle years ago.

"Stewart is finished," Chaz said. "But—"

"No vomiting," Nodin said.

"You have to keep it down, Stewart," Chaz agreed. "Or you start over."

Stewart gagged but managed to keep his stomach under control. "That guy tastes like crap," he said and gagged again. "Is there supposed to be an aftertaste? The other blood didn't taste like, fuck, I don't know, dirt and garbage. What's wrong with you, man?"

Stewart's donor flushed and gave up on the thought of a permanent relationship.

"Donors do not speak," Nodin said. "I would like to know why you feel entitled to complain about the taste."

Emily patted her donor's shoulder in appreciation.

Brett waved a hand and clutched at his donor's chair. He was gasping as though he'd just run miles.

Donovan cast a desperate look around hoping for a more comely donor to offer herself. All the attractive women in range averted their eyes. Miranda took Donovan by the hand and led him onto the stage.

"Portia has completed the challenge," Chaz announced. Portia smacked her donor hard enough to rock his head and stepped back. Her donor let out a final moan and relaxed.

Miranda righted the chair Donovan's original donor had knocked over in his dash for freedom and settled herself on it. She produced a rubber band and thoughtfully secured her hair away from her neck. Donovan took a deep breath and bent down.

"Celeste has completed the challenge," Chaz said.

Celeste and her donor shook hands. "Sorry for biting off your mole," Celeste said.

"It's okay," her donor said. "I always hated that mole."

"*I will kill–*" Edmund began.

"Donors should not speak," Nodin said again.

A section of the audience on the far left started to chant. "*Brett is dying! Brett is dying!*"

Everyone else looked at Brett. He had turned an aggressive shade of red and was breathing in irregular gasps. Hives flowed up his neck, and his eyes were nearly swollen shut.

"What is this?" Delia said.

Chaz shrugged. "Did someone poison Brett?"

"Every fucking season," Delia said.

The other contestants looked at one another and shook their heads.

"Maybe allergies?" Emily suggested.

Brett nodded desperately and then toppled to the stage floor.

"Allergies," Chaz said.

"He might have an EpiPen somewhere in his stuff," Emily said. "Someone should check."

"Does anyone here have an EpiPen?" Chaz said.

Hands throughout the audience produced EpiPens and waved them madly. Several of the cameras zoomed in to capture their images. You could say *As seen on Creature of the Night* all you wanted, but you still had to pay for the footage.

Chaz plucked the nearest EpiPen from the hand of a teenage boy with braces then vaulted over to Brett and plunged in into his thigh.

Everyone watched Brett struggle for breath.

"Hey, guys," Donovan said. "She's bleeding. Look. Can I start my minute?"

"Go ahead," Chaz said.

"Is that her blood or his?" Delia wanted to know. Miranda turned so the judges could see her neck was indeed bleeding.

Donovan resumed sucking. Brett began to breathe more consistently. Emily knelt beside Brett and helped him sit up. "What are you allergic to?"

"Peanuts," Brett said after a moment.

"Shit, man," Brett's donor said. "I'm so sorry. I had peanut butter this morning. And yesterday. Like twice. I fucking practically live on peanut butter. And jelly. You've gotta have jelly too. Unless it's on toast. Then you can just have peanut butter. You okay?"

Brett nodded.

"Did no one explain to them their role as food?" Edmund said. "Why do they continue to verbalize? It's maddening enough that we permit the contestants to speak."

Donovan was still sucking. For lack of anything else to do, most of the other contestants and their donors had gathered around to watch. Emily and Brett remained on the floor as did Lola and her donor.

The audience took it upon themselves to provide the final countdown. *"Five! Four! Three! Two! One!"*

"And that's it," Chaz said. "Donovan has completed the challenge. Let's give all our contestants and their donors a round of applause."

The crowd broke into a rowdy cheer. Chaz signaled for Riley and Kiley to escort the donors offstage. "Don't forget that one," Chaz said. Lola and her donor were well on their way to violating the show's no nudity policy. Riley had to pluck Lola's donor from beneath her, which she did easily with one hand, dumping Lola on her ass. Riley gave the donor a chastising shake and hefted him toward the others.

"We're going to keep the contestants with us while we respond to some members of our television audience and the judges deliberate. Our first question comes from @DonDongGood in Fresno, California."

"Hi, Chaz. Hi, Delia. I fucking worship the ground you walk on. My question is what makes people taste good or bad? And what can I do to make myself appealing?"

"There are many factors," Chaz said, "including diet, health, and age. People who drink heavily, enjoy hard drugs, and even people who smoke have a distinct flavor which is an acquired taste. Because there isn't anything we can't process, Brett would not have suffered his unfortunate reaction to his peanut butter filled donor if he were one of us. However, we do appreciate when you eat organic, and we love vegetarians the way humans value grass-fed beef."

"*They are tasty,*" Delia said.

"*Ever have a virgin vegetarian?*" Nodin said.

"*They're hard to find,*" Delia said.

"*Alvie breeds them,*" Edmund said. "*See him next time you're in Piedmont.*"

"It has been too long since I've seen Italy," Delia said.

"Okay," Chaz said. "Next up, we have a question from Jenny in Lubbock, Texas."

"I was wondering what's going to happen to the guy who escaped."

"Not technically a question," Chaz said, "but nothing will happen. Except his check will be canceled for non-fulfillment of his contract. Since this is a non-lethal challenge, no other action will be taken."

The crowd cheered; why, Chaz had no idea. He spoke over the end of the applause. "Contestants, please step forward."

Emily helped Brett to his feet, and they joined the other contestants in forming a slightly ragged line.

"We have your poll results," Chaz shouted. "And the audience votes have been tallied. Those of you who voted would like to see the last of Donovan, which feels a bit familiar. According to the nearly unanimous poll results, this time it's because he let his donor get away."

Voting based on performance, Cyri thought. *What will they think of next?*

"And it seems you would also like to get rid of Emily," Chaz said, "because she isn't sexy enough. Let that be a lesson to you all: always remember to gyrate."

"*That was truly appalling,*" Edmund said.

"Edmund isn't pleased with how the humans performed," Chaz said. "I'm sure we are all equally shocked."

"I was referring to the poll results," Edmund clarified.

"It was glorious," Vlad said. "So much…"

"Human gumption and resilience?" Chaz said.

"Blood," Vlad said. "So much blood. And sex. I enjoy both these things."

"Yes, it was lovely," Delia agreed. "And the chaos was enjoyable as well. Still, Donovan was a disappointment."

"Not only did he let his donor escape, he succumbed easily to a beating." Nodin steepled his fingers together and looked down on Donovan. "And then he waited for a new donor to choose him instead of taking one like a true predator would."

"Eliminate him," Edmund said.

"He is a brute," Delia said. *"He brings excitement to the competition."*

"What do you have to say about your disappointing performance, Donovan?" Nodin said. Chaz gestured that Donovan should step forward to answer.

"I let myself get distracted," Donovan said. "It won't happen again."

"We must not let it happen again," Edmund said. *"Eliminate him."*

"Which explains how your original donor got away," Delia said. "But we are asking about your failed attempts to secure a new donor."

"I don't know," Donovan said. "The fucking asshole kicked me in the face when I wasn't looking. I think I'm a little off. I still completed the challenge. That should count for something."

"The woman virtually completed the challenge for him," Edmund said.

"We decide what will count," Nodin said. "Step back."

"That one plays with her food," Vlad said, leering at Lola.

"Yes," Delia said. "One can enjoy oneself on multiple levels." Vlad's fangs slid out. Chaz hoped he was only experiencing one level of excitement. "That lesson is one others would do well to learn."

All eyes turned to Portia, who flushed. "She did carry on," Nodin said.

"She did," Delia admitted, "but not without first making a point of displaying her prudishness."

"She finished early," Nodin said.

"Not significantly early." Edmund scowled. "What do you like about that one? There is clearly something."

"Portia, step forward," Chaz said.

"Why were you so alarmed by the signs of your donor's arousal?" Delia asked.

"I'm not a prude," Portia said. "It was just inappropriate. And when I engage in not being a prude, it should be consensual. Also, I was under the impression things of a sexual nature were not considered appropriate for the show."

"It is a gray area," Delia said. "Nudity is not permitted, but your donor was fully clothed."

"She is much like my mother," Vlad said. "I would have her."

"Have her, have her?" Chaz said. This was the kind of unfortunate kink that gave vampires a bad name.

"My mother was beautiful and very skilled." Delia reached out and flicked Vlad's arm. Vlad stopped reminiscing about his mother. Portia looked like she was ready to follow Francis's example.

"She has standards," Nodin said. "Which is perhaps something to be appreciated."

"We should appreciate the one who threw himself into the face of death in order to complete the challenge," Delia said. Brett felt himself flush with pleasure. Or perhaps, he was still affected by the peanuts.

"You are giving him credit he does not warrant," Edmund said. "He had no idea of his peril."

"He may have," Nodin said. "Ask him."

Edmund glowered at the suggestion he should speak directly to a human.

"Brett, did you feel yourself reacting to the allergens in your donor?" Chaz was going to demand more money next season.

Brett cleared his throat. He was able to speak, but his voice was scratchy and his breath shallow. "I could feel my throat getting tight almost as soon as I started my minute. But I didn't want to stop. I didn't know about the peanut butter. If I had, I would have assumed the effect would be diluted, you know, second-hand reaction and all. But I think I would have gone for it no matter what. I want to win this challenge. There's nothing to lose by going for it, right?"

"Profound," Edmund said. "How lucky we are this intellectual giant did not slip from our midst."

"See?" Chaz smiled at Brett. "Edmund agrees completely." Edmund hissed.

"He coped well," Delia said. "You too were once human. You have forgotten what it is like to struggle for bravery under the burden of frailty."

"I have forgotten nothing," Edmund said.

"He won the challenge," Delia said.

"Moving on," Chaz said. "Emily was the second contestant to complete the challenge and the first to drink for a full minute. Thoughts on her performance."

"I see some of myself in that one," Vlad said. "A quiet determination and strength." Emily forced a smile. "You will do what you need to do, I see it. All who stand against you will suffer."

"Let us focus on the challenge at hand," Delia said. "The girl can contemplate the merits of roasting versus impaling her enemies at another time."

"Both is best," Vlad offered.

"She did well," Nodin said. "Very precise. Obviously, she has studied. But there are many who study us who we would not deem suitable companions for eternity. One must have a certain joie de vivre to master the art of being undead."

"Do you believe you have joy for life, Emily?" Delia tilted her head as though Emily were an odd specimen in need of dissection.

"Yes," Emily said. "Of course." She was here, wasn't she? Ready to give up her life to have it forever. If that didn't mean she was full of joie de vivre, what did?

"And Ollie did well," Delia said. "You were both adept and resolute. Congratulations."

"Thank you, ma'am," Ollie said. Chaz snorted.

"Now for Celeste," Nodin said. "Step forward."

Celeste stepped forward and peeked up at the judges from under her lashes.

"Celeste," Delia said. "We do not eat the flesh."

"Like zombies do," Vlad said.

"We do not eat flesh as though we were mythical zombies," Delia agreed. "Your enthusiasm does you credit. Your sloppiness does not."

"Another unfortunate human quality," Edmund said. "Shared by this mole eater and the one who nearly vomited."

Nodin feigned surprise. *"Not all of them?"*

"Of course, all of them," Edmund said.

"You might as well step forward too," Chaz said to Stewart.

"'Nearly' is another way of saying 'did not,'" Delia said. "But it was not impressive. Of course, Stewart could not help finding the taste was objectionable, but there was no need for such drama."

Stewart opened his mouth to defend himself, but Delia forestalled him with an upraised hand. "We are finished with you."

"Celeste and Stewart, step back," Chaz said.

"I didn't eat it," Celeste said under her breath as she stepped back. All the vampires heard, but none of them acknowledged her.

Chaz looked at Delia. The judges conferred silently.

"We would do well to eliminate Lola and Stewart," Delia said.

"No," Edmund said. *"The cowardly brute must go. And the flesh eater. Or we could eliminate four."*

"We will eliminate two," Nodin said.

"We're stuck with Donovan for the time being," Delia said. *"I*

totally get that we all hate him, but his presence fills a need."

"The audience hates him as well," Edmund said.

"Is that you caring what humans think?" Delia wondered.

"I agree we must keep Donovan," Nodin said. *"However, can we agree the mole eater should go?"*

"Yes," Delia said.

"Yes," Edmund said.

"What is a mole eater?" Vlad asked. *"I say, eliminate the prude."*

"We all agree on Celeste," Delia said. *"Which male shall we eliminate?"*

"If not the brute, then the simpering vampire lover," Edmund said.

"He won the challenge," Nodin objected.

"That leaves only the father or the farm boy," Delia said.

"The farm boy smiles too much," Edmund said, feeling terrible about it. *"I will not consent to look at his face for eternity."*

"You are not obligated to spend time with the winner," Delia said.

"We might cross paths," Edmund said. *"He has too much joie de vivre."*

"Fine," Nodin said. *"Let it be those two."*

The band eased into *Mandy* by Barry Manilow.

"Chaz," Nodin said aloud. "Announce the eliminated."

With a bit of flare, Chaz complied. "The judges have eliminated Ollie and Celeste. Never fear, audience. I'm sure you'll get it right eventually."

Those not eliminated avoided looking at those who were. Donovan was trying to wipe the tears off his face without being caught by a camera, but it was impossible to avoid them all. The vampire girls came to take everyone away.

"That was a lot of excitement," Chaz said. "The remaining contestants and your two newest losers will be heading back to the Manor to make their confessionals and hang out for your viewing pleasure. We'll see you soon for more Friends and Family and the fourth challenge!"

"That seemed pretty random," Marv said to his roommate. Marv had never seen *Creature of the Night,* so the whole thing seemed pretty random, but he never turned down an invitation from Ginger to hang out. Marv had hopes.

"Yeah, they just pick the ones they like," Ginger told him. "But, they seem to like the crazy ones. That's how they ended up with the girl who totally went on a blood-sucking rampage after they turned her."

"Hey, the creepy judge keeps mentioning zombies," Marv said. "Do you think they're real too?"

"Yeah. And so are goblins, werewolves, and Tinkerbell," Ginger said. "Don't be so stupid."

Confessional: Donovan

"I just want to say I'm sorry. Tara, I think I miss you, and I might have been a dick. You'll be better off without me; I hope you know that. If you don't, ask your mother. She'll tell you. I'm not giving up. I can't. But if I do win, I'll be coming home. Just to say goodbye. I still don't want to be married anymore, but I could have said it better. Know what's funny? I don't know if I'm weak or finally doing the right thing. It's hard to care right now. That little fuck almost, well, he fucked me up pretty good. You can see that.

"The woman donor reminded me of you a little before we were married. Except fatter. Maybe not fatter than you are now, but...never mind. Maybe I won't come back at all; that might be better for everybody, a clean break. This is my moment of weakness, I guess. It's time to man the fuck up. This challenge, the whole thing just shocked the shit out of me. It's harder than it looks, sucking blood right out of someone's neck. The cup thing was easier. It was gross when you thought about it, but other than that, no problem.

Biting through someone's skin, feeling their pulse beating against your face, it's fucking freaky. Fucking vampires. I just want to live forever. I don't want to get old.

"The way my dad died was fucked up. Pissing himself and drooling and not even fucking together enough to know he was doing it. Am I such an asshole for not wanting to go out like that?"

Confessional: Emily

"Finally, a challenge turned out to be easier than I thought it would. The trick is to find a good vein before you start, no indiscriminate nibbling. That's my advice to the younger generation. No indiscriminate nibbling. Let me counter the awfulness of that advice with the advice to read every day. There. Right now, I'm a bit disgruntled because I should have won the challenge hands down. No muss, no fuss. If not for that ridiculous fainting clause I'd have left everyone else in the dust without spilling a drop. And I get fucking voted off for not being sexy? At least the judges don't abide by you idiots watching. I know these thoughts are pointless. I'm still here, and that's what I need to think about. Just a reaction to the stress, I suppose.

"In other news, I remind Vlad of Vlad. I'm not sure what exactly that says about me, but I am pretty sure it isn't something I would be inclined to brag about. What I want to know now is who turns the winner?"

Donovan wandered around the house until he found Ollie in the theater.

"How's it going, man?" Ollie asked. He wasn't watching a movie. He had been sitting in the dark, bleeding joie de vivre until Donovan hit the lights.

Donovan sneered. He was unaccustomed to sincere inquiries

regarding the state of his being. "Good as can be expected. How are you doing?"

"Just got eliminated, and I'm not sure why," Ollie said. Ollie didn't want to seem bitter, but he was sure it would have been more just to eliminate the guy who lost his donor.

"I think I miss my wife," Donovan told him. "I'm not sure why either. About my wife or you. What movies do they have?"

"Oh, you know, there's *Salem's Lot, Return to Salem's Lot*—not sure why anyone would return, but they're still brighter bulbs than we are. They've got *Lost Boys, Blade* through *Blade Infinity, Daybreakers*; you're getting the idea. No *Dracula* though, which seems weird. I don't understand what I did wrong," Ollie added. He was wondering if Donovan would confess to some bribe or blackmail that had kept him in the running.

"Stop looking at me, or I'm going to kick your ass," Donovan told him.

On a good day, maybe. Donovan was in no shape to kick anyone's ass right now. Still, Ollie said, "Sorry. Why do you miss your wife? I thought you hated her."

"That woman in the audience," Donovan said.

"The one who sacrificed herself to you after you lost your original donor?" Ollie's usual need to consider how his words would affect others had deserted him.

The muscle in Donovan's jaw clenched, and he let out a slow breath before answering. "Yeah, that one," he said. "She reminded me of Tara. How she used to be."

Ollie quickly understood that extended time with Donovan would bring anyone down. "So what?" Ollie said.

"Nothing."

"Want to watch *Dusk 'til Dawn?*"

"Salma Hayek?"

"Yeah."

"Yeah."

Confessional: Lola

"That was fucking hot! When I win this, I'm going to drink and fuck all day long. Well, all night long because that's how I'll be rolling. I haven't had a dry hump like that since I was thirteen. When I was drinking, I kept imagining his blood mixing with mine like I was taking his life and channeling it, so it turned into my life. Fucking amazing. I've never felt so good. And it has to be like a million times better once you're changed. I think my donor was a little freaked out at first. But I am Lola, Creature of the Night, and I seduced him and made him my eager victim. I can't wait to find out what's next.

"And for the record, I could have won, I could have been first, but I think style is more important than speed. That uptight bitch Emily might as well have used a scalpel. Not sexy at all and the audience picked up on that. Everybody else knows vampires are sexy. Look at Chaz for god's sake. Gorgeous. And Delia is too. Edmund is sexy even though he hates us. No, that's wrong. It's *because* he hates us. I'd totally let him hate fuck me. And Nodin is like Clark Kent without the glasses. Okay, so Vlad isn't sexy. Unless you think about all the stuff he's done, then he starts looking kind of hot. I bet he's into some absolutely freaky shit. So, I guess that makes him ugly sexy. We could always turn off the lights."

Confessional: Stewart

"At least I didn't throw up. It was close though. That guy tasted like armpit and garbage. The fair thing would have been to make sure all the donors tasted the same, but fuck them. I'm still here. Halfway through and I'm still in the running. How's that kids? You little bastards. I hope you're enjoying the show. Necks are tougher than you'd think. I always thought of the neck as a vulnerable place on the body, but it wasn't easy to get through. Maybe it is vulnerable in comparison. Maybe if it had been a thigh, I'd still be out there chewing. At least my guy didn't escape. That shit with Donovan was intense. It was really good to see that guy's ridiculously large ego take a blow. Not that I want anyone else to suffer, but I've been feeling this whole time I could never beat the big guy, and now, maybe, I can. Maybe I can beat them all. Maybe I'm the next Creature. Am I smiling? It feels like I'm smiling. That's because I can suddenly picture it."

Madeline was in the sauna with a wedge of Brie and a box of sesame crackers. The steam dampened the crackers and made the cheese sweat, rendering her snack patently undesirable, but it had been time for a break from her duties.

There were far too many people crying around the house, needing her tea and sympathy and Madeline was putting her foot down and taking some time for her. She would be no good to any of her charges if she didn't take care of herself.

She lifted a Brie smeared cracker toward her mouth and began to weep when it crumbled to the floor.

"Okay, what the hell is wrong with the one eating crackers in the closet?" Marv was looking from Ginger to the TV with sincere alarm. Ginger thought he looked like Lassie and wondered if she could get him to fetch her one more hard cider.

"It's not a closet; it's the sauna," Ginger said. "Like a steam room."

"That's so not the issue," Marv told her, thinking Ginger was lucky she was hot.

Confessional: Ollie

"I've never felt so low, but that's not something to focus on, is it? I still feel sure everyone has their path. I thought I'd found mine, but I guess now it's something different. Something I haven't thought of yet. I don't want to hate anyone over this. Donovan, I just don't feel like he still deserves to be here, but it wasn't my call. And he seems like a decent guy. And truthfully, they can take this place and shove it. That's not sour grapes. It's just not for me. I'm not saying I didn't want it to be; it just means I've changed since this thing started."

Confessional: Brett

"Thanks, everybody, for your support. I'm feeling better. I'm not sure if I was more afraid of dying or being eliminated from the show. It's like peanuts are my kryptonite, but it's worse because they're fucking peanuts. It sounds kind of lame, but it's really serious. As you all saw. If I win, after I'm changed, I'm going to eat a peanut butter sandwich just because I can. I kept going though, even when I could feel myself starting to react. Which kind of makes me proud. Maybe I shouldn't say I'm proud of myself, but fuck it. I am. That Lola chick is insanely hot. I can see her being a dominatrix or something, whipping guys for money all the livelong day. I'd let her whip me, and I'm not even into that shit. I would have come all over myself if she'd been riding me like she was riding her donor, even with my pants on. I bet he did too. Yeah, I'm feeling better."

"I tried to avoid the mole," Celeste said. "It was really big though. Fuck."

"You could have tried the other side of her neck," Stewart

pointed out.

"I didn't even think of that," Celeste said, feeling like an idiot. "I bet there were more though. Who the fuck picked these people?"

"I had to eat a homeless person," Stewart said. "Don't look at me for sympathy."

Celeste was past being choosy. She would accept sympathy from anyone, but her housemates ignored her to rain empathy on the stupid homeless guy.

"I think you hurt his feelings," Brett said, "when you told everybody how gross he was."

"Yeah, I noticed that too." Stewart sighed. "I feel bad about it."

"If you win, you should do something to make it up to him," Brett offered. "Let him be part of your stable."

"I don't think that's anybody's aspiration," Stewart said, "even if they are homeless."

"Are we done talking about my mole-eating extravaganza?" Celeste frowned at the room. "Maybe I haven't made clear how disgusting it was."

"Is that a thing?" Lola said. "Not the mole eating. We know that's a thing, thanks to Celeste. I mean the stable thing. I'm going to keep a stable full of hot guys to suck on."

"Don't you already?" Emily said.

"Judgy bitch." Lola flipped her hair and stalked out.

"She should meet my sister," Emily said.

Celeste sighed. It was a dramatic one meant to draw attention. It failed as miserably as Celeste had.

Confessional: Portia

"I don't want to be the one to bring it up, but that was fucking sexist as hell. Who was in charge of picking the donors? This is the most disorganized production I've ever seen. I'm starting to think they don't even care about their own rules. Is there some reason I have to deal with the erection of some hairy asshole when all I wanted was to drink his blood then get on with my day? And Lola? You are not doing women any favors by behaving like a prostitute. You're the reason everyone expected me to suck in silence while some random cock was trying to jump up and assault me.

"And for the record, when I'm a vampire, I will fucking kill anyone who waves an uninvited dick in my direction. But I handled it. Not *it*. I did not handle it. I handled the situation. So hear me fucking roar. I am finished being a fragile fucking flower. From now on, if someone needs a fucking smack on their horny head, I'm going to be the one to give it to them. Forgive the rage; I'm trying to hang onto it to keep me motivated. Also, I want to thank all of you so much for your support!"

Confessional: Jeff

"I admit. I'm glad I broke down and watched the challenge. The mole thing was hysterical, and watching Big D get his ass kicked by a ninety-eight-pound weakling was not to be missed. I'm going kind of stir crazy though, which made me think. When I was a kid, I wasn't allowed to be bored. I had to make my own fun. I've been thinking about that a lot lately. And I've decided I have to find a way to make my own fun."

"This is harder than it looks," Cassie said. She had been fitted with a walking cast, which seemed a bit too optimistic, but at least they'd also given her crutches.

"You'll get the hang of it," Kannon told her. "I've been on crutches a couple times."

"I bet my broken leg story is better than yours," Cassie teased.

"Car wreck and skiing accident," Kannon admitted. "Those might be too tall for you. You're taking it well."

Cassie grimaced. Her armpits hurt more than her ankle at this point. She eased onto a chair and handed the crutches to Kannon for adjustment. She studied his face while he was absorbed in his task. He was still beautiful. Maybe it was because she had spent so much time in a world of costumes and fantasy, but the eye patch didn't bother Cassie. Plus, she would never have expected him to be so kind. "I was done dancing before I got here. And, believe me, I didn't take it well. My grief colored everything in my life for a long time before I could accept what my diagnosis meant. Rheumatoid arthritis, if you haven't heard," she clarified.

Kannon nodded.

"So, this was a Hail Mary for me, *is* I mean, and if it doesn't work out, then I'll go out knowing I tried absolutely everything. For me there wasn't going to be a real life without dancing anyway."

"Do you still feel that way?" Kannon asked. "Now that there's no way out?"

"I'm trying to."

Confessional: Cassie

"We worked out that Kannon has seen me dance. Before we came here, I mean. This endeavor hasn't turned out like I planned, but I can't say I'm unhappy about everything. Thank God for that because I think some of the contestants are unhappy about everything. And as hard as that is to be around, it's got to be harder to live through. Since it's hard to hope for the future, I'm trying right now to enjoy every second I have left. I guess that's a common reaction to almost losing everything. But it's the best reaction, I think."

Confessional: Kannon

"I don't recognize myself. Physically or mentally. I'm not going to talk about silver linings because I am down a fucking eye, but I'm done being defeated. And I'm done being who I was. Sorry, parents, about all the staggering disappointments, but I'm done with you too. I think something must be coming, and I doubt it's anything good."

"Are you guys ready?" Brett said. He only asked because he was ready, and he wanted to talk about it.

"How do we know if we're ready when we don't know what the fuck they're going to do to us next?" Portia was giving him her haughty face, eyebrows slightly elevated, head tilted so she could look down her nose at him. It was exceedingly hot.

"Well, I'm ready," Brett said.

Jeff snorted. He was sitting in the corner with a plate of pastries. Brett was thinking of asking for some; Jeff wasn't even eating them.

Like an answer to a prayer, Jeff said, "Anyone want some of these?"

"Right here, man," Brett said.

Madeline swooped in and hovered over the plate. She picked up a pastry and sniffed it then returned it to its place. She had picked up and smelled five or six of them before she found one that met her ambiguous standards.

When Jeff extended the plate his way, Brett declined.

Confessional: Celeste

"You would think that after spending all this time with people they could show the tiniest bit of compassion when things go wrong. And none of them sees how unfair it was. My donor was flawed, and I got eliminated because of it. I mean, there are millions of people with perfect skin out there. How hard is it to just have one tiny prerequisite? But all they care about is that they weren't eliminated. Assholes. It just sucks when people only think of themselves. I'm not sure what I should do now."

Confessional: Madeline

"Today is a good day. There are lots of extra people outside. There are more every time I look. The chanting is good. It relaxes me. I'm starting to wonder what I'll have for dinner. Maybe I'll make something for everyone. The mailman hasn't come with my cookbook yet. I think that pastry made me a little sick, but they were good. Maybe I can learn to make my own. I can't eat too many more   of   the   others."

The Quality of Mercy is _ _ _ _ _ Strained.

Edmund was in his dressing room watching the last challenge replay. You had to love humans. As had been pointed out so recently by Little P, you also had to keep it to yourself.

His fascination with humanity sprang from the myriad flaws that caused other supernaturals to discount them. Even Edmund couldn't argue the others were wrong to scorn humans. The inconsistencies and cruelties of mankind were too numerous to categorize. But. They did, on occasion, help each other out of fiery pits, even when the one they helped was their competition in a contest which would determine life or death. Or help a competitor survive an allergic reaction when it was much easier to keep quiet.

So, while there was needless cruelty to be found among humans such as had never been seen in another species, there was also compassion beyond all logic. Compassion strong enough to soundly trump self-preservation.

These were things one did not say.

Edmund had fled to a remote corner of the world when the Vampire war began. Not out of fear but out of an unwillingness to participate in the extinction of mankind.

To his delight, human cowardice had won out almost

immediately with the leaders of the world promising an immediate and lasting end to the hostilities.

For their part, the vampires had acquiesced to some restrictions (restrictions that were generally disregarded) on whom and how many could be changed. Which brought them to—

A rap on the door was closely followed by a quavering human male calling, "Five minutes."

"Okay, people," Chaz said. "It's my pleasure to welcome you back on this beautiful night. I see you all made it past the protestors. Before our fourth challenge, we're going to meet the loved ones of a couple more contestants in the Friends and Family segment. Who's ready to hear from Donovan's wife and Celeste's parents?"

Everybody was ready.

"Let's start with Tara, Donovan's long-suffering wife."

Everyone turned to a monitor. Tara did look like Donovan's second donor except for the lack of joy in her eyes. "Hi, honey. I hope you're doing well. We miss you here, of course. The kids are fine. Vincent got an A on his spelling test; they asked him to participate in the bee. We're all so excited about it." Tara looked like she hadn't been excited about anything in at least five years. "I loaned the mower to Bill down the block, I hope you don't mind. We miss you. The kids said to tell you hi. I hope you're having a nice time."

"As you know, this was prerecorded, but I feel like Tara doesn't watch the show," Chaz said. The audience laughed. "Let's hear from Celeste's parents."

Celeste's parents were older than what was obviously predictable based on her age. They were both gray-haired and grim. Celeste's mother was clutching a wad of tissues, and when her father spoke, he addressed some point left of the camera. "We miss you, Celeste," her father said. "You know we didn't want you

to be a part of this foolishness, but you felt you had to do it."
Celeste's mother burst into tears. "We always loved you just the
way you were, we wish that had been enough for you."

"I just want her back," Celeste's mother said, her voice rising to
a wail. Her nose started to run; she took a swipe at it with the back
of her hand. Her husband put an arm around her.

"We both want you back," her father said. "So, we hope you win
this thing. We pray every day you learn to love yourself. We miss
you." A single tear rolled down his cheek while Celeste's mother
lost her shit entirely. The camera stayed on the weeping couple for
a few beats before fading to black.

"Okay, those people have seen the show," Chaz said. "That was
a bit depressing. Let's move on. I think it's time for the fourth
challenge. Contestants, to the stage!"

Emily, Portia, Lola, Donovan, Brett, and Stewart filed out.

"This challenge is special for a couple of reasons," Chaz said.
"Let's bring out the first reason now. There are a lot of fans of the
show—and a lot of you claim to be 'the biggest fan'–but I think
tonight's special guest might be the one who truly deserves that
title. Landon Jones turns seven today. In fact, we tweaked the
schedule so he could be here on his birthday. Landon has been
watching the show his entire life, and even though he can't
remember the early seasons, his parents swear he's never missed
an episode. He's been scheming to make an appearance on
Creature of the Night for **quite** some time, but these things are
sometimes tough for kids to arrange. Luckily for Landon, he has a
grown-up friend who reached out to us and helped make all this
happen. Please welcome Landon Jones and his friend Melissa from
the Grant a Wish Foundation!"

The crowd screamed for Landon, and even the judges put their
hands together. Except Edmund. Landon smiled sweetly and
waved to everyone in sight as he came onstage. The twins wheeled
Landon out in a hospital bed; the accouterments had been
discarded backstage. Melissa walked alongside the bed, holding

the boy's hand. Landon was a beautiful child. He had big dark eyes and tousled brown hair. He was clutching a well-worn stuffed dog. "That's Boogie," Chaz told the audience. "I got to meet him earlier." The crowd cheered for Boogie too, and Landon held up his beloved toy in response.

Chaz reached out to shake hands with Melissa and then more gently with Landon. Rylie and Kylie faded into the background. Landon watched them go. "How are you feeling, buddy?" Chaz asked.

"I'm good," Landon said. "I didn't feel so good when I woke up, but then I remembered what day it was, and that made me happy. Then Dr. Drake came with some more medicine, and I felt better."

"Glad to hear it," Chaz said. "And you got to bring your friend Melissa."

"Yes," Landon agreed.

"We are so happy to have the chance to help a kid like Landon fulfill his biggest wish," Melissa said. "It's been a joy working with him and with all of you on the show to make this happen."

"I do not remember this from last time," Vlad said.

"Perhaps that is because you were not with us last season," Delia told him. "Still, it is true we have not previously had this particular challenge."

"We got to talk earlier," Chaz said to Landon, "but can you tell the audience about yourself?"

"My bone marrow doesn't work, so I'm going to die soon." The audience looked mournful. "I had a transplant, but it didn't help. It's okay though because I'm going to heaven."

Chaz cast a wary glance upward.

"Why they must fill the heads of their children with fables is beyond me," Edmund said.

"No one knows for sure," Delia said. *"Chaz is a believer."*

"Agnostic," Chaz clarified.

Vlad scowled. "Bah."

Chaz managed to smile for Landon. "Good job," he said. "Tell the almighty to go easy on us when you get there."

Landon giggled. "I will. I'll tell him what you did for me."

"Okay, but maybe not in too much detail," Chaz said. "Are you excited?"

"So excited," Landon said. "This is way better than being stuck in the hospital. And now, I'll be famous forever. It would only be better if I could live forever."

"Yeah, buddy, I know," Chaz said.

Melissa bent down, so her face was level with Landon's. "Sometimes, there are bad laws, and the one that won't let them change you is one of those."

Landon nodded. "Some of the people outside want to let me be a vampire."

"And some of them don't want you to be here at all," Melissa said. "But we're here and we're going to do the best thing we can for you."

"I know." Landon flung his little arms around Melissa's neck, and half the audience started to sob.

Edmund vanished.

Just outside:

"This is so fucked." Callie set her sign down to tie her shoe. "Did you see all those assholes walk by without even pausing? Without even looking?"

"People do that," Carson said. "It makes them uncomfortable to consider they might be doing something wrong, so they ignore the people who are trying to tell them."

"So, all of us standing in the cold holding signs are wasting our time?"

"It's never useless to stand up for the innocent," Carson said. "You can't expect victory every time. Don't lose heart, or you will be useless."

"I'm sorry; you're right." Callie wiped a tear off her chilled face. "I just keep thinking about that poor kid. Like it's not enough having cancer, he's going to lose what little time he has left because those fucking *things* romanticize themselves and deluded kids buy into it. The whole thing just... sucks."

"Life sucks, but we do what we can, right?"

"Right."

"You ready? The news guys are here." Callie nodded and picked up her sign. Together, Carson, Callie, and scores of others raised their signs and resumed their chant, *"Let Landon live! Let Landon live! Let Landon live!"*

Light years away in spirit, but physically proximate:

"This is so fucked." Dawn stomped her feet and tried to blow some warmth into her fingers. She was so cold she could hardly feel the sign she was holding. "I hate those idiots. Not that I can even understand them. Enunciate, assholes!"

"I know how you feel." Gavin reached out to bestow an awkward pat on Dawn's shoulder. "The idea that it's better for this kid to die instead of being changed into a vampire is crazy. Instant fucking cure right inside that building, but God forbid we should let them help because vampires are 'evil' or something."

"They're a lot less evil than the hypocrites who've made it illegal for him to be turned. But, I'm glad they're doing this for him, at least," Dawn said. "It's still sad but better than nothing."

"I saw him on *Last Week Tonight,* and he seemed pretty jazzed about it."

"Yay." Dawn made a big deal gesture. "The little boy gets a cool quick death instead of a sterile lingering one."

"What happened to 'It's better than nothing?'"

"It's barely better. This shouldn't be the best we get." Dawn said. "It certainly shouldn't be the best he gets."

"It shouldn't be, but for this kid, yeah, it's the best he gets," Gavin said. "But we're here, raising awareness, so maybe the next kid gets better. Maybe the next one doesn't have to die at all. Okay?"

Dawn nodded. "Looks like they're done filming the loonies."

"Okay," Gavin said. "It's our turn. Everybody! Raise those signs, and on three, two, one!" Signs popped up, and the protestors turned to meet the cameras. Their passionate cries filled the night air. *"Let Landon live! Let Landon live! Let Landon live!"*

"Are they going to eat the boy?" Vlad asked.

Delia smiled. "It is not required."

"No. Absolutely not," Chaz said. "Landon is on some potent medications that it would not be advisable for the contestants to ingest, even secondhand."

"Ask Brett," Delia said.

"Yeah, the medications can make you feel yucky," Landon agreed. Melissa stroked his hair. "But I'm excited to be here. I always watch the show. It's so cool."

"That means a lot," Chaz said. "Do you understand what is about to happen, Landon?"

"Yes, we're going to play a game where I pretend to be a vampire, and they come to get me, and when they do, I'll be in heaven. But I won't have to die like a sick kid in the hospital; I'll get to die like an awesome vampire."

"One might argue an 'awesome' vampire would not allow himself to be killed by an overeager pack of humans," Edmund said.

"You being that one?" Delia said.

"Indeed."

"So glad to see you back," said Nodin.

The audience continued to applaud for heaven, and more tissues were destroyed.

"I agree with Ed," Vlad said. "Such nonsense."

CREATURE OF THE NIGHT

"Hush," Delia said.

"Humans enjoy their fantasies," Edmund said.

"They die so quickly," Nodin said. *"Adhering to a belief is all most of them have time to accomplish."*

"We want the audience to be able to enjoy the challenge," Chaz said. "So tell them how you're feeling."

Landon poked himself in the leg and giggled some more. "I feel good, but my body can't feel anything."

"Who says pharmaceuticals are not the answer?" Chaz said. "Contestants, before we get started, come meet Landon."

Six faces in a row went from grim to grimmer. The contestants made their way to Landon's bed, their reluctance apparent with every move.

"It's okay," Landon said when the contestants had arrayed themselves around him. "I thought about it a lot. It's what I want to do."

Stewart took one of Landon's hands in both of his. "I'm glad to meet you." *They have got to be fucking kidding with this. Are we seriously supposed to do something to this helpless kid?* Stewart thought of how his kids would react to seeing him kill a little boy with cancer on a vampire show in his quest to become immortal, and more importantly, impress them. That's when he made up his mind.

"It's nice to meet you too," Landon said. "I've been watching. Your kids must be excited."

"Yes," Stewart said, "I'm sure they are." He stepped back.

"Hey, man," Donovan said. Donovan was not thinking of his children. He was wondering if this challenge was actually what they were making it look like. The whole thing could be a setup designed to find out who was willing to go to extreme lengths. Even for vampires, it seemed unbelievable that killing some kid would be part of a game. Either way, Donovan was more than ready to demonstrate his willing and able state.

"Hi, honey," Portia said, wondering if she'd ever be able to

CREATURE OF THE NIGHT

perform without some child managing to wreck it in some way. *Jesus, look at the eyes on that kid.* He was cute. No one could deny the appeal of those big smiley eyes. He also hadn't wiped his nose on anything he shouldn't, thrown a temper tantrum, or gotten scared of something totally innocuous and burst into tears. He didn't even seem scared about the challenge. Because Portia was terrified about the challenge, she was pissed at him all the same.

"Did you really get to be Peter Pan?" Landon wanted to know.

"Yeah," Portia said. She wanted to say *Do you seriously expect us to put you out of your misery?* Instead, she stepped back.

"Sorry about your, you know, condition, little guy," Brett said. "Cancer sucks." Landon nodded. He was aware. Brett blinked frantically. *Poor little bastard.* Brett would change the kid if it were up to him. If it were up to him, everybody who wanted to would be made a vampire. They could all just live forever and have lots of sex, not the kids, of course because that would be sick and Brett was horny, sure, but not in a sick way. It might suck for the vampire kids living forever and never getting laid because their outsides wouldn't match their insides, but it would be better than dying of cancer, better than dying period. Brett sniffed deeply and blinked a few more times as he stepped back.

"Hey," Lola said, without approaching. Why the fuck would they bring a cancer kid here? Lola hadn't signed up to deal with anyone's feelings. *Stop looking at me, you little shit.* Lola tried to keep the scowl she was feeling away from her face. She didn't need the whole world to turn against her because she gave the cancer kid a dirty look. Lola hoped the world would be forgiving of whoever ripped his little heart out because that person was going to be her. And not just because she needed to win. The little shit kept trying to catch her eye, and his smile was oddly sympathetic. There was no group more condescending than the terminally ill.

"Is there a challenge today?" Vlad said.

"Patience," Chaz said.

Emily stepped up and stuck out a hand for Landon to shake.

170

"Hi."

"Hi," Landon said. "Do you like kids?"

"As much as I like adults," Emily said. Although this kid seemed particularly likable, and their challenge was to end him. *This is going to be the line I can't cross.* But she wouldn't have to. Plenty of the others were essentially without scruples. Emily hoped it would be done quickly. "I like your dog."

"I like him too," Landon said. "I don't have a real dog. My parents couldn't take care of a dog and me. Do you have a dog?"

"I did," Emily said. "She's gone now. She was the best dog ever. You would have liked her."

"Sorry," Landon said. "Do you believe in heaven?"

"I don't," Emily said, "but most people do."

"I do. What was her name?"

"Sophie."

"If I see Sophie, I'll tell her you said hi."

"Scratch her back and kiss her nose too," Emily managed. "She especially loved nose kisses. Good luck, Landon."

"Are you okay?" Landon said.

Emily nodded and stepped back.

"Landon wants to say a few words before we begin," Chaz said. "Go ahead, Landon."

"I just want to tell my mom 'I love you' because she couldn't come here tonight. And she's the best mom."

Hence her presence, Cyri thought.

"I know you want me to stay longer, but I'm ready now. I think it's cool to do it in an exciting way so everyone will remember. Plus, I want everyone to know it should be up to us, the sick people. And I want to thank Brittany Maynard. Even though she needed to die even before I was born, I know she helped kids and other people like me by letting people know that sometimes this is best for us. And I want to thank the contestants and tell them it's okay, really. And to make it awesome. I hope I get a lot of views."

"You can rest assured you will," Chaz said. "Rylie and Kylie are going to take Landon's dad and Melissa backstage, and we'll get started."

Rylie and Kylie swept up to usher Landon's entourage away. Landon's father hugged him tight and covered his face with kisses. He was shaking with sobs. All the humans onstage averted their eyes; the audience devoured the drama.

"I'm good, Dad," Landon said. "It's okay."

"I'm just going to miss you," his dad said.

"But I'll see you in heaven, and I won't be sick."

"That's right, baby."

"You have to go now," Landon said.

"I know." Melissa had already disappeared backstage, and finally, Landon's father let the vampire girls lead him away. He turned to blow one last kiss in Landon's direction, but his boy was focused on the contestants.

"I have something for you guys," Landon said.

Donovan and Portia immediately took a step back.

"What? Do you think he's going to explode?" Emily said. "Whatcha got?" She asked Landon.

"Behind you," Landon said. "Look."

Everyone turned. The accessories for the challenge had been laid out behind a mid-stage curtain. As the curtain parted, Rylie and Kylie extended their arms and ta-da'd. The band was playing something Cyri found familiar but couldn't place.

"You have choices," Chaz said. "On the table, we have an ax, a flamethrower, a stake, a syringe of Euthanol, and on the other side of the stage is a full bathtub, bubbles not included. If you were counting, that's five. Five ways to help Landon leave this mortal coil. Four of those things are weapons traditionally used against us, and the fifth, the Euthanol, is an injection that will painlessly send Landon on his final journey. Once it's injected into his heart that is."

Landon grinned.

Journey to where? Cyri thought. Six feet under wasn't quite the center of the Earth.

"*Mortal coil! Mortal coil! Mortal coil!*"

"*Inform them that anyone who is not able to identify the origin of the phrase needs to stop chanting immediately,*" Edmund said to Chaz.

In spite of Chaz's warning, seventeen people continued to chant but gave up quickly when Edmund flashed his fangs.

"No one is eating the boy?" Vlad asked.

"We covered that," Chaz said. "Lots of unhealthy chemicals in that adorable package."

"I would not be hurt," Vlad declared.

"True," Delia said, "but you may not eat the boy."

"I am stifled by these myriad of rules," Vlad said.

"That is the purpose of rules," Nodin told him.

"Contestants, go to your marks," Chaz said. The remaining six lined up. "When I start the challenge, you may choose any weapon on the stage. Of course, bare hands are an option as well. The winner of this challenge is the one who releases Landon from his suffering."

"Anyone who brandishes one of these weapons at a vampire will be immediately killed and disqualified," Edmund said.

"Can I say it?" Landon asked. "Can I say start?" Chaz nodded.

"Ready, set, go!" Landon said. The audience roared. The judges snapped to attention. The contestants didn't move. The rowdy cheers started to turn hostile. Landon sat on his bed and waited.

Chaz whispered in Landon's ear. "I mean start," Landon clarified.

"*Kill the boy! Kill the boy! Kill the boy!*"

Emily clenched her fists. *This is what he wants; it's probably what I'd want in his position. But not the flamethrower. Jesus. Talk about overkill. Who's up for the smell of barbecued cancer kid? Not this girl. The ax would be quickest. Cleanest, if one didn't consider the aftermath. One quick whack and the head and body get to go their separate ways. Long goodbyes never made things easier.*

Fucking pussies, Lola thought. *Why is everybody just standing here?* There was no point in crying for some kid who was going to be dead in a week. They were doing him a favor. Lola was going to do him a fucking favor. The flamethrower would be the most badass. The kid wanted to go viral, anyway. Lola managed one step.

Portia was learning things about herself. The most noteworthy discovery was that spending fifteen years hating kids didn't guarantee you'd be raring to chop and char one when opportunity reared its ugly head. There was just no way she could pick up that ax or light him on fire, for fuck's sake. It would be so much easier just to shoot the little jerk. What the fuck had they done with the guns from the second challenge? It would have to be the syringe of Euthanol. Quick, easy, and officially proclaimed painless. Except for the stab through the heart. Still, a needle should hurt less than the stake.

Think about the pussy, Donovan told himself. He just needed to kill the kid, and everybody would be getting what they wanted. The tub was fucking stupid. Like they wanted to drag the kid out of his hospital bed and carry him over to drown. The stake would be nice. Stick to the theme. Donovan was a big, strong guy. A stake in his hand would go right through that little chest. No contest. Just have to get there.

Drowning would make it more special, Brett thought. Everyone knew about stakes and fire and beheading, but drowning wasn't as well-known a method of vamp killing. And it should be special for the kid. He'd done a lot to get here just like Brett had. They were kindred spirits. He could tell this story to *Rolling Stone.* How he knew what the kid wanted, how he looked into his eyes as he put the kid in the water. How he saved Landon from misery and made his wish come true.

It's okay, Landon told himself. *If they chicken out, Vlad will eat me for sure.* But Lola took a second step then a third. Donovan was startled out of his stasis and ran for the weapons. Emily and

Brett started to move with Brett heading straight for Landon. *He wants to put me in the tub,* Landon realized. Melissa had told him they almost hadn't included the tub, too messy and difficult. Landon didn't see how it was so hard. The nurses and his parents were always picking him up; he didn't weigh much.

Stewart watched everybody move forward without him. The weapons would be gone, and he'd be stuck strangling the kid or maybe smothering him with one of his flat hospital pillows. Except, that was never going to happen. Here was the end of his line. Portia was the only one left, the only one still standing and as he watched she took a tentative step forward. But for Stewart, there was no point in pretending. He wasn't going to be the one to let Landon go. Murder or mercy, he didn't have it in him. He hoped his kids wouldn't be too disappointed.

As Brett reached Landon, Stewart sank to his knees.

Twenty yards away, Lola saw Brett pluck the boy out of bed and head for the tub. Lola hefted the flamethrower, but the fucking thing was heavy. She turned to swap it for the ax and found it clutched in Donovan's meaty fists.

Emily reached for the stake, the last decent weapon. She had nothing against the Euthanol; she would have preferred to send Landon gently into the night, but she had some unsourced idea that the injection might take minutes to perform its task. Time was of the essence.

While Emily was lost in her mental debate, Lola hefted the flamethrower up and threw it. It struck Emily on the arm, a glancing blow, but it was enough to slow her down. Lola snatched the stake and took off to intercept Landon.

Emily made a grab for the flamethrower, but it rolled past her and off the edge of the stage. Brett was closing in on the tub with the kid in his arms, and Donovan and Lola were streaking to intercept them. It looked like it was all going to be over before Emily made it near any of them.

Donovan made the interception. He raised the ax over Landon, who was still in Brett's arms. One plunge and it would have been done, but Donovan hesitated. Lola saw only that Donovan was poised to kill the boy, so she adjusted her trajectory and launched herself into Donovan's side. Donovan dropped to his knees but kept hold of the ax while Brett, in a visceral attempt to get away from the huge fucking blade, dropped the kid.

Landon hit the stage and sprawled on his back. He got his elbows under him and managed to rise to half sitting which was good enough to see the action.

Emily broke into a run. Her eyes were on Lola, who was making her way over to the kid. Emily snatched the ax from Donovan almost without slowing and resumed her sprint expecting time to turn from *almost there* to *too late* with each pound of her heart.

And then it was too late. Everyone watched as Lola raised the stake over her head. Emily would not get to Landon before Lola could bring the stake down. The audience held their collective breath as Landon met Lola's eyes and nodded. Lola raised her chin. Emily circled around, one slow step at a time, until she was beside Landon's head, opposite Lola. One good thrust of the stake and Lola would break right through Landon's fragile chest.

Landon remained focused on Lola, who was poised to make his wish come true. Lola had her head tipped back, and her eyes rolled up like she was communing with the stake, and her arms were starting to shake. Emily snapped out of her stake fascination when the syringe hit the floor in front of her. She raised her head to find Portia standing beside Lola. Movement beyond them caught her attention. It was Brett, creeping up as though he were springing an ambush in a dark house, rather than with a spotlight in his face and millions of eyes following him. Donovan had made it to his knees. He was clutching his ribs where Lola had careened into them and struggling to look as though he couldn't rise.

Brett reached up and twisted the stake out of Lola's hands, simultaneously shoving her away from Landon. He dropped into a straddle over the boy and, with minimal hesitation, plunged the stake down.

Landon's eyes went wide. His hand moved to touch the stake in his shoulder.

"Just like a vampire," Landon said. "Except you missed my heart."

"This is a farce," Edmund said.

"Oh my god," Brett said. "What the fuck am I supposed to do now? Do something!"

"He's right," Donovan said. "You have to get him in the heart."

"It's in there pretty far," Brett said.

"Just give it a good pull." Donovan had gotten to his feet and was standing behind Brett with his arms crossed in a supervisory stance.

"He'll bleed."

"We're killing him anyway," Lola said.

Donovan sneered. "You're not."

"Fuck you."

Emily could hardly hear them over the buzzing in her ears. Her grip felt uncertain, courtesy of her sweaty hands. Vlad was going to come down and eat them all if someone didn't do this soon. No one else was poised to strike. *Just pull the stake out and put it in his fucking heart.* Emily felt a deep hatred for Brett. Five or six inches to the right and they would have been done with it. *Stupid fuck-up.* She was not a fuck-up, which meant she had to stop dithering as though she were.

Okay. Good grip, two hands, and everything: check. Upswing: check. Arms locked and loaded: check. *It's okay. It's going to be okay: Check.* She swung down fast and hard, throwing her weight into it. There was a fearful moment of resistance that she pushed through, or maybe it had been anticipation of resistance that never was. Either way, it was done now. Landon's last breath wasn't going to make it out of the head that wasn't attached anymore. Emily's hands were bloody because she'd choked up way too much on the ax. In fact, her fingers were touching him, and she wondered why the head hadn't gone flying; that's what happened in the movies. In the movies, the head never just lolled gently away from its body. It didn't continue to hang out by the body as if, in spite of the recent breakup, the friendship remained.

If his face had been turned in her direction, she might have screamed, but all she could see was the back with his fine, blood soaked curls. She wanted to stroke them, just for a moment, but she was still clutching the ax with its blade still resting between the boy and his head, and stroking the hair of someone you've recently beheaded was odd. Not something a refined killer would do. And she was a killer if not yet refined. It was done, definitively done, and right then, it didn't matter that, to Landon, she was an angel.

Emily wanted to get up, but she was stuck on her knees beside Landon's body. Her hands still clutched the ax. She had thrown her weight so fully into her swing that, in her shaky state, letting go might cause her to topple onto the boy's body. And toppling onto a dead child seemed disrespectful.

The silence in the studio was so overwhelming that she couldn't break it to ask for something as paltry as help. Finally, someone hauled her up by the armpits, and Emily gratefully struggled to her feet. As she rose, the crowd broke into a ragged cheer that built in volume and intensity until the vibrations of it were discernible under their feet. People were stomping and whistling and pounding their approval on the seatbacks in front of them.

"We have to line up," Stewart whispered in her ear, and Emily wondered how she hadn't heard the instruction. She let him take her arm and followed him docilely to take her place in line with the others.

"We have a special Friends and Family with Landon's parents," Chaz said. "They asked that it not be shown until after, so here it is."

Landon's father was on the screens with his arm around a woman who was clearly Landon's mother and who was just as clearly about to be someone else's as well.

Landon's father spoke first. "We want to thank everybody who helped Landon go out like he wanted to. We are devastated, but it's not you who took him from us. It was his illness. One of you spared him his last bit of suffering, and I know he was grateful for that. Not as grateful as he was to meet all you vampires, but you know kids. I don't know if I'll get a chance to explain why Landon's mom couldn't be there, but as you can see, she's going to be having a baby just about any minute. We thought maybe this one could help Landon, but it wasn't meant to be."

Landon's mom put a hand on his father's knee in comfort. When it became clear he couldn't go on, she took over. "We would never bring one child into the world just to save another. We love children. We do. We thought we would want another one even before Landon got sick. But, it took so long to get pregnant, and Landon was too far gone. We hoped he would make it longer. Long enough for this to have a chance, but it turns out it was all for nothing."

"Not nothing," Landon's father said. "We're about to have a beautiful little girl."

Who's going to be able to find this video online someday, Cyri thought.

"Yes," Landon's mother said. "I'm sure she'll be beautiful."

The six contestants were in the green room.

"Okay, guys." Little P waited for acknowledgment, got none, and sighed inwardly. What part of *the kid was already dying* did they not understand? "Take a minute to get yourselves together. And then we have to get you back onstage."

Emily scowled over her shoulder at Little P. Lola had gone straight to the bathroom and locked herself in without a word to anyone, so Emily stood in front of the bar sink. She was scrubbing her hands for the fourth time in as many minutes. There were traces of blood under her fingernails that refused to wash away.

Stewart was sitting on the couch with his head in his hands thinking about missed opportunities. Portia was waiting for either Lola or Emily to abdicate a mirror; she was worried about what the stress of the challenge had done to her makeup.

"Can you wait outside?" Donovan had gone straight for the bourbon. The second shot might have lessened the trembling in his hands; even so, he downed a third.

"Would that I could," Little P said, quite sincerely. "The feeling upstairs is you all could use a friend right about now."

"That is true," Emily said. "Start with Brett. He needs a hug."

In the big armchair in the corner, Brett sat turned toward the wall. His arms were wrapped around his knees holding them close to his chest, and his lips were moving, but if anything coherent was coming out, it was doing so too softly for the others to hear.

Little P opted to wait outside.

"While we wait for the contestants, we're going to answer a couple of viewer questions," Chaz said. "Let's see what Jackson from Lansing, Michigan is wondering."

"Hi, I was just wondering, was there holy water in the tub during the last challenge?"

"Nope," Chaz said. "Holy water would have had no different effect on our special guest than regular water."

"*Or on anyone else,*" Edmund grumbled.

"Next question is from Len in Albuquerque, New Mexico," Chaz said.

"I was wondering about the vampire girls. Which one is Riley and which one is Kiley?"

Chaz was surprised this hadn't come up sooner. "Good question, Len. Girls, come on out." A moment later Riley and Kiley were standing beside Chaz. Side by side, it should have been easy enough to tell them apart. One might have been an inch taller, one

CREATURE OF THE NIGHT

a shade blonder; one might have had an extra freckle or two.

"Riley is," Chaz paused and then announced, "going to raise her hand." Riley obediently held up a hand. "And Kylie is the other one." Chaz thanked the girls and waved them away.

"So that's finally settled," Chaz said. "We're almost ready for the contestants to rejoin us, but let's take one more question from Katie in Lancaster, Pennsylvania."

"Hi, Vlad. Are you single? And if so would you be interested in hanging out sometime?"

"That's her picture on the monitor," Chaz said. Vlad demonstrated he had no idea what a monitor was. Delia finally got him pointed in the right direction.

"She is young," Vlad said. "Pretty. I would consent to dine on her."

"That's a yes, Katie," Chaz said. "Please note, he said 'on', not 'with.' If you would care to hold, someone will take your information."

The crowd erupted into catcalls and smooching noises.

"Power is an aphrodisiac," Cyri's dad explained between whistles.

Cyri shuddered.

"We shall bring the contestants back when the audience ceases to behave like a chaos of children," Chaz told the audience.

The crowd generated a swell of noise then subsided. Chaz signaled, and the girls sent the contestants to the stage.

"That one is eliminated, yes?" Vlad asked as the competitors reached their marks.

"You will ruin the suspense," Delia warned.

"As though we might retain the one who failed to compete?" Edmund said. "The one so craven he managed to make the others shine like beacons of fortitude?"

"Yes, that one will be eliminated," Nodin said. "I believe it is obvious to all, Delia. Don't fret."

"I fret not," Delia said.

"*You fret not?*" Edmund said.

"*Shut up, Edmund.*"

"*Fraud.*"

"I am an entertainer," Delia said. "*One of us should do something besides scowl and threaten to eat them.*"

"*I never threaten to eat them,*" Nodin said.

"*I've never eaten one,*" Edmund said sadly. "*But soon, I believe. Soon.*"

"I simply feel," Delia said, "a sense of ceremony adds much to the proceedings."

"Until a moment of boredom overcomes your sense of ceremony, which we have often seen," Nodin said. "But until that moment is again upon us, let us cater to ceremony."

"Speaking of ceremony," Chaz said. "Let's hear what our lovely audience has to say. Just for fun, let's invite one of them up to help me read the results."

Nodin frowned. "*What is this?*"

"How about you?" Chaz gestured casually at the girl in the audience who wasn't adoring him. "No. No. Not you either. Blue shirt, playing on your phone. The girl."

"Ow," Cyri said when her dad elbowed her in the side.

"He wants you to go up there." Cyri raised her eyebrows at her father who was bouncing in his seat like a three-year-old about to ruin his pants.

Cyri shook her head.

"It won't hurt," Chaz said. "I promise." His fangs gleamed in the light from his spot.

"What won't hurt?" Cyri thought it was a reasonable question deserving an answer. If anyone had one, they didn't share it. Onstage, Chaz waited.

"Go on, honey," Cyri's dad said. He pushed her up and out of her seat. The audience around them helped shove her down the row until she was standing in the aisle with every eye on her.

"Oh my God. I hate you," the chubby guy on the end hissed.

"He's so gorgeous."

"You can go instead," Cyri offered.

"No, no. You're already up," Chaz said. "Girls."

Riley and Kiley swept out and transported Cyri to Chaz's side.

"What is he doing?" Nodin asked.

"Having issues," Delia told him.

Upstairs, Little P and The Voice were throwing back bourbon and watching the monitor.

"Do you want me to stop this?" Little P asked.

"We're insured if he eats her?"

"We're insured if he eats the entire audience."

"So, young lady," Chaz patted Cyri on the shoulder. "What's your name?"

"Cyri."

"Are you excited to be here?"

Cyri looked out at the audience. She spotted her father grinning like an idiot and wondered, if she were killed on this stage today, whether his future retellings of this moment would focus on his tragic loss or his excitement. "How could I not be?"

Chaz put his lips near Cyri's ear and drawled, "Can you read the results for us?"

"I can," Cyri assured him. Delia tittered.

Chaz focused on projecting his appeal. He turned Cyri so she faced him and gazed at her deeply. He envisioned her cheeks pink with the pleasure of being near him, squealing with the excitement of being plucked from obscurity to bask in his regard, quivering with pride to be standing at his side however temporarily. He smoldered.

Cyri got tired of waiting and silently held out her hand for the envelope. She ripped it open with no sense of ceremony and skimmed the contents.

"They want to eliminate Stewart and Portia," she said. "Because Stewart loves children too much, and Portia is a pussy."

"Interesting choices," Chaz said. "How did you vote, Cyri?"

Cyri parroted his game show host intonation. "I didn't vote, Chaz."

Chaz tried one last time for his pride. He put everything he had into his stellar smile. He placed her delicate hand over his heart, even though there was nothing beating in his chest for her to feel, and waited for her to be overcome with longing.

Cyri lifted her indifferent eyes to his and asked, "Is that it?"

"Okay, back you go," Chaz said. He gave her a little push to send her back to the audience.

"That was entertaining," Delia said.

"There's something wrong with this one," Chaz said.

"There, there," Delia consoled. "Perhaps she's a lesbian."

"I was Sexiest Dead Man Alive three years running," Chaz said. "She'd have to be."

"But, as I understand it," Delia said, "not this year."

Chaz scowled before remembering himself. He sketched a bow and threw on his biggest grin. He fucking hated humans. "What would you like to say to the contestants?"

"Many things to each of them," Delia said. "As a group, I would like to tell them the first kill is difficult for many, even after one has transformed, which is why we tried to create an unobjectionable scenario. A boy who is dying slowly and soon, who longed to be a part of our experience seemed an ideal solution. But even the youngest of us left mortality behind long ago. We knew this would be a difficult challenge for you. And like any other challenge, we saw that some were capable of rising to meet it, and some were not."

"I still think we should eat the eliminated," Vlad said.

"Someone fetch an intern for Vlad," Delia said. "Now."

There was a pause in the proceedings while someone procured

an intern.

"*Must we extend these already interminable proceedings simply to cater to his uncontrollable appetites?*" Edmund said.

"*It's faster than cleaning up after if he loses his shit,*" Delia said. "*Besides, they've already got one.*"

Riley and Kiley escorted a girl, who looked eager behind her glasses and freckles, to Vlad. They tossed her onto the altar at Vlad's feet. He scooped her up as Delia said, "Neck, please."

There was an annoyed hiss, but Vlad complied and sunk his fangs into the girl somewhere above her left collarbone. The contestants and audience watched in fascination as Vlad slurped from the intern. She moaned and writhed a bit while her hands clutched at Vlad. When he finished, he set her upright, but her knees buckled, and she nearly toppled off the altar. She said something to Vlad so quietly only the vampires in the room could hear her.

Vlad looked to Delia for guidance.

Delia shrugged. "It's not dangerous," she said.

"*It is ridiculous,*" Edmund said.

The intern took that as permission. Before Edmund could object further, which he was surely about to, she had whipped out her phone and was posing with one arm extended and the other around the old vampire. She tilted her head to display her fang marks.

"How was that for ceremony?" Edmund asked after the vampire twins had retrieved the intern.

"I was a bit surprised you didn't just snap her neck," Delia said to Edmund.

"I want to get on with it." Edmund scowled at Chaz. "Where were we?"

"We are hearing thoughts from the judges about the last challenge," Chaz said. "Do you have any to share?"

"You know my thoughts," Edmund said. "The idea of adding to our ranks any of these—"

"Summon Lola," Nodin interrupted. Chaz motioned Lola forward. "You chose the flamethrower. Why?"

After a quick glance around to see if anyone was going to intervene, Lola stepped forward. "I chose the flamethrower initially because I thought it would be dramatic. And I knew that's what Landon wanted. He wanted to go viral."

"And you didn't think that would happen no matter what method was used to end his suffering? How many hits has the video gotten so far, Chaz?"

"Since the challenge ended earlier today," Chaz said, "the clip has gotten fifty-seven million views."

"That counts, yes?" Nodin said.

Lola cast her eyes down and nodded.

"My concern is that you intended to burn a human child to death," Nodin said.

"But, the flamethrower was there." And Lola hadn't even burned the kid.

"That option was offered as part of the challenge, yes," Nodin said. "We hoped no one would choose it."

"They are all barbarians," Edmund said.

"She thought she was doing what we expected," Delia said.

Nodin rolled his eyes. "Your defense is peer pressure?"

"*We are her superiors, not her peers,*" Delia said. "But, essentially, yes."

"Did you behave as you thought was expected?" Nodin asked.

"Yes." Lola nodded desperately. "I thought it was something we needed to be able to do, to be ruthless."

"Her previous explanation had her doing it to help the boy," Edmund said.

"I believe you thought you were meeting our expectations," Nodin said. "The question of whether we want to turn someone who would behave so abhorrently because they believe it is expected is one we will have to answer amongst ourselves. Step back."

"*Have the youngest male step forward,*" Edmund said.

Chaz raised his eyebrows at Brett, who complied. He stood before the judges shifting his weight, almost imperceptibly, from foot to foot.

"You planned to drown the child?" Edmund said. "Explain."

"*The most mundane option available,*" Delia commented. "*Showmanship is dead.*"

"*You forgot the death by needle,*" Edmund said.

"*Yes,*" Delia said. "*It was forgettable.*"

"I thought it would be more meaningful," Brett said. "Because not as many people think of drowning vampires. Everybody knows about stakes and fire, but drowning doesn't just come to mind. I thought that would make it more special."

"*Why do they always want death to be special?*" Nodin said.

"*As though they don't all end up rotting in the same ground,*" Delia agreed.

"*I've seen many deaths,*" Edmund said. "*Some were special.*" Aloud, he added, "But because he is human and lacks resolve, he gave up."

Brett tried to defend himself. "I did stake him."

Nodin snorted. "In the shoulder."

"Tell us what happened in your words," Delia said.

"I felt like Landon and I were the same," Brett said. "I know he loved vampires the way I do, but he didn't have a chance to be one because he was too young. It seemed like I would be able to honor him by being the one to end his suffering."

Edmund let his fangs show. "*What honor is there in a botched attempt?*"

"You failed both to drown the boy and to stake him," Chaz said.

"I was a little freaked out," Brett said. "It's harder than it looks. Killing someone, I mean."

"*We told them that before the challenge, didn't we?*" Delia asked flatly.

"*We told them,*" Nodin agreed. "*At some point.*"

"*I remember the first one I took,*" Edmund said.

"I don't mean that. I know you've killed lots of people," Brett said. "I'm sure you're all great at killing people. I just meant for me. It was a first. And you know, he was a cancer kid, so there's that. Have you guys ever killed a cancer kid? I mean, not that I think it's required of you. To be good vampires. I don't think anythi—"

To the humans, it looked as if Edmund suddenly appeared with his fangs in Brett's neck. The vampires had been able to track his leap off the altar, the seizing of Brett, and the bite, but they were letting Edmund blow off some steam. Chaz gave it a ten count and intervened.

"Are you finished?" Chaz asked once he'd detached Edmund from Brett's throat.

"If he is finished speaking," Edmund said. "I found him offensive. I required him to contribute something of value as expiation."

"You asked him a question," Delia said. "Leave him be."

"Happily," Edmund said. He returned to his throne in a great swoop and sat. He was as dignified as one can be with a trickle of blood on one's chin.

Brett tried to stagger back into line, but Delia forestalled him. "Why did you not stake the boy in the heart?"

"I meant to," Brett said. He kept trying to look at Delia, but the force of her gaze daunted him. He managed to hold his eyes steady on her left knee. Both hands were on his neck containing the trickle of blood. He was grateful to realize Edmund had barely pierced the skin.

"I'd be shitting myself right now if I was that guy," Mike said. "Grab me another beer, would you?"

"Then you're a fucking pussy." Nick downed the second half of his beer and let out a thunderous belch.

"Stay classy, man," Mike said. He reached up and caught the beer Nick launched at his head.

"It's just a show; it's not like they're going to do shit."

"Seriously, you dumb fuck?" Mike said. "The smart, hot one just beheaded a kid. Be-fucking-headed. How's that for doing shit?"

"There's a smart, hot one?"

"There's a smart, hot one and a slutty, hot one," Mike confirmed. "Emily and Lola. Do you not remember when we went over this? Pay the fuck attention, man." He let out a belch that surpassed Nick's.

"How do you know the slutty one isn't smart?" Nick said.

"I just don't see it," Mike said.

"Like you have any experience with smart girls."

"Because I'm fucking smart."

"I couldn't do it again," Brett said.

"You did not do it the first time," Delia said. "A flesh wound has no significance when the challenge was to take a life."

"A life freely offered," Nodin added. *"They are a disappointment. The task could not have been easier."*

"Do you remember the first life you took?" Delia said.

"I do. What of it?"

"It's significant to anyone who isn't a sociopath," Delia said. *"A milestone if you will. And the challenge was completed. Go easy."*

"This one did not complete it," Edmund said. *"Dismiss him."*

"I do not remember my first," Vlad said.

"I'm sorry," Brett said. "I'm doing my best. I am."

"Aye," Nodin said. "There's the rub." His hope that the audience would chuckle at his reference was dashed.

"Step back," Chaz said.

"Let Stewart come forward," Delia said, "and tell us of his experience."

"I'm a father," Stewart said.

"Yes, he has managed the spectacular feat of procreation, and it has changed him forever," Edmund said. "Fascinating. That was, perhaps, something he might have considered before his arrival here."

Delia turned deliberately toward Edmund and showed her fangs. *"Peace."*

"You're right," Stewart said. "I should have considered. Except I did. I came here because of my kids, because I wanted to make them proud, and I wanted to reach out to them by being part of something they love. But, this isn't the right way. I'm not the right guy to be Creature of the Night. I'm not grand or dramatic, and I don't want to live forever. I don't want ever to watch my kids die."

"You could choose to turn them," Nodin said. "If you were victorious."

"I could," Stewart agreed. "But, I wouldn't. No offense, but I think there's a lot to be said for humanity."

"The implication being he was exercising his humanity when he declined to participate in the challenge," Edmund said. "Now he wishes to sit in judgment of us? Such loftiness in such a low creature is excruciating."

"I didn't put it that way to myself," Stewart said. "I just knew I couldn't do it. I know you see that as weakness, but I don't think it is. And I'm not judging anyone." He looked at Emily. "For me, it was impossible."

"Do you think that constitutes strength?" Delia asked.

"I think it constitutes humanity," Stewart said.

"You humans kill one another indiscriminately and constantly," Nodin said.

"Not like that. Not children," Stewart said. After a moment he added, "Not most of us."

"Get rid of him," Edmund said.

Chaz indicated Stewart could return to his place and that Portia should step forward.

Edmund refocused his ire. *"Ah, the actress. How ever did she find* the fortitude to fleetingly put her hand on the dreariest of implements?"

"Edmund wants to know what you were thinking during the challenge," Chaz said.

Portia flushed. "I know I didn't do well," she said. "But, I think there's so much more to being a vampire than killing children. Please give me the chance to show you I deserve to be the next Creature of the Night."

"Would you do anything differently if you had the chance?" Delia asked.

Portia smiled. "I would do everything differently if I had the chance." *I would be a freaking schoolteacher if I could go back. I would stay in Pennsylvania, marry Brad Smith, and give birth to five goddamn kids who would destroy my body. I would choose to be nothing spectacular, and I would be content with it.*

"Step back, please," Delia instructed. "Donovan."

Donovan stepped forward. "You initially appeared determined," Nodin said. "But when the wild one knocked you aside, you ceased your attempt. It was as though you were hoping for an excuse to fail."

"No," Donovan said. "No, sir. I never hope to fail. It was all so chaotic, and everything was over before I knew it."

"Emily," Delia said. "Step forward. No, Donovan. Stay where you are."

"She is so fucking horrible," Gina said.

"You're crazy." Kip poked at her with a toe. Gina slapped his leg. "She's that kid's hero."

"She didn't do it for him," Gina said. She grabbed a pillow and flung it across the room. It took out a vase that shattered when it hit the floor, sending glass, water, and irises everywhere.

"Feel better?" Kip said.

Gina shook her head. "Sorry."

"Look, he benefited, didn't he?" Kip said patiently. "He was suffering and now he's not. Does it matter why she did it?"

"He's dead," Gina's ire drove her from the couch. "How is being dead beneficial?"

"Count your blessings, darling," Kip said. "The ability to sincerely ask that question is a luxury lots of us don't have."

Donovan and Emily stood side by side in front of the judges. "Explain how you acted so swiftly you deprived this one of his chance to take the boy."

"It didn't seem like that to me," Emily said.

"No," Delia agreed. "It did not seem so to any of us."

Donovan didn't dare glare at Delia, so he settled for Emily, who didn't give him the satisfaction of noticing.

Delia raised an eyebrow at Chaz, who said, "Donovan may step back."

"Tell us about your hesitation," Nodin said.

"I was working some things out," Emily said.

"And are those things now worked?" Delia wanted to know.

"No," Emily said. "But I'll think about them later."

"Or tomorrow?" Delia said.

Emily let out a small laugh and nodded.

"Step back," Nodin said.

"Do not blame us for the lack of suspense," Edmund said. "The two who did not compete are eliminated."

"Portia and Stewart are out," Chaz said. "And as you may recall, in a *Creature of the Night* first, the audience managed to come up with the correct result, also voting to eliminate Portia and Stewart."

The audience cheered their sudden acuity.

"The contestants are going to be heading back to the Manor. Join us tomorrow night for the fifth challenge! And in the meantime, remember to check in with your favorite contestants via the Manor cams!" Chaz paused while Riley and Kiley swept out to claim the contestants. "We'll see you tomorrow night!"

"Let's forget it," Dawn said. "We're never going to get a table."

"Although I usually find your pessimism charming, it is getting to be a bit much this evening," Gavin said.

"I feel a little guilty for being hungry." They stood shivering in front of the *Please Wait to be Seated* sign. Dawn pulled off her gloves and rubbed her hands together.

"Have toast." Gavin handed his sign to Dawn so he could pull off his gloves. His fingers were stiff and pinched with cold. "Besides, I need coffee."

"Toast?"

"Toast is just toast. Dry bread. It's not something enjoyable enough to warrant guilt."

"That's ridiculous," Dawn said. "Plus, I like toast."

"But, you have to admit it's more sensitive than waffles," Gavin said.

"You're a fucking nut," Dawn said.

"Right this way." Dawn turned around to find the waitress standing there with two menus in one hand and the other on her hip. Her nametag read Irma, and the purse of her lips made Dawn think she was sensitive to profanity. Dawn would have expected someone capable of handling the after bar crowd at a twenty-four-hour diner to be made of sterner stuff.

Dawn and Gavin followed in the wake of Irma's yellow polyester uniform and sneakers. They ended up at a large corner booth. It was already occupied. A small pile of *Let Landon Live* signs leaned against the booth. Like Gavin and Dawn, all the occupants of the booth wore tee shirts immortalizing Landon Jones.

The five people already seated scooted to make room for Dawn and Gavin. Dawn nodded at the two she recognized and slid in, making room for Gavin to sit next to her.

"Hey," Gavin said. A subdued volley of greetings came back.

"Rough night, right?" Carson said. Dawn and Gavin nodded.

"Fucking bunch of assholes," Dawn agreed. Irma's lips clenched tighter. She dropped the menus on the table and left.

"Totally." Callie ripped open a packet of sugar and dumped it into her coffee. "I couldn't believe how many people walked by pretending they couldn't see us."

"Yeah, that was shitty," Dawn said.

"You guys want coffee?" Someone indicated the carafe on the table. Dawn turned over a couple of mugs and poured for herself and Gavin.

Irma reappeared with her pen and pad ready for action. "You ready to order?"

"Steak sandwich, please. And a side of bacon," Carson said.

"Gross. Red meat sounds vile." The girl opposite Gavin made a face. "Sorry. I just can't handle any more bloody flesh after seeing that."

"Can you make the sandwich medium well?" Gavin said.

"Wait. You saw it?" Callie was aghast.

"I watched the clip on YouTube." The girl looked around the table and cringed. "I just wanted to see what happened."

"I'll come back." Irma stalked away.

"You already knew what happened," Callie said. "All you did by watching was add to their sacred hit count."

"One view isn't going to make a difference," Dawn said. There was no point in fighting one another.

"That's the problem with the world," Callie snapped. "Everyone thinks whatever they do is okay."

"I'm not like everybody else," the girl said. "I'm sorry. I didn't think."

"No, you fucking didn't. Whatever. Sorry." Callie tried to open another packet of sugar. In her agitation, she ripped it in half; scattering the grains across the table.

"It does make you wonder if the ratings would have been better if they turned the kid," Dawn said. If some big shot was motivated to do the right thing by the possibility of more viewers, she was all for it.

"I'm sure they would be," Callie said. "But the laws won't allow it."

"Not yet," Dawn said. But someday. They could make it happen. Gavin was right. They just had to stay dedicated.

"Yeah," Callie agreed grimly. "Not yet. Sometimes, I feel like I'm ready to give up. Nothing we do makes a difference. Tonight proved how ineffectual protests are. And caring."

"That's not true," Dawn said. She reached out for an awkward pat on Callie's hand. "I mean, I feel the same way sometimes, tonight even, but we do make a difference. It just takes longer than we want it to."

"She's right," Carson said. "And we shouldn't be fighting amongst ourselves."

"I can't believe he's dead," Callie said. Landon's life had mattered. He could have had weeks remaining. Months even. All that time had been stolen.

"I know." Dawn ran her fingers under her eyes, removing tears but smearing mascara. Sick kids were being denied eternal life, and it was heartbreaking. "It's devastating. I feel like we should have done more. Like I should have done more, but I don't know what else I could have done."

"There was nothing else any of us could have done," Callie said. "We don't have the power to make people not be assholes. No one wants to have to think about what's best for that poor kid because then they'd have to do something besides watch TV."

Heads nodded glumly around the table.

"Are we ready to order over here?" Irma tapped her pen against her order pad.

"Sorry," Carson said to the disgruntled server. "We've had a big night."

"So I've been hearing," Irma said. "Are you the ones that are mad because the cancer kid didn't get to be a vampire or the ones that are mad because they didn't leave him to waste away in peace?"

Confessional: Emily

"So that's done. I have no idea how to feel. Besides horrified. Am I an angel of mercy or a murderer? I have no doubt my sister could answer that question. Luckily for me, she's not here. He seemed happy, the kid I mean. Landon. Landon Jones. I'll remember his name forever. I'll remember the blood forever. But if there are others, will I remember them? How many people must one kill before they become nameless? Faceless? Suddenly, I'm more afraid of winning than of losing. It's not because I just killed a kid. It's because no matter how hard I try to convince myself I just did something monstrous, I don't feel it. I feel like I did what I needed to. For both of us. Which brings me back to thinking I must be horrible if I don't feel horrible."

Confessional: Cassie

"Poor Emily. I'm probably going to be the only one saying that, but wow, killing a cancer kid had to be hard. I wish I hadn't watched. I'm sure I would have been a disaster if I'd been there. All I can think about now is, it's almost over. Of course, we all know what they say about 'almost.' Now I've put the thought of hand grenades into my head. I hate to be a pessimist, but in this situation, grenades come to mind more easily than horseshoes. I'll just say, I hope they don't have people chucking either of those at each other."

Kannon wished he hadn't allowed Cassie to convince him to accompany her to the common area to greet the returning contestants. You would think the fact they'd just killed a little kid would be enough to keep the focus off his marred face, but as it turned out, not even close. The kid had died so quickly. Suffering was best enjoyed lingeringly.

Cassie bumped his leg gently with her walking cast and winked when she had his attention. Kannon smiled in spite of himself.

"How are you feeling?" Cassie said to Emily.

"I'm alive," Emily said. "What more can one hope for?"

Kannon could list a few things, but he knew an answer wouldn't be appreciated.

"Do you want a pastry?" Madeline pulled a raspberry tart from a pocket. There was some jam smeared on her palm, but otherwise, the pastry had fared surprisingly well.

Sure she just murdered a child, but at least she's polite to lunatics, Kannon thought as he watched Emily gently decline the dubious offering.

"Should we do something for her?" Emily asked after Madeline wandered away with the pastry safely back in her pocket.

"I think she needs some heavy-duty meds and to get out of this house," Cassie said. "We can't help her with that."

Confessional: Stewart

"I'm done. I know I am, but that's okay. I kept thinking of my Logan and Audrey when we were lined up out there preparing to massacre that poor kid, and there was no way. I couldn't do it. I couldn't even try. I'm not meant to be a vampire, I guess. I'm not judging Emily. In fact, I believe in Landon's right to make this choice for himself, but it couldn't have been by my hand. Not ever. That makes me weak, I suppose. I'm ready to go home; I hope I get to."

Confessional: Jeff

"I can't believe no one ate the pastries. I'm not counting the crazy girl; she eats everything, and honestly adding a little diarrhea to her day was like putting sprinkles on a pile of sugar. Fuck it. These people suck. For the record, I was trying to liven things up for everyone's benefit, not just mine. Do you ever feel like you want to go on a modest killing spree just to break up the day? Don't get me wrong. I know that would be a little anti-social, and I'm not planning on it, but you can't keep the thoughts from coming, can you?"

"I can't believe she did it," Portia said. She was sitting on the floor at the coffee table playing with slices of the orange she'd just peeled.

Ollie watched Portia's fingers manipulate the orange with all the concentration he could muster.

"Of course she did," Lola said. "She's a fucking psycho."

"Maybe we're all fucking psychos," Ollie said.

"It was the challenge," Portia said. "And I'm not sure the person who went for the flamethrower is the best judge of sanity."

"At least I didn't get eliminated for being a chicken shit," Lola said.

"Yeah, we're all in awe of your magnificence," Jeff said. "The kid did sign up for it."

"I know that matters," Ollie said. "But how much? I mean, does it matter enough to make it okay?"

"Are they going to let all of you keep hanging out after you're eliminated or what?" Lola curled her lip. "It feels crowded with all these opinions that don't matter."

"Chill out," Ollie said although he was feeling decidedly un-chill himself. "They could add like twenty more people, and we wouldn't even notice. This place is huge. Where did she go anyway?"

"The library." Lola rolled her eyes. "She's always in the fucking library."

Confessional: Donovan

"Women are vicious. Between the quiet one and the crazy one, I'm starting to think it's not safe to sleep in this house. I'd still bang the actress though. Fucking kid. They should have let us kill a bum or something. I wouldn't have hesitated. But I guess that wouldn't have been much of a challenge. Anyone could kill a bum. Talk about a mercy killing. A cancer kid, though? So fucked up. I don't even care about the kid; I hesitated because I don't think women are going to go crazy to fuck the guy who staked Landon Jones, the big cancer hero. Such bullshit. It's not like he got cancer on purpose, you know what I mean? So, it's not so much I couldn't do it. I just chose not to for the health of my social life. And that's the truth. And if I ever get a chance to pay that bitch Lola back for hitting me with a goddamn ax, I'll do it in a heartbeat, and that's the truth too."

Confessional: Celeste

"That was officially the worst day of my life. I have seen too much shit I'll never be able to un-see. And I know I'm not the only one. Everybody is freaking the fuck out. I mean, of course, they are. Normal people freak out when a kid gets beheaded, right? You freak the fuck out. If they made a manual, that would be page one. But the thing I can't stop thinking about is there's still another challenge coming. And I'm terrified because I'm wondering what the hell are they going to come up with that could top what happened today?"

"They beheaded the little boy?" Tim and Kristen's mother had a bowl of cupcake batter braced on her hip and was stirring vigorously.

"It was only one of them," Kristen corrected.

"Yeah," her brother confirmed. "The rest of them pussied out."

"Language," their mother said absently. "I'm not sure you guys should be watching this."

"Come on, mom," Tim moaned.

"The kid's already dead," Kristen said. "And besides, he had cancer."

"Really?" The heads of her offspring nodded vigorously. "I guess if he had cancer it's okay. Do you guys want to taste the batter?"

"One of us is going to be a monster," Stewart said.

"You don't have to worry about it," Donovan told him. "You're done, remember?"

"I remember," Stewart said. "But, I bet you're about done too. You couldn't kill the kid. Everyone saw you couldn't. Do you think you're going to be able to live by taking life from others?"

"They don't kill people," Lola said. "Not usually. Being a vampire doesn't mean you have to go around killing everybody. But if you want to, nobody is going to stop you."

"Even they have to follow rules," Brett said. Of course, being a rock star and a vampire, there wouldn't be much Brett couldn't get away with.

"They set up a competition where we had to kill a kid," Stewart said. "There's no rule they couldn't find a way around. They're monsters."

"They set it up, but they didn't kill him," Celeste said. She was wrapped in a robe with a towel on her head. She had crawled into a hot bubble bath and cried after watching the last challenge. "A human killed him. And it was legal."

"Yes," Emily said from the doorway. "At least I think I'm human. I don't feel like myself." She wasn't acting like herself. Seeking out the others wasn't like her, and she already wished she hadn't.

"We didn't know you were there," Stewart said. Because she looked so fragile, he added. "Sorry, you were only doing what you had to."

"It's fine," Emily told him. "Is 'had to' really accurate? I don't know. Long term, I suppose. But we always have a choice, don't we?"

Stewart looked around for help. He didn't feel like dealing with Emily's existential crisis. Neither did anyone else.

"Look, whatever you're going through, it's almost over." Trying not to show his distaste, Stewart patted her on the shoulder. "Just focus on that."

"You're right." Emily met his eyes with her big dark ones, and Stewart couldn't remember why he'd ever thought her fragile. "It is almost over."

Confessional: Portia

"I miss doing children's theater. That's how bad this is. I tried. I mean, I believe in the Death with Dignity laws. I honestly do. I just never expected to be the one dishing out the dignity. I thought I could just stick him with the Euthanol, but I was wrong. Death is so final. That's stupid. Of course, it's final except it's not, not if you get turned. But for that kid, it's final. And I kept thinking what if I stick the needle in and push the plunger, and he changes his mind? I'm starting to think maybe I'm not playing the lead. On the other hand, this could just be the part where the main character is hitting rock bottom, which means it's all uphill from here. I'm so upset; I thought about sleeping with Donovan just to take the edge off. Sorry, baby, but what happens on set stays on set."

Confessional: Madeline

"There was something horribly wrong with me. My insides wouldn't stop coming out. I haven't had to go to the toilet for a while now, so maybe I'm better. But who knows? The problem with always being the nurturer is there's no one to take care of you when you need help. People are like pets that way. They just let you take care of them, but they don't give anything back. It's like we have a buddy system, but I'm my buddy. My mom taught me how to do that, you know, be my own buddy."

"Are there more pastries?" Madeline didn't see any, but it was always good to ask. "I think I need to rest. I was sick earlier, but I wanted to check on you guys. Since you all look okay, can someone carry me to bed?"

"Could you please shut the fuck up?" Portia said. "Everybody is fucking exhausted and on edge. We can't coddle a nut job on top of everything else. No offense."

"You're hot when you let loose your captive bitch," Donovan said. "Not that I wouldn't hit it any old time, but I like the edge."

"You're disgusting," Portia told him. She already regretted what she had said in confessional about sleeping with him. "And I'm not a bitch. I reasonably asked her to let us have a little peace the same way I do every time you say something offensive, which is almost every time you talk."

Madeline leaned over and puked on the couch.

"I'm not cleaning that shit up," Donovan said.

Portia refrained, with heroic effort, from striking him. "Take a look around. No one is going to clean it up. You should see what she left in the hall. It's like we're on a fucking cruise."

Little P dared not turn away from the monitor lest he accidentally make eye contact with The Voice.

"This wasn't what I meant when I said things at the house needed stirring up."

"Sorry, sir," Little P said.

Confessional: Brett

"That was amazing and super sad at the same time. I wanted to be the one, but I'm so relieved I wasn't. Today is a day of contradictions. I wouldn't have thought a wooden freaking stake would go in so easy. It must have been sharper than I thought. If my aim had been better, I would have killed the kid. Here's something weird: I don't know if I missed on purpose or not, but I still think the drowning would have been more peaceful. It always looks peaceful in the movies. I wonder if the protestors are still out there. People are all riled up about all this. I never really thought about right to die stuff before, but it doesn't seem like it's any of their business. If someone's sick and they've had enough, I mean I get it. Turns out it's tough being the one who's expected to help them along. At least they didn't get us each a sick kid. That would've been brutal. Fuck. I just realized I won't have that great story to tell to *Rolling Stone*."

Confessional: Kannon

"It feels different today. I mean, I know the kid and all—was a big deal, but something's up. Maybe we get to leave. The show is about done. If one more junior producer sticks his head in to check on us and write notes, there's going to be bloodshed. I understand the utter lack of privacy was always part of the deal, but it's driving me crazy. If everything had gone according to my plan, I would have been there. I would have had to choose whether or not to try to end that little boy, and I honestly can't say what I would have done. Hmm, I can probably guess. I can't stand to look at Emily. I can't look at any of them without being overcome with revulsion. I hate that I have to walk the world with these people."

"Did you follow me?"

"No," Donovan said.

"I call bullshit on that," Lola said. "You've been trying to catch me alone."

"Fuck you," Donovan said.

Lola smiled. "Want to? If you're not too pissed about the ax thing."

"Define 'too pissed.'"

Lola laughed. "Tell you what. I know what you're here for, and I'm up for it. But I want to hear you say it."

"You're completely fucking crazy, aren't you?" Donovan said.

"If you admit it, I'll let you," Lola said. "You're outside my room, Joe Cool. It's not a fucking mystery, and I need to relax. All you have to do is say it."

"Why do I have to say anything? Did someone not get enough compliments as a girl?"

"Okay, bye." Lola swung the door. Donovan stopped it as easily as Lola had imagined he would. He went her one better by pushing her into the room and coming in after her.

"Lock it, why don't you?" Lola said as he pushed the door shut behind him.

Donovan complied. "You don't think this means anything,

right? I'm still going to bury you in competition. And I'm still going to get you back for nailing me with the ax."

"There's a first time for everything," Lola said. She pulled Donovan's shirt off. "But how chivalrous of you to make it clear while my clothes are still on."

"I didn't see a reason to worry," Donovan said.

Lola flipped him off and pulled off her shirt.

I'm going to wreck this bitch, Donovan thought and stuck a finger down the front of Lola's bra to pull her closer. His pull opened the clasp allowing Lola's heaving bounty to spring free. Donovan's inner deviant gleefully began to whack off.

They didn't bother with kissing.

Donovan bent his head, and as his lips closed around her nipple, Lola gasped. When his teeth nipped gently, she moaned. Donovan applied more pressure and—

"Ow! Fuck!" Lola smacked Donovan across the temple. "Too hard, asshole."

"What the fuck?"

"You can't bite that fucking hard," Lola said. "How would you like it if I bit your fucking dick like that?"

"I'll kill you if you bite my dick," Donovan assured her. "It's not the same."

"Whatever," Lola scowled. "Just take your clothes off." She removed her remaining garments and hopped on the bed. Donovan admired the way her tits hopped with her and followed after shedding the rest of his clothes.

"You want to suck it?" Donovan invited, grabbing his penis and waggling it at Lola.

"Only if you go down on me first," Lola said.

"Why do I have to go first?"

"Because I don't trust you," Lola said. "I'm not giving one of my amazing bloweys and not getting anything back." In fact, Lola was terrible at giving blow jobs, mostly due to the lack of practice that was a natural result of her policy of selfishness but partly because she had a strong gag reflex.

"I don't trust you either. Forget it," Donovan said. "Let's just fuck." Since Lola wouldn't do it, Donovan took a moment to bring his manhood to attention.

"Okay, asshole," Lola said spreading her legs. "Make me scream."

"What about...?"

"What?"

"You know," Donovan said. "I just had a baby with some bitch I haven't seen for almost a year."

"Idiot," Lola said. "Tomorrow, you'll be dead, and I'll be immortal. And trust me, if the change doesn't rid me of any internal parasites, I'll take care of it. I think we can cross pregnancy and disease off our list of worries."

It was a good point. Donovan nodded and crawled over Lola until he was in position to insert his throbbing member. She guided him in, and he gave her a nice slow, long thrust. In. Out. Crap. He'd gone too far on the outstroke. He tried to shove back in before Lola noticed.

Lola swore. "Not there!"

"Sorry," Donovan grunted. "Slipped."

"Just start out slow," Lola said when everything was in its place. "Okay, good boy. That feels good. Go a little faster. Harder. Oh, yeah, oh, fuck me, yeah, faster. Not that fast. Keep going—" Lola stopped talking to concentrate on Donovan's rhythm, which included the slap of his balls on her ass each time he thrust. Every time the balls hit her, Lola moaned.

Donovan was dripping sweat. His man rain sprinkled Lola's chest, neck, and a couple drops hit her face as he watched. He hoped she didn't notice. He thrust harder to distract her. Of course, this caused more profuse sweating.

Lola noticed, but she was so fucking close. It didn't matter. She was going to throw the sweaty bastard out and hit the shower as soon as she came. "Yeah, right there, that's so fucking good, go harder, oh my god, I'm almost—"

Lola was a bitch, no doubt, but she looked so fucking hot with her lips parted, and her hair mussed from the pounding he was giving her. When she dug her nails into his back, Donovan was so turned on that he finished ahead of schedule.

"No, no, no, not yet! Fuck." Lola let out a scream of frustration as Donovan moaned and collapsed on top of her. "Seriously?"

Confessional: Ollie

"That wouldn't have made my dad proud. What happened today, I mean. Not that I couldn't do it, but that I participated in the first place. Not that this is the best time to worry about my dad. I love you, dad, but things here are fairly all-consuming, if you know what I mean. I think sometimes, we have to think about what the best thing to do is without trying to figure out what someone else thinks is the best thing if that makes any sense. Probably not. Sorry. I'm still a little shell-shocked."

Confessional: Lola

"So, I didn't chop a kid's head off. Who the fuck cares? I'm still going to win this thing, and I'm going to do it after avoiding the fucked up part. So, who's fucking stupid now, Emily? I hate her. I hope the next challenge is to stake that bitch. People think I'm unfeeling, but look at what happened out there. And don't think for a second she was doing it for the kid. She just wants to win. I mean, she just beheaded cancer boy like it was nothing. Fuck. I fucked up. I know I should have just done it because someone else was going to do it if I didn't, but what can I say? It turns out I'm not the kind of girl who's comfortable chopping up a kid with an ax. Does that make me a terrible person? I don't fucking think so.

More like old fashioned. You know what makes you a terrible person? Being a premature ejaculator."

"This is getting boring," Penny said.

"It is possible to turn it off," her daughter informed her.

"Nah, it'll get better soon. That stupid girl is trying to stand on her head or something. They should show some blood, that's all."

"I'm sure they will." Allyson snuck a peek at the screen in spite of herself. "She's doing yoga, mother."

"Yoga?" Penny sneered. "Who does yoga?"

"Millions of people," Allyson said. "Maybe billions. I do it myself."

"Why do you do that?"

Allyson sighed. "It's good exercise. And it helps relieve all those little stresses caused by life." And mothers. Allyson watched Emily bend and stretch on the TV and for a moment breathed along with her. Then they switched to someone else, and she turned her focus back to her work and tried to block out her parent.

Emily rolled to her feet. Half an hour of bending and breathing and she felt no more relaxed than she had before she began. At least she had managed to alleviate some of the soreness in her muscles.

Although she had trained for this, she hadn't fully anticipated the beating her body would be taking. Somehow, the aches made her feel accomplished. She'd never been a fan of gratuitous physical activity, but it felt good to lose herself in the flex and stretch of her muscles.

Maybe she'd do more after. If she had an after. Although by then, it would be so easy she'd be cheating.

...Let _ _ _ _ Sort Them Out.

Welcome back and good evening," Chaz said. "Here we are again. We've learned quite a bit about our contestants during our time together, and coming up next, we'll learn a little more from some Friends and Family. We're going to hear from a friend of Madeline's. Have you all been keeping up with Madeline? Interesting stuff. After that, we'll see Ollie's dad. Take a look at Jessa."

Jessa was exactly what one would come up with if trying to conjure a mental picture of a friend of Madeline's, assuming one had only seen Madeline on Creature of the Night. In fact, a costumer with a sense of humor had seen the two together at some point and imitated Jessa's look when putting together Madeline's wardrobe for the first show. Jessa gave the camera an awkward wave. "Hi, Madeline. I hope, by the time you see this, you're totally kicking ass. I want everyone to know I'm proud of this girl. We auditioned for the show together, but they picked Madeline. I guess she just looks like she's more into vampires. But for the record, there are lots of people who wear normal clothes and want to be undead. I'm just saying. I mean, Madeline is special. Just so, so special. And she's been my best friend since we were, like, seven. I'm just really glad I can focus on supporting her, instead of being disappointed I wasn't chosen or feeling like it wasn't fair. Because there's no point in negativity. And I totally think Madeline that, even if you don't win, you'll totally make it out of there alive."

"Always great to get a positive message from home," Chaz said. "Let's see if Ollie's dad can top Jessa's astounding message of support."

The screens had been taken over by an attractively weathered man in a blue chambray shirt. He looked like he spent his life outdoors. "Hi, son," he said. "You know I wish you weren't where you are, but I hope you know how proud of you I am. I know you're not a farmer, and you never were going to be one. Going after something new is never easy; don't think I don't know the strength it took for you to get there. Good luck, Ollie, and know if your mother were still with us, she'd be just as proud as I am. I hope I get to see you again." Ollie's father waved his hand at the camera but not before the audience saw a tear roll out of his eye.

Ollie, too, started to cry.

"*I thought the mother was alive,*" Nodin said. "*I remember the farm boy greeting both his parents.*"

"*Maybe she was alive then but is dead now,*" Delia said.

"*Do we care?*" Edmund snapped. No one bothered with an answer. Edmund hoped the death of Ollie's mother had been unrelated to the show.

"When we come back," Chaz said, "we'll be all set up for the next challenge. See you all soon!"

"That's exactly what I had in mind," The Voice said.

"Thank you, sir." Little P flushed with pleasure. He thought he had been quite ingenious in his arrangements. "I appreciate you saying so."

"Well, you did a good job," The Voice said. "You can never go wrong with a dead mother. Touching stuff."

Nodin set his book down and sighed. Eighty-six pages in, and so far *How to be More Charismatic* was a big disappointment.

A more charismatic vampire would have flung the book at the wall, perhaps even through the wall. Such a being would never have ended up pinned beneath that mad vampire **Vlad**.

Perhaps he should go back out there and tear the throat from some scantily clad *Creature* fan. Sex and death were what the producers were all about; albeit, the sex wasn't officially condoned.

Nodin tried to imagine behaving like Vlad and shuddered. He longed for the days when one could have a quiet meal in a dark alley without feeling pressure to make it look sexy for the benefit of bystanders. Just the other night, someone had approached him and asked if he sparkled. Truly, it was exhausting.

That the others seemed to thrive on the adoration didn't make Nodin feel any better about what he was beginning to suspect were permanent inadequacies on his part.

"Did you miss us?" Chaz shouted. The crowd screamed affirmation. "Of course you did, because we're amazing. But we're back and ready for the next challenge."

The stage had been transformed into an old gothic graveyard. Sod had been laid across the entire stage, half a football field's worth. Littering the grass were coffins, tombstones, and chipped stone angels.

Dominating the center of the stage was a mausoleum. Most of the tombstones surrounding it were old and reeked of the grave dirt from which they had been recently plucked. Many of them were chipped or cracked, but ten of them were new, created for this night. The lights had been changed, set at odd angles to cast shadows while still making it possible for those watching to catch most of the action. Cameras lurked, their electronic eyes waiting to catch whatever the naked ones could not.

Only the bodies were missing.

"Let's bring the contestants out," Chaz said.

Donovan, Emily, Lola, and Brett made their way to Chaz's side shepherded by Rylie and Kylie.

"Give your final four a big round of applause," Chaz said. The crowd roared.

"Bury them! Bury them! Bury them!" The crowd punctuated their chant with fists thrust into the air.

Sick fucks, Donovan thought. Of course, sickness was to be expected from a bunch of losers who lost their shit over a bunch of dead creeps.

"We're not burying them again," Chaz said. "Be quiet now." The crowd refused to settle until Edmund reinforced Chaz's instruction with a flash of fangs.

"Hidden in our beautifully constructed graveyard are various weapons," Chaz said. "Two of the remaining contestants will move forward from this challenge and will be turned, made like us."

Brett felt something inside him jump at the news. He could be turned and gifted with a mate. And a vampire girl would probably be cooler about stuff like orgies than human girls.

"Not so like us," Edmund said. The crowd ignored Edmund and went berserk at the news that two would be turned. Chaz held up a hand, and eventually the crowd responded.

"Many will die today," Vlad said.

"Die! Die! Die!" The crowd chanted.

"As Vlad has pointed out, this is a fatal challenge."

Edmund preempted the crowd. "Do not chant."

"Does that count as speaking to humans?" Delia wondered.

"Only two will come out of this challenge alive," Chaz said, "and we have a special surprise. Since we are woefully low on contestants, the eliminated will be brought back to participate in this challenge. They too will have one last chance to grasp immortality. Because we at *Creature of the Night* are either victorious or we are dead, except when we are both."

In spite of the silence, the glee of the crowd was palpable. This was what they had come for.

"Let's get the others out here," Chaz said. The eight eliminated contestants made their way onto the stage. The crowd jeered. Donovan, Brett, Emily, and Lola seethed with various degrees of resentment.

Attuned as he was to the emotions of the humans around him, Chaz said, "Life is not fair nor is death. We see no reason to hold ourselves to a higher standard."

"That's so not fair," Dylan said. Joey the cocker spaniel whuuffed in agreement.

"He just said it's not fair; that's the point." Bekka loved her brother, but sometimes, he was such a moron.

Dylan flipped his sister a middle finger, following up with a glance over his shoulder to make sure their mother hadn't noticed. Bekka was a pain in his ass. "I don't get it."

"You're such an idiot," Bekka said. "Hey, are those the contestant's names on the tombstones?"

"Quiet," Dylan told her, irked he hadn't noticed. "They're starting."

"Any contestant who attempts to exit the stage before we call a halt to this challenge will be given to Vlad," Chaz said. "When only two contestants remain, this challenge will be considered complete."

Jesus, Cyri thought.

Rylie and Kylie herded the contestants into a line. Kannon fidgeted with his eye patch, and Cassie shifted her weight on her crutches. Eye contact was avoided. At this moment, every kind word the contestants had ever exchanged became a Monday morning liability.

"Before we begin the challenge, we have a special batch of confessionals to show you. As you know, confessionals broadcast live, but we were concerned there might be a lack of candor if the contestants were forced to confess in front one another. So, these we filmed about fifteen minutes ago when the contestants found out they were all participating in the final challenge. Emotions were high as we recorded."

"Human emotions always run high," Edmund said.

"Take a look at the screens," Chaz instructed. Stewart's face was first to flash across the screens. Along with the eleven other contestants and fifty million viewers, Stewart watched as he said his last words.

Stewart:

"I hoped I was done. I want this to be over, but that would be too good to be true. I want to say I'm shocked, but I don't think it would be exactly true. I'm still reeling from the last challenge, even though I wasn't a big part of it. I think I gave up on winning this thing a long time ago, but now that's changed. All I want is to go home and see my kids, and they've set it up so the only way for me to do that is to go through everyone else. I thought I wanted to win at the beginning of this competition, but that feeling was nothing compared to where I'm at now. It's the difference between wanting to win at Monopoly and wanting to escape a burning building. They've taken the simple luxury of caring about others away from us. By the end of this, dead or alive, we will all be monsters. So, Marcy, if I do make it thought this, you would be wise to stop trying to turn my children against me."

"He is an uncomfortable combination of despair and rage," Nodin said. *"And he may not be the only one."*

"The more unstable they are, the higher the ratings," Delia said. *"There is no reason to worry."*

"We cannot have the winner rampage every season," Nodin said.

"I do not think it will come to that," Delia told him. *"I have hope."*

"Based on what?" Edmund filled his mental tone with the scowl he wore.

"I remember the massacre," Vlad said. *"It was a good day."*

Cassie:

"I'm excited, of course, to have another chance. At the same time, because I'm not stupid, I know it's a slim chance. I'm still on crutches. They say everyone roots for the underdog. I don't know if it's true, but I know wishes don't make horses. And suddenly, I'm channeling my grandmother. She would have talked me out of this if she were still alive. But you never know. Right? It's not like I'm going to be the one to beat out there. Maybe I can slip under the radar. Whatever happens we're almost to the end of this. I'm not scared. I don't know if that's good or not because this seems like a situation in which any rational person would be terrified. But mostly, I feel peaceful. And I am ready to unleash my inner badass."

"She's cute," Delia said. *"It's almost a shame."*

"That she has no 'inner badass'?" Nodin said.

"A vampire ballerina would be a fantastic thing," Delia said.

"Yes," Nodin agreed.

"If we were interested in promoting the arts, there are several contestants we would have done well to avoid."

"Thank you, Edmund," Delia said. *"Without you, we would have had no idea of their flaws. We need diversity. Humans like to root for people who they think are like them."*

"Perhaps you will explain the inner workings of larvae next," Edmund suggested.

"Perhaps I will tear your head from your body while I do so," Delia answered.

Brett:

"I don't get it. This is supposed to be a competition about who is the best, about who deserves to be a vampire, a goddamn Creature of the Night. Don't get me wrong. I'm sure there's a great fucking reason for letting the people who've been *eliminated* come back and compete, but I don't fucking get it. I mean, this is unfair as fuck, isn't it? Not that I'm saying they're wrong. They're vampires, and who am I to question them, but it seems a little arbitrary. It's like you climb a mountain, and there's another mountain on top of it. Shitty. I just need to understand.

"I need to win. That's all. I'm still the guy who believed, the guy who was right all along. They could add a million other contestants, and none of them would have anything on me. I'm focused. I'm motherfucking focused, and I'm going to go out there and do whatever. If there's a fucking flamethrower, this time the bitch is mine."

"But there is no flamethrower," Vlad said.

"No matter," Edmund said. *"It would sit untouched. He exaggerates his audacity."*

Portia:

"I couldn't kill the kid, but I'm pretty sure I can kill these assholes. I have to if I don't want these assholes to kill me. What the fuck was I thinking? Babe, I'm sorry. I should have been happier, I shouldn't have ever been jealous of you. Miss me if you don't see me again, okay? And don't you ever hook up with that little bitch Marilyn. I don't care how long I've been dead. Oh, my god. I just realized something. This is like the highest rated show ever. I'll be in the In Memoriam presentation at the Emmy's. Or I'll be a vampire. I'm still freaking out, but that was the best realization I've had in years. The best thing would be if they played a clip of me from right now talking about being in the In Memoriam clip. I need to say something deep. Hmmm. Fuck it! I'm going to be on the Emmy's! Suck on that, Charles!"

"*Actors,*" Nodin said. "*They are a most interesting breed.*"

"*It is nice to see her so happy,*" Delia said. "*I enjoyed her film.*"

"*Does she speak of Marilyn Monroe?*" Vlad asked.

Donovan:

"Fuck these pussies. I beat them once, and I'll do it again. If I have to kill every one of these loser shitheads, I will. And I guess I do. There's no way I'm losing ground now. I want to shout out to my co-contestants. Emily, you bitch, I'm going to rip you apart with my bare hands. And Brett, you've always fucking annoyed me, you puny fuck. Can't wait to kill you, you creepy vampire loving freak. Cassie, you're so pathetic I can't even bring myself to comment on you. Who else do I hate? Kannon, you rich, one-eyed fuck, money won't buy you immortality. Ollie, stop being so fucking earnest; it's disgusting. Be a fucking man. Lola, you're fucking welcome for last night, but I will kill you without thinking twice."

"*I do not believe anyone would mind if I ate that one,*" Vlad said.

"*I do not believe you are mistaken,*" Nodin said.

"*Please do not take that as permission,*" Delia told Vlad. She shot a look of admonishment Nodin's way. "*We are close to the end. This isn't the time to start eating the contestants.*"

"*It is never a good time,*" Vlad grumped.

"*I have a virgin in my dressing room,*" Delia said. "*If you don't eat anyone without permission, I'll share.*"

Lola:

"This is bullshit. I cannot believe they are fucking us like this. What was the point of all the other challenges if they were just going to throw us into a pit so we could be all Thunderdome about it? But I don't give a fuck. That shit with the kid was stupid. *This* is what life is about. Kill or be killed. A real fight. Take what you want. And if there's anyone who thinks I'm going to let any of these shitheads deprive me of what I want, then you have no idea who I am. But I'm going to show you. I'm as ready as I've ever been, and I will never hesitate again. I feel good today. Relaxed. Luckily, I'm an expert at polishing my own pearl. By the way, you guys are welcome for the sex scene. Too bad Donovan is shit in bed. Sorry, D, but it's called confessional for a reason."

"I feel like Lola had an unfortunate childhood," Delia said.

"How many times must I beg you to stop reading human psychology?" Edmund said. *"She's not a particularly damaged human; she is a particularly average one."*

"'Particularly average' sounds redundant," Nodin said.

Jeff:

"Here we are again. Now that it's happened, it seems obvious they planned to throw us back into the mix at some point. I'm glad I didn't realize this was coming. I know these people. I have no desire to kill any of them, but oh, how quickly scruples fly out the window when it truly is them or you. Stewart was right about us being monsters. I keep imagining the things I might do when I go out there, and I realize I already am one. I'm just missing the immortality. This seems like time I should spend listing regrets or beating my chest, but all I have to say is I want to get started. The whole thing seemed like such a waste of effort when I got myself eliminated in the first round, but now I'm back, and I've had lots of time to watch the others. When I said I know these people, that's what I meant. Not that we share bonds, or I know their pain, or even what makes them tick. I know how they behave."

"*I wonder if having them drinking blood so soon gave us an inaccurate measure of their potential,*" Nodin said.

"*He's in it now,*" Delia said.

"*Perhaps a system of points would give us a more effective idea of who is worthy,*" Nodin said.

"*No eliminations?*" Edmund said.

Nodin shrugged.

"*I take that to mean you like this one, Nodin,*" Delia said.

"*As much as it is reasonable to like any of them.*"

Emily:

"So. This is happening. If I disregard the gratuitous bloodshed that's about to occur, I feel like this might make the challenge better. Easier to survive. Easier for me, of course, because who else could I be thinking of at this point? I'm trying to remember everyone else must be in the same place, that I'm no worse than anyone, and probably still better than Lola. Okay, I heard it; I can see why she called me judgy. They say the first time you kill someone is the hardest. I'm not sure if that's true. Now that I think about it, I realize that sentiment may have come entirely from old detective novels. For obvious reasons, I hope it's true. And for obvious reasons, if it is, I have to thank Landon. Landon, if any part of you is still coherent, I hope your pain is over. And I will spend the rest of my life remembering your magnificent composure. I hope I manage to do as well. And if you are in heaven, don't forget to kiss my dog. I don't always talk to dead kids, but when I do, I say something obnoxiously sentimental."

"*Why does she think more foes will be better?*" Delia said.

"*For all you are, my dear,*" Nodin told her. "*You are not a strategist.*"

"*If you take offense to that,*" Vlad said. "*I will kill him for you. But I would like the virgin now.*"

"*If I wanted him killed,*" Delia said. "*I would take the pleasure for myself.*"

Madeline:

"I'm back. I don't want to sound like some new age moron, but this feels a bit preordained. I don't mean by God or anything; I'm an atheist. Maybe more of an agnostic. Point is I had a panic attack in the coffin, and I said some things I shouldn't have. But it won't happen again. And when I said preordained, I meant by something more like Fate. It's like I'm meant to be the *Creature of the Night*. I missed all the hard stuff. No flying bullets, or eating kids, or whatever. Some of the other contestants are so pissed. It's pretty funny. I mean, I would have more compassion for them, but they wouldn't take care of me, would they? Maybe all along the plan was to keep the contestants with the most potential out of harm's way by eliminating us early and then bringing us back for the last challenge. And best of all, they let us dress ourselves. Obviously, I'm not one of those shallow girls who only cares about how they look, and that was a reference to Portia if anyone missed it, but I feel better when I look like myself. Like my true self isn't being obliterated by pink wool."

"*Her true self,*" Edmund said. "*Does she even know her true self? Why must they all be so self-obsessed? They always assume their true selves are worth knowing.*"

"*I must admit,*" Delia said, "*that does seem to be the case. And I have read extensively on the subject.*"

Ollie:

"This has been the ride of a lifetime. Not in a good way. I don't know why I tried to phrase that positively. What's the point? I thought it was over for me, and now I find out it's not. I have another chance to win this thing, but if I had a choice, I think I'd rather go home than have to hurt these people. Some of them are good people. And it won't be just hurting. It'll be killing. My dad, he was disappointed in me when I wouldn't help him round up the cattle for the slaughterhouse. I've felt like a disappointment to him ever since. And that cancer kid. I couldn't do it, even though he wanted us to. Shit, I'm not making any sense. I guess I'm trying to say even though I want to win, I'm not sure I have it in me to do what I'm going to have to do. But they put our backs against the wall, and if I don't have it in me, someone else will. I think what I have to remember is, people aren't cows or cancer kids. Except the cancer kid was a person."

"*Did any of you have any inkling that cows are not people?*" Nodin said.

"*Actually,*" Edmund said. "*I did not.*"

"*Cows,*" Vlad said. "*Bleh. Even if they are virgins, not so good.*"

Celeste:

"I was wrong to come here. Fuck. I don't want to be here, but I can't just go home. It says so in the contract. Now, everything's changed. I need to win. I'm going to win this fucking thing because I have no choice. You know how sometimes you want something for so long and then maybe you get it, or maybe you don't, but you suddenly realize it's shit? That you don't fucking want it? That it, this thing, is the last thing in the world you want? This sucks. But, I need to win. I can do this. I'm fucking back. In every sense. I'm going to rain destruction out there. When I got here, I wasn't a person who could have won. I wasn't a person who wanted to win. But I got a look at what comes from the kind of weakness I was lost in, and that's all it took. I was okay with the thought of being sent home, but home only exists for the winner. And I will do anything. I'm scared though. Look at my hands shake. I mean for fuck's sake, you can't just ask everybody to confirm the contact information for their next of kin and leave with no more explanation. That producer is a prick. And the way things have been going, how did they not have those numbers on speed dial?"

"Did they not know we would see these confessionals?" Nodin said. *"That we have seen all of their confessions?"*

"They don't behave as if they knew," Delia said. *"Although, common sense would dictate anything that was said or done might come to our attention."*

"Expecting humans to behave sensibly," Edmund said, *"in itself demonstrates an absence of sense."*

Kannon:

"I'm going to say it. I'm happy to have the chance to inflict some pain. The thought of killing some of these people thrills me. It's possible I have some pent up rage. But if this isn't the appropriate place to bring it, there isn't one. By the way, fuck you, Dad. For making me prove myself to you and for pressuring me to do it in a way you thought would benefit you. Don't misunderstand; I'm not any better. But I am finished. With you, that is. If I do manage to win this, don't wait around for me to bestow immortality on you. And if someday, I do darken your door, you would be wise not to invite me in."

"I would take that one," Delia said.

"He is marred," Nodin said. *"You have a reputation as one who demands perfection."*

"Rage translates well when one is seeking pleasure," Delia told

him. *"And most of him is still beautiful."*

"Okay, people," Chaz said. "That was that. You know what was on each contestant's mind just before the final challenge. Contestants, listen up. These are the rules: do what you must. Whether you will be held accountable is a worry to savor another time. If you can."

"So now, let's count it down," Chaz said, and the crowd joined in with gusto. *"Three, two, one!"*

The contestants swept into the graveyard. Many of them went for distance, trying to disappear into the set. Some were more intent on arming themselves, but within seconds, everyone had vanished from sight except for Cassie and Lola. Cassie would have been last, but Lola purposely lagged behind her. Lola watched the former dancer struggle across the stage on her crutches, and when Cassie drew near to the nearest tombstone, Lola used a foot to hook Cassie's good ankle from behind. Having her one useful leg swept out from under her sent Cassie sprawling face first into a stone cherub. Cassie tried to pull herself up. She threw her arms around the little stone angel but only managed to bring it down on her head. Lola snatched the crutch that had fallen from Cassie's grasp and proceeded to beat her about the head with it.

"I don't think that one is a nice girl," Mildred said.

"I don't think they pick the nice ones to be on reality shows," Hal said.

Mildred considered the point but soon moved on to bigger things. "Are those nachos?" She shoved the beagle off her lap.

"Chicken wings too." Hal set the food on the table between their burgundy leather recliners. Mildred shooed the dog away.

"I just don't like her," Mildred reiterated. "She's a bad sort. You can tell."

"Now," her husband chided her, "we don't know anything about her."

"Well, I can see they have knives and swords and a couple hatchets hidden in the graveyard," Mildred said. "I think it would be kinder to do it quick, don't you?"

"Maybe she wanted the first thing she could reach so she could protect herself," Hal said. He thought it was a reasonable argument, but Hal had developed a fascination with Lola over the course of the show that inspired him to give her the benefit of any doubt. He loved Mildred, make no mistake, but she was a God-fearing woman who lacked what Hal saw as Lola's dark sexuality. Hal was pretty sure Lola would enjoy getting on top. He scratched his stomach and reached for the basket of chicken wings.

The contestants were pursuing victory with a fury that was new to most of them. Those that had been eliminated were seizing their chance at redemption, fueled by the knowledge that their lives hung in the balance. Those that hadn't been eliminated already knew this on some level, but the return of the vanquished incensed them. Not to mention, they were desperate. So, they scrambled for weapons and strategy, ducked behind oversized tombstones that may have held their own names, and when the bodies began to fall, they counted down.

The first blood of the challenge had gushed out of Cassie's crushed nose and hit the stage. Cassie was no longer resisting, but Lola swung a few more times for good measure. Satisfied for the moment, Lola tossed the crutch aside and scrambled along the edge of the graveyard until her search yielded a hacksaw. There would be no chance for the tiny dancer to overcome her wounds and rise to victory in the final moments. Lola laboriously worked the saw, to-ing and fro-ing across Cassie's neck and cursing for want of an ax. Finally, Lola lifted Cassie's bloody head up and waved it in the crowd's direction. They rewarded her with an enthusiastic and barbarous chant, but the judges gave no acknowledgment, apparently planning to stay out of it until the bitter end instead of calling it death by death.

When Lola realized the tickling on the inside of her arm was Cassie's blood running down it, she tossed the head away. It hit the stage with a squishy thump and rolled toward the audience, coming to rest a few feet away from the edge of the stage. Eager hands reached out for the head, but it hadn't rolled quite far enough to be accessible to the questing fingers. Reclaiming the crutch with her free hand and gripping the saw in the other, Lola set off looking for a more immediately lethal weapon, stepping over Cassie's body as she went.

A few yards in, she found a short sword behind a cherub. Lola dropped down behind the chubby little statue and wrapped her fingers around the blade. When she peeked around the cherub's behind, Donovan plunged a fileting knife into her jugular.

Lola turned to gape at her lover and competitor, and Portia popped up from behind a tombstone and took her head off with a scythe. Unlike Landon's, Lola's head got some distance from her body. Helped on its way with a kick from Kannon, it sailed into the crowd. After much swearing and wrestling, Lola's head ended up in the possession of Marlie Foyil, the nine-year-old pride and joy of Stacy and Beth. After the show, the head would go home with Marlie to occupy a place of honor on her dresser. It would stay there until she went off to college, and her mothers would gratefully let it go at a garage sale for seven dollars, even though the sticker clearly said eight-fifty.

Portia took a swipe at Donovan, who jumped back then easily caught her arm and took the scythe from her on the backswing. Portia yanked her arm free and ran.

In the middle of a bouquet of pansies adorning the tombstone of Xavier Marks, Stewart had discovered a butcher knife. Thus armed, he made his way to center stage where the crypt was located. He'd climbed atop it while most of the other contestants were still scrambling for weapons. Now, he was stretched out flat and quiet, hoping to stay alive by devoting himself to the *out of sight, out of mind* school of combat.

Ganged up on by the height of the crypt and gravity, Stewart had struggled long enough that he had managed to catch Kannon's eye. Armed with a hunting knife Kannon made a running leap at the crypt. His scaling skills surpassed Stewart's, and he had both hands and a foot on the crypt roof when Jeff came up on his blind side and stuck a sword through his back. Jeff pulled the sword, tugging on Kannon from the inside until it slid loose. Kannon toppled off the crypt and hit the floor.

Jeff ran the one-eyed rich boy through a couple more times for the sake of safety and then heaved the body up. He propped Kannon's back against the crypt, arranged the lifeless limbs for maximum support, and used him to climb onto it. The extra boost he got courtesy of Kannon made cake of his upward scramble. In seconds, Jeff saw his prey crouched fearfully atop the crypt.

Stewart closed his eyes and used both hands to thrust the knife at Jeff's face. Jeff cried out and fell. He avoided the blade, but landed on Kannon's lap and, after some hysterical moments spent untangling himself from the dead man, scrambled to his feet. He thrust the sword at Stewart, who ducked back onto the roof of the crypt and out of reach.

On the other side of the crypt, Emily and Ollie had come face to face. Emily was clutching a broadsword that was too heavy for her to wield effectively but had the virtue of being long enough to ensure optimum personal space, at least in front of her. Her back was pressed against the wall of the crypt. She made an occasional thrust at Ollie but hadn't come near to touching him. Ollie was armed with an antique dagger that looked Japanese, and he hadn't wasted any energy taking swipes while she was still out of reach. But Emily knew she wouldn't be able to hold the sword up for much longer, and when it became too heavy, Ollie would dash in and skewer her someplace vital.

Today's lesson, too late as the most important lessons always are, was that time spent training the body can be just as important as time spent training the mind.

Emily was almost done. This current dynamic was not going to end well, so there was nothing to do but change it. She firmed up her failing grip and hefted the end of her blade as well as she could so the tip was pointing slightly up and aimed at Ollie's chest. If she couldn't swing the fucking thing, she would just run it into him.

Ollie's stance changed; Emily knew he could tell she was preparing to move. The fact that he knew it was coming didn't mean she could change her mind. There were no other options. She had just pushed off the crypt when Ollie clutched his throat. From between his fingers, a spearhead popped through, the shaft coming dutifully behind it. The weight brought the end not still buried in Ollie's throat down within Emily's reach. She watched it bob around for a second and finally thought to look up. An arm had been extended over the edge of the crypt, its hand grasping around for the spear.

Emily found it was easier to swing the broadsword straight up than to hold it extended out from her body. She lopped off Stewart's arm near the elbow, sidestepping as she did to avoid the resulting spurt of blood and the plummeting appendage.

Emily had no idea what other weapons of human destruction might be wielded from above, so it seemed relocation was a good idea. The broadsword wasn't much use to her, but she didn't want anyone else to have it. She slid the sword under Ollie's body in exchange for his dagger. Then, she pulled the spear out of his neck and took it too.

She crouched down and stole a glance around the corner of the crypt to make sure the side was clear. It was. Emily took a silent breath and crept along the wall to the next corner. The coast around the second wasn't clear. Emily jerked back and dropped down when she saw Portia peek out from behind a tombstone. Emily gave herself a second or two then forced herself to take another look. This time, she could tell Portia wasn't looking at her, but she couldn't see who was holding the actress's gaze.

Portia transferred her knife to her left hand long enough to dry her other palm on her pants. She edged out from behind her tombstone and crept toward Jeff. His attention was directed at someone on the roof of the crypt. Portia was two steps away from plunging her knife into Jeff when he sensed her behind him and turned around swinging a sword. The sword only sliced halfway through Portia before getting hung up on her spine, but it was enough. Portia toppled to the stage, tearing the blade from Jeff's grasp and taking it with her. Jeff made a frantic attempt to retrieve it, but Emily was on him. She snaked an arm around Jeff's neck and drew the dagger across his throat.

Brett was near the edge of the graveyard. He'd been crawling around the periphery and had collected a couple of knives and a garrote wire. He'd seen Jeff fell Portia with the Samurai sword, had seen Jeff lose the sword to the grip of Portia's corpse, and he knew he needed it. Donovan was running around with a scythe, and Brett couldn't take him if he had to fight in close quarters.

Brett scuttled from tombstone to angel to coffin. He dropped to the ground and pressed his face to the stage when Madeline darted across the end of the row he was working across. She was on her hands and knees, moving at the speed of a demented toddler, with a knife clenched between her teeth. By the time he'd worked up the courage to resume moving, someone had beaten him to his goal. Celeste had appeared seemingly out of nowhere and was crouched beside Portia's body see-sawing the sword back and forth in an effort to detach it from the spine. Celeste hadn't actually appeared out of nowhere; she had been hiding in the coffin Portia had sprawled against when she'd been nearly halved.

Brett swore. He was trying to work out his next move when Donovan thundered across the stage toward Celeste. Between his heavy steps and his war cry, Donovan made such a racket Celeste saw him coming and would have had plenty of time to put a sarcophagus or two between them. It was her desire for the sword that was her undoing. Just as she pulled the blade free from

Portia's bloody bones, Donovan brought the scythe down on the top of her head.

Madeline had crawled around to the far side of the crypt, intending to sneak up behind Donovan. She came upon Emily first. Madeline considered briefly. Her head tilted, her brow furrowed, but she didn't let a sound escape her because this was important. Finally, she shrugged, plucked the knife out of her mouth, and sunk it into Emily's back.

Emily felt a hard thud somewhere between her shoulder and her spine, and suddenly her right arm didn't work. Still in a crouch, she whirled to find Madeline clutching her knife and looking rather shocked.

"Fuck," Madeline said. "I'm so sorry. That is not how a housemother should behave."

"No worries," Emily told her then with her left hand buried her dagger in Madeline's neck. She jumped when something hit her face, but it was just blood trickling over the edge of the crypt. She forgot all about that when Donovan stepped around the corner with a Samurai sword in one hand and a scythe in the other. She didn't realize she'd dropped the spear when Madeline stabbed her until the impulse to use it on Donovan hit her.

Emily took a step back and felt her heel hit Madeline's body. She tried to step around, but in death, Madeline was taking up an unreasonable amount of room.

Donovan wore a madman's grin, alternately hefting the sword and the scythe.

Emily saw Brett creep around the corner. She kept her eyes on Donovan's and took another step back. She almost lost her balance when she stepped on Madeline's torso and some ribs gave way beneath her. She tried to catch herself on the wall, but her arm remained uncooperative. She lurched and hit the crypt with her shoulder. Donovan swung the sword, and Emily tried to duck but instead toppled backward and hit the ground on the far side of Madeline's body.

Brett raised something above his head, and Emily saw he had picked up the spear. With none of the hesitation that had marred his performance in the last challenge, Brett brought the spear down. Emily screamed her encouragement as Brett made contact.

Brett's failure to kill Landon Jones had affected him profoundly. Yesterday, his qualms had nearly ended his dream. But today, he was different, and Donovan was no innocent. Brett had no reservations about killing Donovan. Truly, his heart had grown willing. His body, however, had not grown more competent. Brett drove the spear in, landing a flesh wound in Donovan's side rather than a killing thrust. Donovan whipped around and caught the protruding spear on the wall of the crypt, snapping it off about halfway down its length. Brett was left defenseless and had only a moment to realize that, for him, the competition was over. He was about to die and that it would be Donovan's hand wielding the sword that killed him was an added insult.

Emily had a flash of a second to be glad when Donovan's bulk came between her eyes and Brett's. While Donovan pierced Brett's heart, Emily scrambled to her feet and ran to the downstage edge of the cemetery.

Donovan came tearing after her waving the sword. Emily turned at the edge of the graveyard and thrust her arm out, her fingers working nervously on the knife. Her right arm was still just taking up space.

Donovan kept charging. He was going to knock her off the playing field and run her through in the same thrust. Emily flung herself to the side, losing her balance in the process. *When the fuck did I become some bimbo who falls for no apparent reason?*

She was still in bounds when she hit the ground but only just. As she struggled to get her feet under her, Donovan bore down on her from behind. She kicked at him, and he raised his foot and stomped her ankle, putting all his weight on the joint.

Some part of Emily noted the odd combination of crunch and grind happening in her ankle. She let loose a roar that had more to do with rage than pain, but it was close. She hoped the whole thing would be over before her adrenaline normalized, and the pain became everything.

In spite of his general boorishness, Donovan had the sense not to pause to gloat. He bounded to Emily's head and brought the sword up. Emily thought that was an interesting thing because really, how many people got to experience beheading from both sides?

"The challenge is ended," Edmund announced. Donovan hesitated in the middle of his upswing. The moment lasted long enough to allow Emily to hope, and then whether through incomprehension or spite, he was disregarding the instruction to stop, and Emily was again about to die.

Before she could, Edmund was standing over her, and Donovan was groaning on the other side of the stage where he'd landed after Edmund had flung him away from her.

"Three still live," Chaz countered with a questioning look at Edmund.

There was a whoosh and a blur and then Vlad was on the crypt roof having a snack and bringing the challenge officially to a close.

Edmund said, "It is ended. The next to move will be ended as well."

"It was close enough," Vlad said when the final spark had gone from Stewart's eyes. "Is it not true we need only two for the end? And I was hungry again; although much of this one's blood was wasted."

"I cannot believe this shit," Mandy said. "Did you see what just happened?"

"I've been here the entire time," Seth said. He ruffled her hair. "It would have been hard to miss a dozen people hacking each other to bits."

"Wasn't it the most amazing thing you've ever seen?" Mandy

said.

"Well, there was the birth of our child," Seth teased.

"I felt that more than saw it." Mandy swatted his leg.

"Well, it was far more amazing," Seth assured her. "And only slightly gorier."

Mason pulled his thumb out of his mouth. "What's gory?"

"Okay, then," Chaz said. "Let's give Vlad a round of applause for clearing up that little ambiguity. And keep it going for our final two! Emily and Donovan have fought hard and triumphed over some impressive competitors!"

Edmund snorted, but the humans couldn't hear him over their noise.

"Donovan and Emily," Chaz said when the audience stilled. "Come join me." Donovan went to stand beside Chaz while Emily struggled to rise. Vlad bounded from the crypt to Emily's side and hauled her to her feet. Emily went white; the feeling in her ankle was intensifying, and the stab wound wasn't helping, although it was the lesser problem.

Vlad made another leap this time with Emily in his arms. He set her next to Chaz; Donovan was on the host's other side. When Emily turned to thank Vlad, she saw he was back on the altar sucking blood from his fingers.

"How's the ankle?" Donovan said.

Emily ignored him and smiled when Chaz yanked the spear shaft out of Donovan's shoulder. A fresh gush of blood accompanied Donovan's yelp.

"You insisted we keep him," Nodin said. *"I trust you will turn him."*

Delia nodded. *"Then who will turn the girl?"*

"Vlad." Nodin considered his answer and nodded to confirm his choice.

"If he gets carried away–"

"Must you always suspect my control?" Vlad said.

"You bite someone almost every show," Delia said.

"You understand why Vlad should be the one," Nodin said.

"Rylie and Kylie are going to take our final two to prepare," Chaz said. "And for the rest of you, we have another Friends and Family segment. We'll be hearing from Kannon's parents and Portia's husband, Charles. I believe we have Charles coming up first."

Charles appeared on the screens. There was some excitement in the audience from those who watched *Hours of Our Existence*, a soap opera on which Charles had been a recurring presence for the past seventeen years. "Hey, babe," Charles said. "I hope you know how proud I am. We always knew your big break would come, and now that it has, I want you always to remember I'm here for you the way you've always been there for me. And I want to tell you how sorry I am for saying that you shouldn't do the show. I was just scared, but I was wrong. I know you're going to be amazing because the girl I love is always amazing. I'll see you soon. Break a leg!"

"That means 'good luck' in actor," Chaz said. "Hard to believe she's gone. Let's see what Kannon's parents had to say."

The screens produced an image of a young woman who couldn't possibly be a parent of Kannon's. "At this time," she said, "Kannon's parents would like to express their support of their son. They wish Kannon the best in this endeavor and look forward to visiting with him when said endeavor has come to fruition. Thank you."

"I think that was the most heartfelt Friends and Family segment delivered by a junior associate we've seen all season," Chaz said.

"Junior ass! Junior ass! Junior ass!"

"It is not too late for me to kill them all," Edmund offered. The crowd shut up.

"I have one more viewer question and here it is! Courtesy of James in Royal Kunia, Hawaii."

"Do you ever feel bad for feeding on humans? As though you shouldn't be feeding on fellow sentient beings? Especially since you used to be us?"

"I can only speak for myself," Chaz said. "But no. Delia?"

"No," Delia said. "Nodin?"

"Never," Nodin said. "Vlad?"

"I do not understand the question," Vlad said. "It seems absurd."

Chaz tried to clarify. "James wants to know if killing humans leaves you torn apart by remorse."

"He only said feeding on humans," Delia said. "No one said anything about killing."

"Feed without killing?" Vlad said. "Ridiculous. I am as distraught when I feed on a human as they are when they crush an ant underfoot. As much as they might mourn a cut rose, do I mourn any human loss of life."

"He means blood," Delia said. "Loss of blood."

Vlad went on. "As much—"

"Let's call that another 'No,'" Chaz said. "Edmund?"

Edmund waved a hand in dismissal. "I do not respond to queries from my food."

"There you have it, James," Chaz said. "Now, let's take a look at the last round of confessionals. Here they are in their own words, Emily and Donovan!"

Confessional: Emily

"I want to get on with it already. Of course considering I was two seconds away from being dead, perhaps I shouldn't be so eager for what's to come. But Donovan just fucked up. Though, probably not as much as I did in the last challenge. I should have attacked Donovan at the same time Brett did. Because right now, I wish it was Brett still in this with me instead of Donovan. Not to mention,

Brett probably wouldn't have crushed my fucking ankle. It's like a bag of sticks in there. I can't wait to kill him."

Confessional: Donovan

"I crushed that bitch. Literally. I could almost feel bad; I mean, what fucking chance did she have anyway? None. No woman is going to be able to take me out. Shit. Look at me. It's almost over, and I'm going to be coming for you, world. Parents, lock up your daughters, not that it's going to stop me. They should have just let me kill Emily. It's not like there's a lot of suspense about what's going to happen next. Emily is going to fucking die, and I'm going to be the Creature of the Night."

"If anyone else gets beheaded, I'm buying shots for everybody," Nick roared.

Everyone in the bar cheered.

"You're crazy," Mike said. "You don't have any money."

"It's okay." Nick belched and threw another dart. "The final fight isn't until tomorrow. I just won't show up. Besides, you should have thought of that before you dragged me to a *Creature* night." Some of their friends had been coming here for a couple of seasons now. The bar went all out during *Creature* week, doing the place up in fangs and fake blood.

"That's *Creature of the Night* Night to you," the bartender said. "Can I get you another round?"

"Absolutely, Stacey," Nick said, leaning forward to make a show of reading the nametag pinned over her breast. "I don't have money, so he's buying."

"Yeah, whatever," Mike agreed, hoping to impress Stacey who was new and cute. "Great challenge, huh?" he said.

"That was the best challenge ever," she agreed. "It was the first time one of the judges ever killed someone onstage."

"I think it's against the rules for the judges to kill contestants," Mike said.

"They make their own rules," Stacey argued. "And the guy was almost dead."

"So, is she on board?" The Voice said.

Little P flinched but held onto his composure. He was accustomed to going from basking in praise to weathering sudden onslaughts of hostility. "I don't know if she will. She wanted me to show her where in the contract it said she had to."

"How did someone who read the contract make it onto the show?"

"She was in the stack approved by you," Little P managed. "Unfortunately, they all read some of it. Every season. Although by the time section 3.24 paragraph 12 comes along, most of them have given up."

"Did you specifically point out to me her proclivity for reading?" The Voice was giving Little P the Look.

"I'm so sorry, sir," Little P said. "I didn't realize you didn't know."

"You have to always assume—" The Voice stopped talking. "Never mind."

For the last time, Emily had taken refuge in the library. She had found a lot of comfort here over the course of the show. Emily had always enjoyed books, not only the reading but the physical presence of them, the heft in her hand, the various scents, and the feel of pages under her fingers. As a bonus, most of her competitors hadn't set foot in here since their initial tour.

Sometimes, Emily read. Sometimes, she sat in one of the overstuffed armchairs. Sometimes, she perused the shelves, dipping into a page here, a page there, unable to make a decision, a pleasant torture that could occupy her for hours.

Today, she was stretched out on the loveseat, her feet on one arm and her head on the other while she contemplated the ceiling. It was the closest she could come to comfort. There was an ice pack balanced on her traumatized ankle and another under the hole in her shoulder. They'd dosed her with pain meds, but since they weren't going to bother patching her up this close to the end, she had refused to stay in the infirmary.

"Fuck it," Emily said to no one; although watching in The Voice's office, Little P heaved a sigh of relief. As surprised as Emily was to find herself arriving at this conclusion, it seemed it was indeed possible to indulge in too much thought. Luckily, the remedy for too much thought was right downstairs.

She was doing it because she wanted to; that's all.

"What do you want?" Donovan said when she finally discovered him in the sauna.

"Is there any reason you need to be naked in here?" Her search had included more walking than was advisable (none had been the amount of walking recommended by the guy who'd fed her the pain pills) and the throb in her ankle was awakening her temper.

"Yeah. I fucked Lola before I killed her, and I thought you might want the same courtesy."

"Word on the street is you suck in bed," Emily said. "And I didn't think being delusional was one of your myriad flaws."

"That's why people don't like you," Donovan said. "Why not just say 'many' flaws?"

"Go fornicate yourself," Emily said.

"What are you doing?" Donovan sat up and gawked as Emily began to shed clothes. "You want me to—"

"No." Emily stopped undressing when she was down to her bra and underwear. "As painful as it is to admit, I wanted company."

"And you thought this was a good time to bond?"

Emily shrugged then winced at the effect on her shoulder. "I'm not worried about getting attached to you."

"Why not?" Donovan flopped back down on the bench. "Lots of people like me. What the fuck do you want to talk about?"

"I don't know," Emily said. "It's a little counterproductive, but you could tell me something that makes you seem like a real person."

"I don't think everyone realizes how shitty you are," Donovan said.

"Since I'm the one with the broken ankle, I'm not sure where you get off calling me shitty." Emily tossed one of the towels she'd brought to Donovan. "But I meant about you, not about me."

"I hate fucking whiners," Donovan said. "And I'm not going to feel bad for understanding there are no rules, even when someone says there are."

"Profound," Emily said.

"You weren't the only brain invited to the party."

"Where's the other one?"

"You want to talk?" Donovan crossed his arms over his chest. "Tell me what all that bullshit about college was."

Emily had been surprised that this hadn't come up sooner. She'd decided to chalk it up to the self-absorption of her castmates and been grateful.

"They don't give a shit about who went to college, so there was something else going on there. So fucking spill it," Donovan said. "I want to know about you. My friend. My compatriot. The only remaining piece of ass."

"I'm going to kill you." Donovan was the second man to whom Emily had made that promise. The first one was still alive, but he hadn't been conscious since the night before Emily dropped out of school. Donovan was just another predator, not worthy of her secrets. Emily leaned forward. "That's all you need to know about me."

Donovan opened his mouth, and the lights went out.

Vlad could still taste the intern. The hard part about being on the show was all the restraint it took. The purity of the relationship between a creature and his prey was something that was misunderstood in these times. So, Vlad was forced to feed sparingly, leaving them alive whenever eyes were watching, depriving hunter and prey of the ultimate experience.

Part of him wished he could drain this one. He felt sure the spill of her blood past his lips would be an exquisite experience. But it had been made clear by everyone that draining a contestant was forbidden. So instead, he focused on the lesser pleasure to be gained from watching her sleep.

Humans liked to make fun of vampires' fascination with watching people sleep. They didn't understand how enjoyable it was to contemplate all the things that could be done to a human body without the distraction of screams or worse, insipid conversation. Although, contrary creature that he was, there were other times when he missed the screams, the futile struggles, and the tantalizing reek of fear.

And Emily was lovely. She didn't give the impression of caring much about her womanly charms, but they were there, rising and falling gently beneath her bra. But even more than that, she seemed like a woman of substance, a woman who could withstand some torture and still be up for sharing a serving girl for supper.

There was a tap on the door. Vlad could smell the blood pulsing through the man from here. They were usually careful not to send humans alone to him. Usually, it was Riley or the other one.

Perhaps, while he waited for Emily to wake, he would have a snack.

Emily awoke stretched out on her bed, brought back to the world entirely by the throb of her pulse in the injured ankle. She tried to hold onto the pain, use it to stoke her rage because rage was always a useful weapon. But she was so tired, and the blood loss wasn't helping her energy level. And she was going to lose more shortly. Or rather, now.

Vlad was standing by the bed. He was wearing a tuxedo and a cape.

"You look nice," Emily said and Vlad inclined his head. "You can take someone with you when you poof?"

"I am very old and have many abilities," Vlad said.

"I'm taking that as a yes," Emily said.

"Is that what you would ask?"

"I would ask if there are any abilities of yours that pertain to me at this moment."

"I have much control over my fledglings," Vlad said. "Over how easily they turn. That is why my brethren searched so relentlessly for me when the war broke out."

"So it won't hurt?"

"If lack of pain is your measure of success, we would have done well to eliminate you in the first round," Vlad said. Emily flushed. "Multiple exchanges will strengthen the bond of my blood to yours. Although other exchanges would alleviate the pain you will feel in death."

"Other exchanges? Like sex?"

"I have given such pleasure to countless lovers, and that is only in the recent years when it has become vogue to worry about such things."

"That is a really good offer," Emily said. "But this doesn't seem like a great time to start a relationship."

Vlad let out a roar of amusement. "Then you are ready? You know what is coming?"

"We exchange blood. And then I die."

"Three times," Vlad agreed. "And then you die. When you come back, you will be your new self and the last challenge will have begun. You will fight to the death once again, and then you will be

CREATURE OF THE NIGHT

one of us, or you will be gone."

"I understand," Emily said. "Why did you kill Stewart?"

"Moments only remained for that one," Vlad said. "And none can be sure why I do what I do."

Emily laughed and wished she hadn't. Even a bit of movement set her injuries screaming. "You want me to win."

"What anyone wants pales compared to what you achieve," Vlad said. "We begin." He took her head in his hands and turned it to expose her neck. Emily took a deep breath and tried to relax. Her eyes found the ridiculous chandelier hanging above the bed, and she began counting its crystals.

If she had been whole, the pain of Vlad's fangs penetrating her neck might have bothered her, but compared to everything else her body was dealing with, a couple of practiced punctures were negligible.

"Now you," Vlad said and Emily's eyes popped open. Of this whole experience, knowing she had drifted off while Vlad the Impaler sucked on her neck would forever remain the most surprising thing. No wonder so many humans lined up to be donors.

Emily opened her mouth and accepted Vlad's wrist. He had thoughtfully opened a vein, so there was no need to bite. She latched on and sucked. Vlad's blood wasn't the same as the humans'. She could feel her body thrum in response. The more she drank, the more the thum intensified until she felt she was vibrating from within.

The thrum faded when Vlad drank from her the second time, and she nearly fainted from relief when his fangs sunk through her flesh yet again.

She felt she might shake apart from the vibrations that shook her when she tasted her maker's blood for the third time, but to an onlooker she would have already appeared to be dead. There was a peak after which the thrumming faded away, and she noticed her pain had faded away and then finally her consciousness went as well, and Emily died for a while.

Donovan had been pacing around his room for hours, or if one was going strictly by the clock, for twenty minutes. Emily had disappeared from the sauna almost an hour ago. Donovan had waited for someone to come for him before finally going back to his room. He had tried watching TV, but he couldn't focus for shit. He suspected the wait was just to fuck with him, but that was ridiculous. They had no reason to screw with the goddamn champion. Punctuality probably wasn't a thing to creatures who measured their time in centuries. He was ready. He was hoping he'd get to fuck Delia, but maybe that would be something better done after he was changed. He didn't want her throwing him around like he was the bitch.

Donovan jumped when the tap on the door came. He had half been expecting Delia to materialize or fly in as a bat. But when he opened the door, there she was, smiling demurely.

"May I enter?" Delia said.

"Oh, because you can't come in unless you're invited, right?" Donovan moved back and waved her inside. "Come in."

"This Manor is more mine than yours," Delia said. "I was being polite."

"Right. Of course." Donovan bobbed his head at her. What the hell was wrong with him? He was acting like Brett. He had been occasionally distracted by Delia's beauty throughout the competition, but he had never been this close to her. She was perfect. Her skin was flawless, her eyes were the hot blue of a summer sky, and her lips, her lips would be on him and that thought sent all the others scurrying out of his head. The images of him destroying Emily were gone, and all he could do was yearn for Delia's touch.

"I will drink from you now," Delia said. Donovan continued to nod. "Then you must drink from me. When you awake, you will be changed, and the last challenge will be upon you. Do you understand?"

"I do." The last time Donovan had said those words he was marrying Tara, but he said them now with far more sincerity.

"Good." Delia turned his head with the touch of one cool finger. "Sit." Donovan fell into the nearest chair. His anticipation turned to panic when Delia's fangs pierced his skin bringing pain instead of the expected pleasure. But she wasn't savaging him. She drank steadily, and Donovan began to relax. Then her wrist was at his lips, and he drank. Donovan could feel the power building in his veins, that and Delia's nearness intoxicated him so he put an arm around her waist and pulled her closer. Delia took him by the wrist and removed his arm, snapping it almost as an afterthought. Donovan was too far along for the new pain to have much of an effect, but before he went away, he experienced a flash of disappointment that things hadn't gone as he had imagined.

Emily and Donovan, Sitting in a Tree, _ _ _ _ _ _ _.

 thought you were never going to forgive me," Brad said.

"I haven't." Although, Gina had realized Brad wasn't much worse than anyone else. She ran a hand up Brad's thigh and snuggled closer. "But I missed you."

"You've been watching, right?" Brad wanted to forestall the possibility of Gina asking a bunch of annoying questions once the finale started.

"Yeah." Gina was a little embarrassed she'd made such a big deal about what was a pretty entertaining show. After all, the contestants were surely on board, so who was she to quibble?

"I can't believe it's finally happening," Brad said, and he wasn't thinking of Gina.

Gina reached for the remote and handed it to Brad. "You do the honors."

Emily opened her eyes. She reached out to confirm the sense of enclosure and sighed at the knowledge she'd once again been stuffed into a coffin. She realized then it must be dark, but, in fact, she could see the silk lining, a soft peach that was quite similar to the color of her kitchen at home.

Emily hated the color of her kitchen, but there was always something better to do than paint it. Like become a vampire.

"Our contestants will be waking up shortly," Chaz was saying, and Emily realized she could hear him as though he were sharing her coffin. And she was hungry. She gave an experimental push on the lid of the coffin and found it had been secured.

Outside Emily's twenty-eight by eighty-four inches of heaven, the audience was chanting.

"Creature fight! Creature fight! Creature fight!"

Emily could smell their excitement. In fact, some of them smelled almost, nearly, definitely like dinner. She suddenly understood why Vlad was always having such a hard time keeping his fangs to himself. Emily smiled in the not-really-dark of her coffin and ran her tongue over her teeth. No fangs. But they would pop out when she needed them surely.

Emily heard something creak nearby. It was the same creak her coffin had produced when she'd tested it. Donovan. He would be beside her, similarly contained, which meant not contained at all, not really. It was time. Emily placed both hands on the lid of her coffin and shoved hard. The lid separated from the coffin completely and cartwheeled over the stage. Emily jumped to her feet and laughed. She turned to throw Vlad a kiss (she could feel where he was without even looking, which was fascinating), and Donovan crashed into her and they both went sprawling across the stage.

Donovan hit the bitch with a flying tackle. Unfortunately, he didn't fly, but the breadth of his leap made that almost irrelevant. He thought he had a good grip, but she twisted around so she was facing him and bit off his nose.

Yes, the fangs were there when you needed them. All her teeth seemed sharper, or perhaps her jaws were stronger. Emily spat out the nose and almost forgot what she was doing when the hole in

Donovan's face immediately began to close over, and holy shit, he was growing a new nose. Emily extended a finger; she needed physical confirmation. Donovan grabbed her questing digit and snapped it.

Emily snarled and shoved the great oaf away. Donovan sailed into the air and came crashing down on the first row, many of whom now doubted the wisdom of paying extra for those seats. Donovan pushed himself off the hapless audience members and sprang back onto the stage. Emily grabbed him by the arm and spun, flinging him again toward the audience, but this time, his momentum sent him past the first rows and all the way to the altar.

"Bitch," Donovan hissed.

Vlad flashed his fangs, and Delia put a hand on his arm. "Be still, friend."

Donovan pushed off the altar and landed on the edge of the stage. Before Emily could fling him again, he sprang across the stage, ripped the lower lid off his coffin, and launched it. Emily caught the lid, but the force of its flight caused her to stagger back, and before she could recover, Donovan was on her. He clamped a beefy hand on either side of her head and spun her around. Emily hung onto the coffin lid and managed to bring it down on Donovan's skull.

Donovan threw her down. The force of her impact cracked the stage. Emily swept Donovan's legs out from under him with her own and brought the lid crashing down on his head again. Donovan drew his legs up and kicked her in the stomach, sending her flying upstage where she hit the curtain and disappeared under it when it fell.

Emily was still trying to rid herself of the engulfing fabric when she felt Donovan grab her legs. She managed a good kick, but he came back, and now she was being hefted in the air and slammed down with shocking force. Her face hit the stage, and she felt a fang snap off.

"That is fucking it!" Emily screamed. She was already quite fond of her fangs. The first few rows started to gather their coats and purses in preparation for flight.

"They are very strong now," Chaz said.

No shit, Cyri thought. She was grateful to her father for cheaping out on the seats. They were something akin to safe in the tenth row.

Yes, very strong now. And perhaps a bit stupid. Emily grabbed the curtain in both hands and ripped it in half. The first thing she saw was Donovan's boot coming at her face. She caught it and pushed. Donovan's ass hit the floor and Emily sprang, landing in a crouch over his chest. She jabbed his new nose with her palm and felt it crunch. That reminded her to check herself, and she was pleasantly surprised to find her missing fang had already regrown.

Donovan punched her in the jaw. She tasted blood and then she didn't. She needed a stake. Emily drew back her fist and brought it down, but before she could connect, Donovan rolled and she ended up on her back with his bulk pressing her into the floor. She wriggled around, so she was face down and heard the smug beast say, "So that's how you like it."

Emily leveled her torso up, allowing herself room for a good swing, and brought her fist crashing to the stage. She felt the vibration of the blow beneath her, but the wood didn't splinter. She heard a crack when she struck the second blow, and the third yielded a visible fissure. Donovan finally realized what she was up to and tried to pull her away. Emily dug her fingers into the crack and pulled, bringing an entire floorboard along with her.

She flipped onto her back and kicked at Donovan again. He was dragging her by one ankle toward the coffins. She broke the floorboard over her knee and flung half of it into the audience. She snapped the remaining half in half again lengthwise and ended up with something approximating a stake. Donovan screamed with rage and threw himself on her. His careless leap would have saved her the trouble, but since they were now chest to chest, she might have impaled herself as well. One never considers how dangerous small pieces of wood are until potentially eternal life comes a-calling.

Emily had moved the stake out of Donovan's way when he landed on her, and now she tried to bring it around to penetrate the heart from behind. Donovan bit her. Emily stabbed Donovan repeatedly in the back, but since he just kept sucking her neck, she had to assume she wasn't reaching anything vital. *Time for something else.* She adjusted her aim and drove the makeshift stake into Donovan's ear. He released her neck and jumped off her, which was all according to plan, but what came next was not.

Donovan yanked the stake out of his ear and charged. Emily rolled to her feet and skipped back. She almost tripped over one of the coffin lids. She stomped, and the thing snapped into pieces. She snatched the smallest. It was about the length and width of her arm, and then Donovan was on her. She threw up an arm, and such was the force of Donovan's rage, the stake went right through it. She yanked her arm away so he couldn't get the stake back, and part of her reflected that these things hurt just as much as they would have had she still been human. *All things hurt the same.* She kicked Donovan in the balls.

Donovan had been kicked in the balls more than once; it was a natural consequence of being a philandering misogynist. But he had never been kicked in the balls by a vampire. He went down. But super healing works on even the most delicate parts, and he was ready to come up swinging in three seconds flat. And up he came as Emily thrust down with her coffin lid stake, finally pulling off her stake through the back maneuver and landing her **killing** blow.

Then Chaz was beside her, carefully prying her fingers off the stake, and the twins were there scooping Donovan off the floor for disposal. They disappeared offstage, leaving Emily with one hand in the air courtesy of Chaz, who was declaring her the victor, the new *Creature of the Night.* Vlad appeared beside her, so she turned

CREATURE OF THE NIGHT

to plant a kiss on his cheek while she wondered how such a fearsome historical figure could be so darling in his bloodthirsty way.

"Like you, I am many things," Vlad said.

Emily started.

"It is a talent of some of our kind," Vlad explained out loud. "Although, I have been informed not quite 'the rules.'"

"So, those were your thoughts in my head?"

"You were lucky to have been chosen by me," Vlad told her. Still on the altar, Delia hissed at Vlad. "No offense meant to the loveliest of our judges," Vlad told her.

"I cannot take offense when I am pleased with the outcome," Delia said.

"Did you break the rules, Delia?" Chaz said.

"I would never."

Nodin smiled. "We are all pleased with this outcome."

"It is a pleasure," Edmund said. "To meet you, Emily."

"The pleasure is mine," Emily said. She flashed Edmund a huge smile. It was endearing in the manner of a gap-tooth smile on a child. The audience cheered. "They feel weird," Emily said. "It reminds me of when I got braces."

"You got used to those," Chaz told her, and she nodded.

Marv doled out two more shots from the bottle of tequila on the coffee table and offered Ginger the saltshaker. "You've been watching this for how long?"

"Since the first season," Ginger said. She licked the inside of her wrist and salted it liberally. "Years. What did you think?"

Marv thought if Ginger's lips were less full or her tits not as perky, he'd be having second thoughts about his plans to get her naked. "I loved it," Marv told her tapping her glass with his.

"A few more things," Chaz said. "First, we're going to take a look at some of the highlights of our fallen contestants. When the contestants were chosen, each was asked to give us their last words in case there wasn't time later on."

The audience chuckled.

"Those last words will be what you see at the end of each montage. Enjoy their final words of wisdom. Or whatever."

The music swelled, and a small montage of Donovan began to play across the screens. There was a picture of Donovan as a child holding a cat who seemed to be trying to escape. A couple's picture of Donovan taken at a school dance. A shot of Donovan covered in his own blood after the escape of his donor. The music faded away, and Donovan's video played. "If you think I'm going to die, you can go fuck yourself. The world is going to be my bitch!"

"Perhaps he was referring to another world," Edmund said.

"The look on his face when Emily kills him is priceless," Delia said.

"It was the best moment of the season," Edmund said.

The music faded, and the montage ended with a shot of Donovan holding a football, arm back, preparing to pass. Shots of Celeste replaced Donovan onscreen. She appeared as a cherub in pigtails then an awkward adolescent with a hint of sullen. In some of the later pictures, scars could be seen traveling Celeste's arms in opposition to whatever smile she had pasted on her face. "Thank you all for being a part of my journey."

"She came wanting to die, that one," Edmund said.

"Yes, she did." Delia tapped her fingers on her throne.

"You feel sympathy because she changed her mind?"

"No. I wonder if she ever did change her mind," Delia said.

Kannon replaced Celeste. The crowd cheered for immortalized moments of two-eyed Kannon: there he was taking his first bath, riding his first bike, drinking a wine cooler the night he would first have sex with his math tutor.

"I didn't know he had been a Boy Scout," Delia said as a picture of young uniformed Kannon flashed on the screens.

"Isn't their motto *'Be Prepared'?*'" Nodin asked.

Cyri snorted.

"Don't be insensitive, honey," her father said.

The crowd cheered even harder for one-eyed Kannon and his bloody eye socket. "I guess I'd want to say to my parents I'm sorry I disappointed you again."

"That one experienced true growth," Delia's attention was focused on Kannon's laughing image. "It's almost a shame."

"Seriously?" Nodin wondered.

Delia shrugged. *"I thought someone should say something."*

Now, Cassie's image smiled down. "If I die, I guess I'd need to apologize to my family for letting my brother die for nothing. So, I refuse to believe it will come to that." Even as a child, her smile had been joyous, a smile that managed to wipe away the memory of her suffering and defeat.

"Refusing to believe is always the best way," Nodin said.

Delia rolled her eyes. *"Were you so eager to believe in your imminent death before your change?"*

"I did like the dancer," Delia said aloud.

Through pictures, Cassie grew to adulthood as the audience adored her. The images of Cassie clawing her way out of the coals juxtaposed with a close-up of Lola hacking away at her neck provoked a thunderous, if slightly mixed, reaction.

"Rudyard Kipling knew of what he spoke," Nodin said.

"Yes," Delia said. "He did indeed."

"Who is Rudyard Kipling?" Vlad asked.

"He was a writer," Nodin said. "He said the female of the species is more deadly than the male."

"I don't know him," Vlad said. "Or did I eat him?"

"He's dead," Nodin told Vlad. "He was much younger, so no. I don't believe you ate him."

"At least they're together now," Cyri's dad said. He wrapped an arm around her for a comforting hug she could have done without. She wondered if Rudyard Kipling had been eaten.

"As always," Chaz said. "Prints or posters are available for order on the *Creature of the Night* website. That beheading shot is a thing of beauty, and it is available now along with a ton of other shit you must have."

"There were no beheadings last season," Edmund said.

"I think you might be right." Delia considered. "I cannot recall."

"You cannot recall whether there was a beheading last season?" Nodin lifted his eyebrows. The audience chuckled.

"You're ruining it," Delia said.

"She is attempting to give the impression that things are so exciting here it becomes impossible to keep an exact tally of how many heads have been abruptly severed from their host."

"I remember so many beheadings," Delia said. "The difficulty is placing them in their proper time and space."

"First world problems," Chaz said.

"And perhaps third," Edmund noted.

Cassie with a head was back onscreen, smiling and waving. Her clip ended with a few seconds of Cassie dancing, the frame freezing on a shot of Cassie mid-leap with pointed toes and graceful arms as close to flying as she had ever come.

"Where is the chronology?" Nodin said.

Lola's childhood self had been ragtag. In one childhood photo, both front teeth had gone AWOL, and she wore an improbable dress with a pair of jeans underneath. It was impossible to tell whether she had been allowed to dress herself as a matter of self-expression or because of a lack of parental care. This uncertainty made the picture both sad and adorable.

Teenaged Lola had been the kind of girl mothers warned their sons about while those sons could think of nothing else. That Lola had already possessed the eyes of a forty-year-old. Of course, no pictures of Lola engaging in self-abuse could be shown, but a shot of Chaz beating on the lid of her coffin to stop her was included. The crowd tittered.

The picture of Cassie having her head sawed off by Lola

reappeared, but now it was a picture of Lola. "Last words? Fuck that. I'll give you my winning speech instead. I told you assholes I was going to win this thing! Now bow the fuck down, bitches! Lola's ready for eternity."

"*Didn't someone bet on that one?*" Delia said all innocence. "*I believe I am owed virgins.*"

"*You'll get them,*" Nodin sighed. He didn't know what he had been thinking risking so many. This sort of thing always happened when he tried to be charismatic.

Jeff had been a cute kid with a love of Halloween. There, he was dressed as Superman, then as a bunny, and inevitably as a vampire. His plastic fangs and bloody chin did nothing to distract from his open smile.

Edmund grumbled at the sight of the fangs.

"He did go on to march for vampire rights," Delia said.

"*As if I need or desire anything that could be granted by humans,*" Edmund said.

Delia snorted gently. "*You mean besides your salary?*"

Grown up Jeff threw his cap at his college commencement ceremony. Bearded Jeff sported a big grin while he posed with a largish and quite dead fish. The final shot of Jeff showed him throwing up blood.

Then there he was again, smiling as he said a goodbye he never thought would be shared. "I know vampires like to maintain their image, but I'm not worried. I've come to believe they're a lot kinder and gentler than most people think."

To the surprise of everyone, Brett had been a great looking child. Things didn't go wrong until some point between the tee ball championship and First Communion.

And then there was headgear, Emily thought when she saw Brett's middle school picture. *No wonder.*

Brett's headgear and braces gave way to images of a skinny teenager with pimples and beautiful teeth. According to his prom pic, Brett had gone alone. He shone with exuberance in early stills from the show, and his voice was gleeful in the clip. "I'm so excited. I feel like I've already won. But my imaginary last words for the world are... wait for it... wait for it... just kidding. Because I just can't imagine dying. I just don't see it."

Portia had been in tap shoes at three. In her seventh birthday photo, she was wearing an ornate princess dress and a tiara. Preteen Portia rehearsed a production of what looked to be *Who's Afraid of Virginia Woolf?* Portia's wedding dress had resembled her princess dress in all but color. Shots from the show included Portia smacking her donor in the third challenge and Portia standing over Landon, frozen in the photo as she had been during the challenge. "If I must have a legacy so soon, I hope it will be this: that my death will be a wake-up call for Hollywood. That they will realize older female actors are still valuable and desirable. I want the world to know those of us in our late twenties still have a lot of talent to offer the industry."

"Wasn't she in her early thirties?" Chaz said.

"If she was a day," Delia, who had died in her late teens, agreed.

Madeline had been a redheaded cherub. Her green eyes were bright with happiness in her early photos; apparently, the world had conspired successfully to keep the truth from young Madeline about what a dark and depressing place it was.

By high school, Madeline had found the truth behind that conspiracy. Madeline scowled out from different pictures taken in different places, now always appearing in her signature Goth getup. The photo of Madeline in her *Creature of the Night* sweater set flashed onto the screens, just before one of her dead yet comfortably attired in her own clothes. "I can't die. I am the one. I know. So, I'm excited. I can't wait. And I think, Mom and Dad, when you see who I am, you'll finally understand."

Ollie as a child brought to mind dirt and sunshine. The pictures of young Ollie included dogs, horses, and cows. "If I die, I want to say to my parents that I love them. And also, one more time that I'm sorry. I set out to make you proud, and if you're watching this,

I let you down instead. I love you." Unlike Madeline, Ollie smiled in every picture, the only exceptions being the still taken of him with Landon and the candid shot of him dying.

"He was nice," Emily said then clapped a hand over her mouth.

"You are one of us," Edmund told her. "You may speak whenever you choose."

"Yet I may not have the same courtesy?" Vlad said.

Emily smiled at them both.

Stewart's school photos showed him in a simple uniform of a white button-up shirt and blue shorts. He had played baseball, basketball, and football throughout the years as well as the trombone. The trombone had been a brief experiment designed by Stewart's mother to make him a more well-rounded child, and it had failed miserably.

High school pictures highlighted a laughing, boisterous Stewart and in his prom photo, he was paired with another attractive teenager. "This only gets played if I die, right? So, what I want to do is say goodbye to Audrey and Logan. I love you guys literally more than life itself, and I hope, that whatever else happens, at the end of all this, I've earned back your respect. And, Marcy, fuck you." There followed a single shot of Stewart and Marcy, although Marcy had never consented to appear on the show. A fact which someone from legal realized when the image flashed across the screen, setting in motion events that would end his association with *Creature of the Night* and cost the show something in the low six figures.

"Who needs a tissue?" Chaz asked the audience who responded with whistles and cheers. "Now joining us by Skype to share their final goodbyes with us are the friends and family who held our beloved contestants so dear."

Donovan's wife Tara appeared on the screens.

"I hope you're happy," Tara said then laughed. "You're dead; I almost forgot. I watched your confessional, you shit. I don't know how you could humiliate me like that in front of the whole world. I did everything for you. I cooked, I entertained, I gave you two beautiful children who you never appreciated, and I had relations with you once a week even when I didn't feel like it. And you know what, Mr. Donovan Juan? I haven't felt like it for years."

"At least she's not bitter," Delia said.

"Don't judge," Nodin said. *"She lacks your ability to easily exsanguinate an offending spouse."*

"I watched you die about twenty minutes ago," Tara said. "That's normal now, right? Your cheating fucking husband dies on a game show trying to become a vampire, and there's a camera crew on standby to get your reaction. Well, here it is. You'd think I'd have some grief, but I don't. If it weren't for the kids and the life insurance, I would call our relationship a twenty-year mistake. I guess I should thank the nice people from the show. Because now, my dreams are going to come true. And my dreams include lying on the beach with anyone who isn't you."

"Wow," Delia said. *"Everything does happen for a reason."*

"I'm confused by that inanity uttered in such sincere tones," Edmund said.

"Fuck off, Edmund," Delia said.

"I think we're more of a reality show than a game show," Chaz said.

"Re-al-i-ty! Re-al-i-ty! Re-al-i-ty!" The audience chimed.

Celeste's parents replaced Tara. This time, her father wept while his wife held his hand and spoke. "I knew this would be our outcome. I also know God has a plan for us all, and now I know this was His plan for you. I don't understand it, and my heart is broken, but I know we will see you again one day."

"See?" Delia said.

"You don't believe in God," Nodin observed.

"I believe in serendipity," Delia said. *"If my father had not done unspeakable things, I would not have fled. If the humans had not panicked and declared war when vampires revealed themselves, I would not have been found and changed so I might join the fight to*

oppose their madness. I would not have had my glorious revenge and become the powerful and beautiful creature here today. Instead, I would have died centuries ago after living a sad life as a cook and broodmare to some brute."

"Now I'm a believer," Edmund sang, in a surprising tenor. "There is minimal to no doubt in my mind."

"Edmund!" Delia was surprised into a grin that was not in keeping with her regal façade. In her delight, she sang a few words aloud. "I'm in love…"

Edmund grumbled. "Now you're a believer?"

"I couldn't drain her if I tried." Nodin had joined the game enthusiastically, forgetting for too long, that he couldn't sing.

Cyri's dad was humming along. Cyri tried to nudge him silent.

"What honey? Everybody loves The Beatles."

"That's not…" Cyri stopped. It just wasn't worth the effort. She pointedly turned her attention to the stage. Her father did the same.

Charmed, if slightly confused, the audience had begun to chant. "Believer! Believer! Believer!"

"In loftier times," Edmund said, "women were to be seen, rather than heard."

"Later, I will hurt you," Delia said. "But I promise to do it silently."

"It was fond memories of the last time you hurt me that brought me back to this ridiculous show."

"Flatterer."

"I thought your presence was needed to prevent the changing of someone unsuitable," Nodin said.

"Let us agree my reasons are my own." Edmund glowered. The audience roared its approval of the vampire banter.

"Here to represent Kannon's parents in their final farewell is that nice official looking person we saw earlier." Chaz waved the audience's attention toward the screens.

"The Balls would like to express their sorrow at the loss of their son. However, despite their earlier expression of support, they did not condone his association with *Creature of the Night* or any affiliate company. We would like to remind everyone Kannon was of age and the family is not responsible for any action taken by Kannon during the course of the show."

"I forget," Edmund said. *"Was any action taken by Kannon during the course of the show?"*

"This is a tragic loss," the associate said. "And Kannon will be missed. At this time, we have no further comment."

"Here comes Cassie's friend Milay with another touching goodbye," Chaz said.

"So you're dead," Milay said beside Cassie's image on the screens. "And you would think they would give me your solo now, but I just heard from Jenna they're looking to bring some bitch in from a Russian company. And if that's not enough, I'm getting threatening emails." Milay burst into tears. "People are saying I'm not a good friend. I think we both know what a good friend I am. I mean, you did know, but now you're dead because you're selfish, even though everyone thinks you're wonderful. But you're not wonderful.

"You had to go on that show and die when the least you could have done was stay and coach me so I could have your solo once you got all crippled. That's what a friend would do. I just think it's not fair, that's all. How people don't understand how self-centered you were. And I want everyone to know I loved CassCass like a sister, and this has a profound effect on me. I'm suffering, and I need support. So don't be evil to me."

"Let's send Milay an edible bouquet," Chaz said.

"Let us make her an edible bouquet," Vlad suggested.

Chaz introduced Lola's ex-boyfriend who arrived via electronics in the middle of it.

"Sorry, I'm kind of shocked. You never know, do you? I would have bet on Lola to win it. Obviously, now I'm glad I didn't. It's too bad though. It's always a sad day when a hot chick dies. I remember the night we met. We ended up fucking on the hood of my Impala."

"And the beauty of the world is less than it was," Edmund said.

"Is that the quote?" Nodin said.

"Ask Delia."

"Fuck you, Edmund."

"We must take the first opportunity to work on your banter," Edmund said.

"Shit. I don't know what else I can say. Except, Emily, if you want to look me up, I'm cool with that. I think you and Lola might have been sisters under the skin, you know? We can have some good times."

Emily looked pained.

"Remember, you could make a date and tear his head from his body if you wanted to," Delia told her.

Emily started and snuck a smile at Delia. It might not be advisable to start out her new life by ripping someone's head from his body. But it was reassuring to know she could.

"Joining us now," Chaz said, "is Jeff's mother."

"I'm not sure I'm doing the right thing," Jeff's mother said. "I don't think things like this need to be so public. But, I wanted to say goodbye to my baby. For some reason, this was important to him, so I'm saying my goodbye here. You were the world to me, and I've felt pride in you every moment from the second you were born. And what I think is my Jeff was too good for this show. I think he was a person who wasn't accepting of violence or domination, and that's why he didn't win. That's why he died. Because he was the best person there."

"Something else that should have been considered before his agreement to appear on the show," Nodin said.

"I'm sure everyone remembers Brett's friend Jonas," Chaz said as Jonas's image replaced that of Jeff's mother.

"Jesus, man," Jonas said. "I fucking knew you were gonna die. That sucks. But your mom said I could have your video games, so..."

I'll think of you every time I play them, I swear. Unless I forget which ones were yours and which ones I already had. Maybe I can label them or something. Your mom is pretty bummed. She wouldn't talk to the show. Man, I'm talking like you're going to be able to hear me. Stupid, right? I think your mom was pissed when I asked about the video games. Fuck. I just realized you're not going to be able to hook me up with hot girls. It's like I already miss you, man."

"It's almost like we'll miss him too," Chaz said.

"Let's hear from Charles, Portia's husband," Chaz said, and Charles came onscreen.

"I love you, Charles," a woman in the audience screamed.

"I love you too," Charles said. "I love all my fans. But tonight is not about me. My wife was an amazing woman," Charles said. "She was a great talent who never got the recognition she deserved. My greatest regret is she felt she had to risk her life to attain the professional stature she felt she lacked. I never minded she hadn't made it big. I loved her for who she was, and I'll always remember the girl I married. I want to dedicate this monolog to my beautiful wife; I'll miss her always."

A single tear rolled out of Charles' eye and trickled down his cheek as he let the recitation take him. "She should have died hereafter."

"I know I haven't been human for a bit, but this is weird right?" Nodin said.

"So weird," Delia agreed.

"Completely inappropriate," Emily chimed in. *"And I was human about twelve hours ago."*

"There would have been a time for such a word," Charles continued. "Tomorrow, and tomorrow, and tomorrow..."

"This one talks too much," Vlad said. *"Can I eat him?"*

"I would let you eat this one if he were here," Delia said.

Charles droned on. He had begun to writhe. "...Out, out, brief candle!"

"*Surely, someone has an address on file?*" Nodin said.

"*Am I appalled or impressed?*" Delia said.

"*It could be worse,*" Nodin told them. "*The actress could have won and decided to change this one.*"

All the vampires, including Emily, grimaced at the same time.

"...an idiot, full of sound and fury, signifying no—"

"That's enough," Delia said.

"*That was the entire bit,*" Nodin said.

"—thing." Charles stopped reciting and wiped the single tear that still clung to his cheek. "We always loved the Scottish play. To be honest, it's not my favorite, but today isn't about me."

"You are amazing," Chaz said. "Even compared to the rest of the humans."

"That means the world to me," Charles said. "On a more personal note, I just signed on to play the title role in the live-action reboot of Plastic Man, so don't forget to see it next summer."

"*I have to agree with Vlad,*" Edmund said. "*I could visit that one on a dark night.*"

"*You are not allowed,*" Nodin told him. "*Friends and family are protected by the terms of the contract.*"

"That was a tribute I, for one, will never forget," Chaz said. "But for those of you who want to try, Madeline's friend Jessa is up next."

"I can't believe how wrong I was." Jessa twirled a lock of hair around her finger as she talked. "I told her she was going to make it out alive. I feel like it's my fault because she relied on me so much, and I gave her bad information. But you can't say, 'You're totally going to die; get out of there.' That wouldn't be supportive. I hope it's clear I always supported Madeline; she was my best friend. And best friends are like sisters. Sometimes they have little issues, but I always wanted the best for her. I'm going to miss her so much. I love you, Maddie.

"When I think about how much I wanted to be on the show and

how jealous I was… I mean, it was so lucky I didn't get picked. Although, I mean, I might have won, so that could be different, but what if I hadn't? That would be terrible. Of course, it's terrible now. I'm just so upset about this I might not even audition for next season."

"So many little tragedies today," Delia said.

Edmund snorted.

"Now appearing on your screens is Ollie's dad," Chaz said.

"That damn boy never thought I was proud enough of him," Ollie's dad said. "But I was. I'll admit I wasn't crazy about this show nonsense, no offense, but that doesn't mean I wasn't fond of him. It doesn't mean I didn't consider him a man. And now he's gone. I don't look forward to living with that. I'm glad his mother had passed before she had to watch him die.

"I guess he finally did succeed in disappointing me." Ollie's dad paused as if to consider his next words. "I know you don't care what I think, but I want you all to know I don't think your show is a decent thing. I don't think anything that causes pain to satisfy some shallow taste for entertainment is a decent thing."

"Who is entertained?" Edmund said.

"There are rodeo trophies behind him," Nodin said. "I assume he thinks we should all endeavor to enjoy the nobility of watching grown men ride protesting cows for the entertainment of others."

Delia tilted her head. *"Do they ride the cows?"*

"At least our cows consented," Edmund said.

"Cows aren't people," Ollie's father said.

"And people aren't vampires," Edmund answered. "Let us all pause to search for profundity in those statements."

"Let's give Ollie's dad a round of applause," Chaz said. The crowd clapped obediently and somewhere backstage a tech took the cue to bring the visitation by Skype to an end.

Stewart's kids popped onscreen.

"This is so embarrassing," Audrey said. "I don't want to do it. What are we even supposed to say?"

"Hi, kids," Chaz said, alerting them to the fact that they were already conversing with the world. "Thanks for being here to say goodbye to your father."

Logan waved at Chaz. His sister gave a cool flip of her hair and nodded.

"We can't say anything to him; he's dead." Audrey scowled. "So fucking lame."

"Tell me I did not just hear you swear on television," someone yelled from off-screen.

"It *is* lame!" Audrey turned away from Chaz and the audience to engage with her mother. "This show is fucked up, and I don't even like vampires anymore."

Logan looked anxious. "I still do. Dad said there was no shame in not being first."

His sister refocused her savagery. "He didn't just lose, moron," she said. "He's fucking dead, and those assholes watching cheered when he died. It's fucking ridiculous."

"Why was that so much cuter when it was Jake?" Chaz speculated. The audience laughed in agreement.

"I want to say goodbye to Dad," Logan said.

"Hurry up," Audrey snapped.

"I love you, Dad," Logan said. "Father Dominick said we get to see you someday in Heaven, but mom said we won't because—"

"Logan!"

Logan threw a fearful glance over his shoulder. "I miss you, Dad."

Chaz paused to allow Audrey to speak, but the girl turned her head and remained silent.

"Thanks for being here today, kids," Chaz said. "I'm sure if your father could see you he would be proud. Let's give them a hand."

Stewart's kids disappeared as the thunderous applause dwindled.

"Our last friends and family participant isn't here to say goodbye to a departed loved one but to congratulate a sister on her leap into immortality."

Chaz paused to allow the audience to express their glee. As the audience pounded their hands together, Emily muttered, "Fat chance."

"Yes," Vlad said. *"She will surely have her objections."*

"Please look at the screens to see how Emily's sister is feeling about today's momentous events."

Emily's sister was holding a bible to her chest as though it were a shield against the metaphorical darkness that was her sibling.

"Today, I mourn my sister," she said. "Finally, for the last time."

"Hello, Evelyn," Emily said.

"I have been grieving my sister's loss for years; today, that grieving will end. The demon that now inhabits the body that used to belong to Emily is nothing to me, and I will from this moment strive to forget she ever existed."

"I think you have some of the old photo albums," Emily said.

Evelyn sketched a cross in the air with her hand. "Your evil knows no bounds, yet it will be bound by the faith of the devout."

"I'm sure you'll be praying for us all," Emily said.

"It would be amusing to turn her," Delia said.

"God helps those who help themselves," Evelyn said. She leaned forward and picked up a pitcher of water which she flung not quite at the camera.

"Do you think that was holy water?" Chaz said.

Emily nodded. "Undoubtedly."

"That's it." A man thrust his dripping face into view. "I'm out of here."

"Which is why we sent a human," Chaz said. "Although, to be honest, we were expecting something a little more problematic than water."

Evelyn's feed ended as the tech that had drawn the short straw packed up his camera and microphone and went home.

"Let's all give a hand to Riley and Kiley, who did a fantastic job and exercised an immense amount of self-control." Riley and Kiley came out and exchanged hugs with Chaz. "Let's hear it for the girls!"

The judges applauded for the vampire twins as well.

"Check out the *Creature of the Night* website to find out how Emily is enjoying eternal life, to apply to be a donor, and to audition for next season."

"My duty is met, is it not?" Vlad said.

Chaz nodded. Emily started to object.

"You will soon discover that I will not be a secret to you," Vlad told her.

The audience gasped then cheered for the huge bat that hovered above the stage where Vlad had been. Then even the bat was gone.

"Remember, folks," Chaz said. "When you go to bed tonight, there will be one more creature out there watching from the dark, ready to come scratching at your door. Or perhaps, silently through it."

"I like that," Vlad's disembodied voice wasn't loud, but not a soul in the theater missed it. "It is sporting to give them warning."

"So, please," Chaz smiled around at the audience finally settling on Cyri. "Do sleep tight."

"I got express shipping." Mildred was gathering the remnants of the evening's snacking. Dishes went into the sink for the morning, trash was tossed in the can, and the dog chipped in by taking care of any leftover crumbs. "Our commemorative glasses will be here in two business days."

"So, in three days?" Hal said.

"I don't know," Mildred said. "Sometimes they deliver on Sunday."

"What glasses? And how much did they cost?"

"Drinking glasses, Hal. And they hardly cost anything." Mildred wiped her hands on a dishtowel. "They have cute little fangs on them and they say *Drain Me*. Isn't that adorable?"

"Maybe we should get a poster." Hal was thinking of Lola.

"Don't forget to check the locks," Mildred said. She called for the beagle to follow and headed for the bedroom.

"Do I ever forget?" Hal was feeling a little regretful about Lola's death. Lola wouldn't have nagged him about the locks.

"If you never forgot, I wouldn't have to remind you," Mildred said.

"What now? Emily asked. She and Chaz were still on the stage smiling and waving the audience away. The judges had removed themselves from the altar but were somewhere nearby, still able to participate in the conversation.

"Now is whatever you want," Delia said.

"Home?" Chaz asked.

Emily thought of her apartment. It was part of a small community, working upscale, and it had adequately housed Emily and her belongings for six years. Home seemed anticlimactic, although she did have a neighbor or two who could use a good eating.

"Not there," Delia said. *"Your new home."*

"The Manor is yours," Chaz said. "Traditionally, the new creature hosts a gathering."

"The show supplies the virgins," Delia added.

And They _ _ _ _ _ _
Happily Ever After.

"Yeah, I tweeted a question and they answered it and even showed my picture." Cody was talking to his mother who had expressed an overabundance of interest in the fact that his question had been chosen to be read on air. "You didn't watch it, did you?"

"No," his mother said. "You know I don't like things like that."

She wouldn't like what he was going to watch next either. He was in the process of fast forwarding to the good part. "Gotta go, mom." Cody had finally struck gold. Cody's mother wanted to talk Sunday breakfast followed by church, which was only one of the perils of having a mother who **lived** too close.

Cody agreed, knowing he would regret it Sunday morning, but he wanted to get off the phone. It was way too awkward masturbating with your mom chattering in your ear.

His mother agreed to hang up just in time, allowing Cody free reign to express his appreciation. Since her death, Portia's "art" film had been downloaded several hundred thousand times. Cody, who was a purist, had ordered a hard copy, but since his order wouldn't arrive for two business days, he was getting started with the digital version.

There she was. Ten years younger, twenty times hotter, and rapidly achieving nudity. Cody groaned through his release while Portia cavorted onscreen, immortal in a sense.

"Good season," said The Voice.

"Definitely," Little P said with more than a little relief. They were sitting on opposite sides of The Voice's desk, both with their feet propped up. "There were a lot of tweets about the girl eating the mole."

"I do like the idea of getting donors who are as unappealing as possible," The Voice said. "Makes it more fun."

"We had a homeless donor, too," Little P said as though it had been planned. You had to take opportunities for self-promotion as they presented themselves.

"That was good thinking," The Voice said. "Maybe we can do all homeless next season. Just no one too literate. Donors or contestants."

"Of course," Little P said.

"And we'll need a couple more sluts. This season's livened things up quite a bit."

Little P agreed. You could never have too many sluts. "We could have a slut themed shirt," Little P suggested. "Maybe with fangs?"

The Voice nodded. "Maybe. Speaking of merch, how is the new line of kids' shirts selling?"

"Like hotcakes," Little P assured The Voice.

It was near dawn. Emily and Vlad had just polished off the last virgin.

"*So, no dramatic falling into the sleep of the dead when the sun comes up?*" Emily asked.

"No. That is a superstition based on the belief we are soulless and evil. Creatures that are undone by the light."

"Sunlight doesn't hurt us?"

"You will not want a beachfront home," Vlad said, "but it is manageable. Our skin suffers with prolonged exposure, but we do not burst into flames. The young ones cry they are unable to tan."

It had at no point occurred to Emily that vampires might share traits with gingers.

"If you wish to lose a day of your immortality, Delia can tell you more."

"What else?" Emily said. "The drowning thing. Is that true?"

"People drown for want of breath," Vlad said. "That is not an issue for us."

"So...?

"So?"

"So, they include things like the drowning, implying it is something that would hurt us, to distract humans from realizing what really will?"

Vlad bowed in acknowledgment.

"Is Chaz going to hunt the girl from the audience?" Emily asked.

"What difference would it make to the state of the world?"

"I think she's different," Emily said.

"Different is something that does not work well for humans."

Emily considered. "Depends on how strong you are, I guess."

"Perhaps he will turn her. Make her strong."

"She's a child," Emily said.

"Not such a child." Vlad leered.

Emily flashed her fangs; she liked the way it felt. "Is that your insightful comment on the arbitrary age restrictions we like to place on our youth before we deem them ready to enlist, imbibe, or fornicate?"

"What we? You are no longer that 'we.' You are something new," Vlad said. "To answer your question: I merely observe; comment is futile."

"As is resistance," Emily said.

"As, they say, is searching for a black cat in a dark room."

"Especially if there is no cat," Emily finished.

"Yet, there is always something to be found in the darkness," Vlad said, as though that were the final word on darkness.

Emily supposed it was.

ABOUT THE AUTHOR

Anne Stinnett was born in Los Angeles where she spent most of her first decade reading books and playing in traffic. Eventually, she learned the foolishness of frolicking amongst moving vehicles, but she is still a voracious reader of multiple genres.

After growing up in California, she moved around a bit, eventually landing in Albuquerque. She graduated from the University of New Mexico, with a major in English and a minor in Theater Arts.

She now lives in Palm Springs, California with her freeloader canine friends Sirius (yes, Black) and Midge, who occasionally allow her to get some writing done.

Made in the USA
Middletown, DE
12 June 2022